... of some sort, having spent my career ... porter, anchor or producer in television news. ... is a lot more fun, since you don't have to deal with those pesky things known as facts.

I spent fifteen years as a television news reporter and anchor. My work has taken me from the floors of the Democratic and Republican National Conventions to Ground Zero in New York to Jay Leno's backyard. My stories have been seen on NBC, ABC and CNN. I still work as a freelance network field producer for FOX, NBC, CBS and ABC.

I grew up in the New York City metropolitan area and now live on the Gulf Coast where I will never shovel snow again. I'm happily married to a math teacher and we share our wonderful home with our tortoiseshell tabby cat, Gypsy.

You can follow me on Twitter @NicTatano.

Praise For Nic Tatano's Debut
Wing Girl

'One of the top 20 books of 2013'
I Heart . . . Chick Lit

'E-book novel of the year'
Chick Lit Chloe

*'I truly adored this novel . . . One of my favourite
books this year, for sure'*
Chick Lit Reviews

*'The heroine is sassy, the dialogue is razor-sharp and the
romance is sweet. Well worth a read'*
Chick Lit Club

'Fast and funny'
Wondrous Reads

The Lost Cats and Lonely Hearts Club

Book One

NIC TATANO

A division of HarperCollins*Publishers*
www.harpercollins.co.uk

Harper*Impulse* an imprint of
HarperCollins*Publishers*
1 London Bridge Street
London SE1 9GF

www.harpercollins.co.uk

A Paperback Original 2016

First published in Great Britain in ebook format by Harper*Impulse* 2016

Copyright © Nic Tatano 2016

Nic Tatano asserts the moral right to
be identified as the author of this work

A catalogue record for this book
is available from the British Library

ISBN: 9780008212186

Set in Bembo by Palimpsest Book Production Limited,
Falkirk, Stirlingshire

Printed and bound in Great Britain

For Gypsy, Pandora, Bella, Buttons, Snoopy, and J.R.,
my furry companions through life . . .

Chapter One

The tortoiseshell kitten with one good eye and a limp awoke first, emerging from the ball of fur comprised of his three siblings. Light from the setting sun filtered into the abandoned room as he moved toward his mother, eagerly awaiting the quick bath she gave him every day. She was still asleep so he nuzzled her chin.

She didn't move.

He bumped her with his head. Still nothing.

Her mouth hung open. She wasn't breathing.

And she was cold.

His heart rate spiked as he went back to wake his siblings.

The three kittens stirred from their slumber and moved toward their mother.

The tabby knew it was in trouble.

The black and white tuxedo kitten felt pangs of hunger.

The Russian blue kitten's eyes filled with fear.

Suddenly a nearby noise grabbed the tortoiseshell's attention. His ears perked up. He couldn't see very well or jump, but he was blessed with a very loud voice.

He began to cry.

My face tightens as the construction crew chief hands me and my photographer a hard hat each. "Do I really have to wear this?"

The construction foreman nods. "Sorry, Miss Shaw. Unless you want a block of concrete falling on your head. The stadium is about to come down *without* the help of our demolition crew."

I roll my green eyes as I put on the plastic yellow hat, mashing my salon-perfect copper curls. "My two hundred dollar hair appointment this morning, shot to hell."

My burly, middle-aged photographer shakes his head. "Awww, poor Madison and her six-figure salary. Careful you don't break a nail, *Network*."

Yeah, that's my nickname, which I hate. Even though I'm a network television reporter.

The foreman laughs as he puts his hard hat atop his thick gray hair. "High maintenance, huh?"

The photographer nods. "She's raised it to an art form. Who else wears four inch heels to a demolition story?"

My jaw clenches. "I wouldn't even be covering this if Joe wasn't out sick. I am a national *political* reporter in case you forgot."

"How could I forget when you remind the newsroom every single day?"

I shoot him my patented death stare as he moves in front of me and aims his camera. He turns on his light, walking backwards as I follow the foreman into the condemned structure, navigating my way through oily puddles. (Hey, don't give me that look. Fine, so he was right about the heels. But they take me up to six-foot-two and since I'm one hundred forty-five pounds of solid muscle I like being the Amazon of the newsroom.) "Okay, we're rolling. So, Mister Richards, tell me why demolishing a building with explosives is such an art?"

"Well, you've gotta place the dynamite just right—"

He stops walking so I do the same. "What?"

He puts up his hand and points at a door. "Hang on. You hear that?"

I lean toward it and listen. "Yeah. I think it's coming from that room. You think someone's in there?"

"Not some*one*." He pulls out a flashlight, turns it on and opens the door to a dark office. The high-pitched noise gets louder. "Well, well, we still have a few residents, I see."

"What, rats?"

"Nope." I follow the beam of light and see an old cardboard box filled with a bunch of crying kittens.

And a mother cat that is obviously dead.

The photographer aims his light at the box, brightening the room so we can see better.

I move forward and crouch down to take a closer look. "Poor little guys. The mother cat died." I look around, find a clean box and start to place the kittens inside. "You're a lucky bunch of kittens. You almost got blown up."

And then one of them claws my brand new Prada jacket, pulling out a thread.

"Sonofabitch! My brand new jacket!" I put the kitten in the clean box and shake my head. "Can this day get any worse?"

"Uh-oh," says the photographer as he turns to the foreman. "You might not need the explosives. Mount Madison is about to erupt."

"Bite me, Ed." I lift the box and stand up, then hold it out toward the foreman.

He furrows his brow. "What do you want me to do with these?"

"Find homes for 'em. Your construction site, your kittens."

He shakes his head. "Sorry, young lady, but I can't stop this project to take care of a bunch of orphaned cats. I love animals as much as the next person and I've got two cats at home, but I'm stuck here all night. And it's obvious they need to be taken care of right away. I'll bury the mother cat but as far as those kittens go, you're it."

My face tightens. "What am I gonna do with four kittens?"

He shrugs. "I dunno. Take 'em to a shelter."

"On Friday night of a holiday weekend?"

"What can I say?" He starts to laugh.

3

"What?"

He points at my hand. "I just noticed you don't wear a wedding ring."

"That's because I'm single."

"You live by yourself?"

"Yeah. Why? You want my phone number?"

"Nah, it just hit me. Thirtysomething unmarried woman who lives alone." He points at the box. "You've got yourself a cat lady starter kit."

Stuck in traffic with four crying kittens is not my idea of a fun Friday night. I keep staring at the pull on my jacket, wondering if it can be fixed. And even if it can I would still *know* it's there.

Meanwhile, I have more pressing problems to deal with. I need someone to take said problems off my hands.

I hit the hands-free button on the steering column to access my cell phone, then ask the robot with the clipped female voice a question. "Find all animal shelters on Staten Island."

Beep. *"There are three animal shelters on Staten Island."*

I pump my fist. "Yes!" Back to the robot. "Find an animal shelter on Staten Island that is currently open."

I drum my fingers on the steering wheel as the traffic begins to move. Beep. *"There are no animal shelters currently open on Staten Island. The next shelter opening is at eight a.m. on Monday morning. Would you like directions?"*

"Sonofabitch!"

Beep. *"I do not appreciate your language. Please rephrase in a more dignified manner."*

Just what I need, a snooty cell phone. "Why is this happening to me?"

Beep. *"Your question needs to be more specific. Please re-phrase it—"*

"Oh, shut the hell up!"

Beep. *"I do not appreciate your language. Please—"*

4

I pound the steering wheel, turning off the phone.

There's only one option left as I head for home.

"Please, God, let him be home."

I bound up the steps of the house belonging to the veterinarian who lives next door. The kittens are still crying as I jam my finger into the doorbell several times.

"Coming! Keep your shirt on!"

"Thank you, God." I hear footsteps and see a figure moving toward me through the beveled glass. The door opens and I exhale as I see my neighbor. "Jeff, so glad you're home."

The fortyish vet with short salt-and-pepper hair looks at the box of kittens. "Madison, you shouldn't have. What's going on?"

"I was doing a story on the demolition of the stadium and we found them in one of the offices. The mother cat was dead and they won't stop crying and I know they're hungry and I'm leaving on vacation tomorrow and could you take them—"

"Whoa, hold on. I've got a plane to catch in a couple hours for my own vacation."

"Is there a shelter open?"

"Not at this hour and kittens this young need to be bottle fed." He takes the box from me. "C'mon inside, I've got some formula and bottles."

I follow him and shut the door. "Wait a minute . . . *bottle fed*?"

The short, slightly built vet nods. "It's pretty common for orphaned kittens. Same as feeding a baby. You'll get the hang of it in no time."

"Me?"

"Like I said, I've gotta go but don't worry, it's simple. From the looks of them, they need to be fed right now or they won't survive."

He leads me into the kitchen, then pulls a cardboard box from a cabinet. He opens it, revealing half a dozen cans. My eyes widen as he pulls one out and I read the label. "There's such a thing as formula for kittens? Can't you just heat up some milk?"

"They need special nutrients. This stuff is close to cat's milk as far as what it will do for kittens." He grabs a couple of tiny plastic bottles from a drawer. He opens the can, fills both bottles, then hands one to me. He gently takes the kitten that looks like a tiger and holds the bottle to its mouth. It latches on with tiny paws and begins to eat immediately. "Poor little guy is hungry. Go ahead, Madison, grab a kitten and feed it."

"Well, okay." I reach into the box and gently pick up the kitten with all the colorful markings, then follow the lead of the vet. I can't help but smile as the tiny kitten doesn't take long to start draining the bottle. If only a photographer was here because this image is beyond cute. "Wow, he picked that up pretty quick."

"See how easy it is? You're a natural."

"I've never done this with a baby. I'm an only child and didn't work as a babysitter. I wouldn't even know how to change a diaper."

"Well, now you're a cat foster parent." His kitten finishes the bottle. "And you can't forget to burp your kitten."

"You gotta be kidding me."

"Watch. Very gently." He places the kitten on his shoulder and softly taps it on the back with two fingers until it lets out a tiny burp.

I follow his lead with my kitten. It responds with a burp, then begins to purr, gives me a lick on my neck, then rests its head on my shoulder as it looks up at me. My anxiety seems to drain in an instant. "Awww."

Jeff cocks his head at the kitten. "He just thanked you."

I turn to look at the kitten. "You're very welcome, little guy."

We feed the other two kittens and put them back in the box where they quickly move together into a ball and fall asleep. "Okay, Madison, there's enough formula here to hold you for a couple of days. You need to feed them every few hours."

"Huh? Two a.m. feedings for cats?"

"They need constant care. Right now they're helpless. And keep them in a warm place. If you have a stuffed animal put it in the box and it will make them feel more secure. A ticking clock helps to take the place of the mother's heartbeat." He reaches into another drawer and pulls out a bag of cotton balls. "You also have to encourage them to answer nature's call after you feed them."

"Excuse me?"

"The mother cat stimulates the area where they pee and poop with her tongue. You'll have to do it with your finger."

Okay, that makes my face tighten. "Huh? I have to touch . . ."

"You also need warm water and some cotton balls. I'll show you how it works, and how to clean them when they're done."

It tightens some more. "I've gotta bathe them too?"

"No, but you have to keep them clean. It's simple, Madison. Anyway, you can adopt them out in a few weeks."

My face has now reached the point where I look like a woman who's overdosed on Botox. "*Weeks*? Did you say *weeks*?"

"Yeah. Once they learn to take care of themselves."

"Jeff, don't you know anyone who can take them? I'm supposed to be leaving for a vacation in the Hamptons. My boyfriend is picking me up first thing in the morning."

"Sorry, no foster homes for four orphaned kittens on a Friday night of a holiday weekend. Take 'em with you. You'll do fine." He studies my face for a moment, then takes my hands. "Madison, they'll die if someone doesn't take care of them. Honestly, I'd do it but—"

I look at the ball of fur in the box and the guilt I feel reminds me where I came from. "That's okay. Listen, thanks for your help."

"That's the spirit. C'mon, you carry the kittens back to your house and I'll get the supplies. Then I'll write down all the stuff you need from the pet store and what else you need to do."

10:13 pm: First Feeding/Nature's Call

Jeff told me it helps to keep a log of feedings, so here we go.

I have decided that my storm coverage gear is perfect for what I'm about to do next, so I don my rubber yellow slicker and matching hat. I add a pair of safety goggles as I have no idea how far a kitten can shoot.

I've lined up the cotton balls and warm water.

Four hours ago I was in a Prada suit ready for a vacation in the Hamptons. Now I look like a member of a Hazmat team about to rub my finger on a kitten's . . . hell, I don't even wanna think about what I'm going to do.

I take a cotton ball and dip it into the warm water and grab the colorful kitten from the box. I take a deep breath, hold the kitten at arm's length and turn my head as I have no desire to actually see what I can feel. Ugh. The grimace I see in the mirror is off the charts as I start rubbing the area in question with my finger and within a few seconds I feel something warm which smells really bad.

"Ugh. Oh my God, this is so disgusting. I am never having kids."

I take a peek and see the kitten is done while my finger is covered with (too much information) so I toss the cotton ball in the trash, grab a fresh one and clean the little furball. Back in the box it goes, then I rush to the sink and pour a decent amount of rubbing alcohol on my hands.

"One down, three to go."

Twenty minutes later I'm done.

Twenty minutes after that, the Silkwood shower I'm taking runs out of hot water.

12:02 am: Second Feeding/Nature's Call

I had just drifted off to sleep when the loud one started crying again.

Jeff was right. They're on schedule.

At least I don't need another shower for this part.

Oh, wait. I have to clean them after feeding them. Curses, foiled again.

I prepare four bottles with the formula and line them up on the kitchen table. As I sit I grab the colorful kitten from the box. He already knows the routine as the moment I put the bottle to his mouth he latches on and drains it. "Awww, you were hungry again, huh?" I put the little guy on my shoulder, burp it, and repeat the process with the other kittens.

I feel a twinge of maternal instinct as I look at the adorable tiger kitten sucking on the bottle, but the memory from two hours ago blows it out of the water.

Because I have to do the Hazmat routine again.

The hot water in the shower runs out after eight minutes, apparently not having had enough time to re-load.

I have got to get a bigger water heater.

3:14 am: Third Feeding/Nature's Call.
I must look like an extra from *The Walking Dead* as I shuffle into the kitchen to prepare the bottles. Bleary-eyed I get the kittens fed. The colorful one gives me a soulful look when he's done with his bottle and for a minute I feel guilty about complaining. The poor little thing has lost its mother and I've only lost sleep.

Hazmat suit. Alcohol. Shower.

4:20 am: Bad Dream
Not me, one of the kittens. The colorful one started screaming and shaking. I held him close so he could hear my heartbeat. He calmed down after five minutes. Not sure if kittens have nightmares or if he woke up, couldn't find his mother and freaked out.

That feeling is so familiar to me . . .

5:44 am: Fourth Feeding/Nature's Call

I'm too tired to stand up in the shower so I take a bath. I glance in the box and see them all looking at me.

"Guys, don't do that. You're too damn cute."

They keep looking at me.

"Stop it."

They don't.

They're just too cute.

And something tells me they know it.

8:01 am: Fifth? Sixth? Who the hell knows. I've lost count and can't focus on the log.

The sun woke me up this time before the kittens started crying so I'm actually semi-awake while on my third cup of coffee. I can't help but smile as I look at the kittens huddled together in a ball, fast asleep.

"Well, guys, we made it. Through the first night, anyway."

I can't believe it, but I actually feel some pride in what I've accomplished.

The fact that I've saved four lives gives me a warm feeling.

Which is good, because the water heater gave up the ghost.

8:29 am

I trudge toward the front door to answer the bell. I open it and see my boyfriend's face immediately drop. "Geez, Madison, you look like hell. You can't go to the beach party this afternoon looking like that. I thought you were going to get your hair done yesterday? I mean, there are going to be supermodels there."

It should be noted that my significant other of the past eight months often has no filter and says things that embarrass me in public. According to my best friends this is a major problem, but one I deem fixable even though he has on occasion made my face match my hair. He also tends to gawk at pretty women when we're together, even commenting on them, but I'm working on that one as well. Actually, there's a pretty long to-do list. But as you know, some guys take longer to mature. So let's go with that. "Thank you, Jeremy. And good morning to you too." I shake my head as he comes inside.

My tall, lean boyfriend takes my shoulders, studies my face with his pale blue eyes. "You sick?"

"Nope. Been up all night."

"Well, you can sleep in the car. We'll find a salon when we get there." He reaches for the suitcase that I packed days ago and stops. "What's that noise?"

I point toward the cardboard box with the kittens. "The reason I was up all night."

He walks over to it and takes a look, then runs one hand through his thick, dark hair. "Okay . . . why do you have a bunch of kittens?"

"Long story." I give him the quick recap. "Anyway, they can't take care of themselves so we've gotta take 'em with us. And stop at a pet store along the way for their groceries."

He puts up his hands. "Whoa, hold on a minute. You want to take four orphaned kittens to the Hamptons? And we've got to bottle feed them every few hours? Which means getting up in the middle of the night?"

"No choice. Can't find anyone else to take them and the vet next door is out of town on his own vacation."

He shakes his head. "Madison, I rented a great place and have reservations at some incredible restaurants. The whole week is planned out. We've got an invite to *the* best beach party of the summer in the Hamptons. We can't take a bunch of cats."

I put my hands on my hips. "So, what, we're gonna just leave 'em here?"

He shrugs. "They're just a bunch of strays that no one would want."

Okay, the lack of a filter just crossed the line with the one thing that sets me off. "You *do* know that *I* was basically a stray."

11

"What, because you were an abandoned baby and grew up in foster homes? We're talking about cats, Madison, not people. They would have died anyway if you hadn't found them."

"Are you serious? Leave them here and let them starve to death?"

"Let nature take its course."

A large red flag starts heading up the pole. "I cannot believe you. Are you that cold?"

"Madison, be serious . . . we've been looking forward to this vacation for months. This is *the Hamptons* we're talking about. Think of the celebrities we'll meet and the accounts I can pick up. C'mon, let's go. You'll forget the whole thing once you see the beach."

I can't believe it. My boyfriend is selfish and actually lacking in compassion. Just as my best friends have told me. How did I not see this for myself until now? *Because the incredible sex had your rose-colored glasses firmly in place, dumbass.* A loud meow distracts me and I turn to look at the box of kittens. Four desperate sets of eyes, filled with hope, seem to look right into my heart, like no person ever has. The colorful one meows again and locks eyes with me if to say: *You're all we've got. Please don't leave us.* How could anyone throw away precious lives like that?

And why would I want to keep dating someone who would?

As a reporter, I often see things in black and white, and this is one of those times.

I turn back to Jeremy, narrow my eyes and point at the door. "Get. Out."

"What?"

"You heard me. Get out of my house."

"Madison, c'mon. Calm down—"

"Oh, I'm very calm. You just showed your true colors. And now I owe those kittens for showing me what kind of person you really are."

"You're serious? Madison, we've made *plans.*"

"So go find a new girl at *the Hamptons* and make *plans* with her. Someone selfish who doesn't like responsibility or respect life. Considering your bikini radar, it shouldn't take you long. We're done, Jeremy. Out. Now."

He throws up his hands. "Fine. Enjoy your week-long vacation with a bunch of strays." He spins on his heels and leaves, slamming the door.

I stare at it, my relationship closed like the door. "I'm a stray. We stick together." I feel my eyes well up but the sharp meow grabs my attention. I quickly move to the box and see the colorful kitten standing in front of the other three. "Oh, the loud one again. I guess you're the spokesman for the litter." I pick up the box and bring it in to the kitchen, setting it in a sun square. "C'mon, guys. Time for breakfast. And thank you for showing me what I couldn't see before."

I hear the whispers from the next aisle as I wheel my shopping cart through the pet superstore.

"I'm telling you, it's her."

"No way."

"Molly, that's Madison Shaw."

"Get real, Joe. You think someone on network TV goes out in public like that? The woman looks like she just rolled out of bed and combed her hair with an eggbeater. Trust me, that is NOT the redhead you drool over on the evening news."

I can't help but laugh as I push the cart around to the next aisle. The young couple in front of me studies my face. What the hell. I stick out my hand and flash a big smile. "Hi, I'm Madison."

The woman's eyes widen as she turns beet red. "Oh my God, I am so sorry—"

The man's jaw simply drops and hangs open like a trophy bass. "Uh, I, uh . . ."

I laugh as I wave my hand like I'm shooing a fly. "Pffft, don't worry about it. This is the real me. Pretty scary without the hair

13

spray and makeup, huh?" I pat the guy on the shoulder. "Sorry to blow up your fantasy, dude."

The man looks down at the floor, his face matching his wife's. "You're still . . . naturally beautiful."

"Thank you."

The man looks up and shoots me a sheepish grin. "I'm, uh, a fan."

The woman rolls her eyes. "I think she got that part, Joe."

"Yeah, thanks to your big mouth." He turns back to me. "Nice to know you're a real person."

"Well, that's the first time I've ever been referred to in that manner. Though we do have quite a few plastic androids in the business, so I get it."

He looks in my cart and spots the formula. "Ah, you're taking care of an orphaned kitten."

"Four of 'em. Found them while doing a story yesterday."

"Wow. And you're taking care of all four?"

"Yep."

"Well, your stock just went up. Our cat was an orphan. They make the best pets. It's like they know you've saved them. You gonna keep all of them?"

"Just until I find homes for them in a few weeks."

The guy starts to laugh. "Yeah, right. Trust me, there'll be one that you just can't give away."

"Whoa, fright night."

I shrug as my best friend Rory stares at my disheveled hair, formula-covered t-shirt and sweatpants featuring cat hair, her hazel eyes wide in disbelief. "Yeah, I get that a lot lately."

The slender brunette moves forward and hugs me hard. "Freckles (her nickname for me), why didn't you call me yesterday when you broke up with Jeremy?" She pulls back and takes my face in her hands. "God, you look devastated. You're a wreck. Have you even slept?"

I usher her inside. "That's not why I'm wearing the Raggedy Ann summer collection and have designer bed-head."

"Wait, hold on. You're *not* upset about Jeremy?"

"Nope. Let me show you why." I lead Rory over to the box of kittens.

"Oh my God, they're adorable!" She kneels down to get a closer look. "And they're so little. Whoa, wait a minute. Why do you have all these kittens?"

I tell her the story, how they actually led to the breakup. "So, I sort of owe them for showing me the light about Jeremy."

"Well, I can't tell you—"

"Please, don't give me the *I told you so.* You warned me enough times about him. You were right."

"Maybe next time you'll listen to me when I tell you the guy you're dating is a selfish, superficial sonofabitch."

I nod as she sits on the couch. "I defer to your feminine radar in the future as mine obviously isn't in working condition."

Rory has always been spot-on about men since she became my best friend in high school and saved me from some bad decisions. (Though obviously I don't always listen to her.) She's a half foot shorter than me, about five-four, and has that girl-next-door thing going, fresh faced with never a spot of makeup. Couldn't care less about appearances. But she makes up for that with an incredible personality that attracts men like moths to a flame. And she's quite the wordsmith, working as an advertising copywriter out of her home across the street. It's like having a sister a hundred feet away.

I may as well tell you the story of how she saved my life.

Life began for me, at least the part I can confirm, in a New York City park restroom, where I was abandoned shortly after being born along with a note.

I am unable to take care of my child. Please find a good home for her.

My name comes from the two police officers who followed

the sound of a crying baby and found me. Two cops whose last names were Madison and Shaw brought me to social services, where I began the journey of being shuttled between six foster homes over the next eighteen years.

Some good, some not.

A few of my foster parents were decent people who actually wanted children. Others simply wanted the financial stipend the state provided in return for taking care of me.

That I could live with. The bullying in school I could not.

Children can be cruel, and so the taunting about being "unwanted" began at an early age. By the time I was sixteen, I was bitter and angry at the world.

Until Rory came into my life.

The most popular girl in school, head cheerleader, prom queen, co-valedictorian, saw a tall redhead wearing a death stare on a daily basis who ate alone with her head down in the school cafeteria. When she heard another student taunt me about being a foster kid, she came over during lunch, slid her tray onto my table and sat across from me.

"Hi, I'm Rory."

"Yeah, I know."

"You got a name?"

"Madison Shaw."

"Ah. I was getting tired of referring to you as the angry redhead in my class who's smarter than I am."

"Doubtful. I'm a straight C student."

"But you're smart as hell. You're never wrong when the teachers call on you. You come up with answers faster than I do. You figure out stuff in your head in math class before I can do it on paper."

"Is there something you want?"

"Nope. You just look like you could use a friend. Though I could use the competition for valedictorian. I don't wanna win because a smarter girl didn't give her best effort."

"Why do you care?"

"Like I said, I don't want to win by default. Unless you think you can't beat me." She locked eyes with me as she threw down the gauntlet.

"I could beat you if I wanted to."

"Prove it, Freckles. C'mon, let's rock."

"Why aren't you sitting at the table with all the cool kids?"

"I am sitting at the table with the cool kids. To me, brains are the coolest thing on the planet. And I suspect there's a decent human being behind that Great Wall of China you've put up." She shot me a look that went right to my soul, one that told me she was sincere. I can't explain it, but a wave of calm instantly washed over me.

And when the most popular girl in the school accepts you, the bullying stops. It's like being a made man in the Mafia. I also discovered that Rory's friends, who I assumed were the cool kids, were actually very normal as she had no tolerance for phonies. They accepted me with open arms as well.

We became inseparable, Rory taking me under her wing even though I towered over her. My grades shot up (we tied for the valedictorian thing) as she became the sister I'd never had. She set an example for me, using her popularity for good. Upon being crowned queen of the prom, she immediately took the thing off and placed it on the head of a girl in a wheelchair. She was the least pretentious person I'd ever met, when she could have easily been the queen bitch of the mean girls. A teenager with a forty year old brain, she taught me stuff about life that wasn't in any book.

Most important, my anger and bitterness slowly dissipated, replaced by a passionate desire to succeed and be more successful than anyone else. I dreamed about future high school reunions when I could show up and brag about having the best career and a spectacular life. About being so rich I could write million dollar checks to charities. I ate dinner at her house most nights, her mother and father becoming the parents I desperately needed.

The day I turned eighteen in the middle of my senior year Rory handed me a small gift-wrapped box. "Happy birthday, Freckles."

"Thank you. This is the only present I'll get."

"Well, then, I sure hope you like it."

I tore open the box. I furrowed my brow as I saw a simple key inside. "Okay, this is one of your clever treasure hunts. I suppose I have to find the lock this fits."

"It should be easy. The location is on the card in the box."

I pulled it out and saw Rory's address. "I don't understand."

"You're moving in with us. I want you out of that foster home and so do my parents. This is not up for discussion. As of today, you are living with me. So after school we are going to your house, pack up everything you own and get you the hell outta there."

I became a member of her family, the first one that felt real. Her parents treated me like their own daughter, grounded me with values I desperately needed. We shared a three bedroom housing unit in college, as our friend Tish became our other roommate.

But the qualities Rory had drawn out of me had slowly disappeared in the world of television news, a superficial industry that asks you to check your soul at the door.

And often doesn't give it back.

Thankfully, the kittens came into my life and reminded me where I came from.

I point to the kittens as she sits next to me. "So, you want one?"

"Sure, I could use a fur baby to keep me company. You're really gonna take care of them for a few weeks?"

"Yeah, but I'll need help when I get back to work next week. I was wondering . . . since you work at home if you could pop by during the day and feed them while I'm at work?"

"Sure, no problem."

"You have to clean them too. Y'know, encourage them to go to the bathroom. It's not exactly pleasant."

"Yeah, I had a friend with an orphaned kitten when I was a kid. Again, not a problem."

"The colorful one is really sweet."

"Oh, you mean the tortoiseshell."

"Is that what it's called?"

"Yeah. You've also got a tabby, a tuxedo cat and a Russian blue."

"That kitten is not blue, it's gray."

"That's what the breed is called."

"Oh. Well, anyway, I've got them covered all this week, so if you could start next Monday. It's just for a while, then I can find homes for all four."

"Something tells me you'll be finding homes for three of them."

"Rory, I can't have a cat. I'm gone too much."

"Cats are great pets for people like you. They're independent, take care of themselves. Self-cleaning. A lot like you. Though right now you're missing the self-cleaning part." She starts to laugh.

"What?"

"You know, this is a good look for you."

I point at my face. "Seriously? With hair that looks like I stuck my finger in a light socket, no makeup, clothes covered in formula and cat hair?"

Rory nods. "Yeah. The look of a girl who blew off a vacation in the Hamptons for a bunch of helpless kittens. You were the girl who never had a hair out of place, who wore hundred dollar jeans to a charity car wash, who put on makeup and heels to go to the grocery store. Today you look like the rest of us."

"You don't look sloppy and disheveled, Rory."

"I didn't mean that. While I have always loved you dearly since we met, your career has changed you . . . made you . . . well . . . obsessed with outward appearances and high maintenance. And

Jeremy made you more superficial. You used to be this cute freckle faced redhead who was comfortable in old jeans and a sweatshirt and the network tried to turn you into a smoking hot babe with the hair and the ridiculous makeup and expensive clothes. And now I can see a little change."

"I know, I look like a slob."

"Not in your clothes, in your eyes. There's a little something I haven't seen in a while that you always had before your job. What you did last night for those kittens . . . well, that's the real you. I mean, think about it. You get stuck with a litter of orphans, you're up all night, you break up with your boyfriend . . . and you're not remotely upset."

I cock my head at the kittens. "I guess I'd forgotten where I came from, and they reminded me."

"Well, good. Tell you what, we'll do our usual Sunday brunch here today. I'll call the girls. They don't even know you're in town."

I start to get up. "Okay. I'll go get cleaned up."

Rory grabs my hand and stops me. "No. I want them to see this."

Chapter Two

"Put. The cameras. Down."

The other two members of my tight circle of friends, Tish and A.J., lower their cell phones as Rory laughs. "Aw, c'mon," says Tish. "One for the scrapbook."

I put my hand in front of my face. "Yeah, right. You'd post it on social media and my boss would have a fit when it went viral."

Tish raises her hands, then slowly spreads them apart as she looks up at the ceiling. "I can see it now. Network info-babe revealed as frumpy cat lady. Film at eleven."

"Very funny. And I know A.J. would use it to blackmail me at some point in the future."

A.J. twirls a lock of her raven hair. "Well, I am Sicilian. But seriously, when will we ever have a chance to see you in this condition again?"

Rory nods. "Really. It's like spotting a unicorn."

I start to dish out some food onto my plate. "Oh, leave me alone. Can we just eat?"

Tish brushes her shoulder length blonde hair behind her ears. "Okay girls, we've tortured her enough."

I smile at her, our college roommate who is the smartest of our group and was top of her class in law school. She also has the coolest office I've ever seen, as she rents space in the Empire State Building. Alas, her courtroom shark persona and seriously high IQ are often intimidating to men. Tish is another of those girls who would be really pretty if she tried, with huge blue eyes she hides behind thick horn-rimmed glasses and a good five-foot-eight body she keeps under wraps. But she's all business and doesn't spend much time on appearances, relying on very conservative outfits and hairstyles for the courtroom. She only seems to let that hair down around us. When I need someone for pure logic, she's my first call. She's also an incredibly loyal friend and would drop whatever she was doing if any of us needed help.

She reaches for the pitcher of mimosas and starts to pour everyone a glass. "We do have another topic to discuss besides kittens and Madison's current aversion to soap."

I glare at her. "Bite me."

A.J. furrows her brow. "What topic is that?"

Tish locks eyes with me. "The little matter of Jeremy getting his exit visa. Which deserves a celebration, in my opinion." She holds up her glass. "Cheers!"

I roll my eyes. "I know, I know, you all didn't like him."

A.J. pops an olive in her mouth. "I wouldn't say that. I hated the sonofabitch and wanted to kick his ass."

"Fine, he's gone. Just be happy I didn't walk down the aisle with him."

Rory takes a bite of chicken. "You never would have exchanged vows. There would have been a chorus when the priest did that *speak now or forever hold your peace* thing."

"Right," says Tish. "You would have had to take a number."

A.J. shakes her head. "It wouldn't have gone that far. I would have had him whacked." It should be noted that while A.J. does not have family in the Mob (at least I don't think so), she is fond of using Sicilian stereotypes.

A.J. runs her family's delicatessen here on Staten Island, which is appropriate since she is obsessed with food. Though amazingly

22

while working in a place where she's surrounded by stuff loaded with calories, the petite woman never seems to gain an ounce. I met her as a customer and we immediately hit it off as I pointed at her nameplate and asked her what A.J. stood for. She refused to tell me so I asked her brother who also works there. Get this: Antoinette Josephine. Yikes. (You can see why she goes by A.J. as a spunky attitude doesn't go with a name like Antoinette or her Noo Yawk accent.) She of course threatened to have me whacked should I ever speak her real name in her presence. A.J. is a spunky little thing with zero tolerance for bull, both from her dates and customers. But if you want someone in a foxhole who will take no prisoners, she's your girl. Behind those dark eyes lies the soul of a gunslinger. But the heart is pure gold.

I take a sip of my mimosa as I consider her offer to wish Jeremy into the cornfield. "Very funny. But there's nothing to discuss."

"Sure there is," says Rory. "We've got that *bridesmaids dress from hell* wedding next weekend and now you need a *plus one*. Either that or spend the day dancing with the usher you're paired with."

The image makes me cringe. "Oh, crap. I forgot all about that. I'm not hanging out with the groom's fifteen year old nephew."

Tish smiles at me. "Hence, we must find you a *plus one*. Lest you do the *Bunny Hop* with a pubescent kid's hands on your ass."

I exhale in disgust. "Well, this will certainly be a quick rebound. I'm not wild about a blind date to a wedding, but considering the alternative I have no choice. So, who've you guys got?"

A.J. perks up. "My cousin Joey—"

"No!" Everyone shouts in unison.

Tish shakes her head. "Once and for all, please stop trying to fix up that particular relative. He's un-fix-up-able. We can do better."

A.J. folds her arms. "Fine, Miss legal eagle. Who are you bringin' to the table?"

"There's a guy who just rented the office next to mine. He seems nice."

"What's his name?"

"I don't know."

"What's he do?"

"Don't know that either."

"You wanna fix her up with someone and you don't even know his name or what he does?"

"He smiled at me when he moved in and said hello. And he's got a great ass."

A.J. rolls her eyes. "Gimme a break." She turns to Rory. "You got anyone?"

Rory taps her chin with one finger. "Well . . . there's this guy from a commercial production house I talk to on the phone a lot but I've never met him. He's funny and seems nice. And I know he's single."

"How old is he?" asks A.J.

"Don't know."

"What's he look like?"

"Don't know that either."

A.J. slowly nods. "So, let me get this straight . . . you guys shoot down my cousin and yet all you can come up with is a nameless guy with a great ass and a commercial producer who gives good phone but might be seventy years old, fat and bald."

Rory pulls out her tablet from her purse, taps it a few times. "Fine, let me go to his company website. Maybe there's a photo." She waits a beat, taps the screen a few more times, then smiles. "Ooooh, I think he'll do." She turns the tablet around so the rest of us can see.

My eyes widen a bit as I take in the photo of a hot, dark-haired guy who looks about thirty-five. "Uh . . . yeah."

"Fuhgeddaboudit. He's doable all right," cracks A.J.

Rory smiles as she turns back to her food. "Okay, I'll make the call."

I pat Rory on the shoulder. "Thanks." I start to eat but suddenly it hits me. "Uh-oh. We've got one more problem."

"What?" asks Tish.

"Since we're all going to the wedding, I need a sitter for the kittens. And speaking of *permanent* cat sitters—"

"I'll take a kitten," says Tish.

"Me too," says A.J. "Hell, with a deli downstairs, the thing will never starve."

The teenage girl's eyes bug out as I open the door wearing a bridesmaid's dress that was obviously designed during a power failure. "Wow, Miss Shaw. You must be a *really* good friend to someone to wear that."

"Kelly, remember this phrase when you start being included in bridal parties. *You'll be able to wear this dress again.* Biggest lie you'll ever hear." I usher her in to my home, giving her enough room to get by my ridiculously puffy sleeves that look like they're filled with helium and ready to explode. "I really appreciate you doing this."

"Hey, I love cats. And we actually had an orphaned kitten years ago. I know the routine." I point out all the cat supplies on the kitchen table. The tall, skinny seventeen year old brunette is the incredibly normal daughter of a neighbor who lives down the street, a teen who actually speaks instead of having her head buried in a cell phone. But she can't stop giggling as she looks at my outfit. "I'm sorry, I don't mean to be rude—"

"Oh, you should have heard me while I was putting on this monstrosity." The orange dress (ghastly color for a redhead, or any woman for that matter) is made of this incredibly itchy fabric with a tight waist that makes my ass look like I've had a Kardashian upgrade and an angled hemline that starts at the knee on the right and ends at the ankle on the left. With lovely matching ballet slippers. Then for some bizarre reason there's a circular thing sewn onto the waist that looks like the hand warmers football players wear during cold games. We're supposed to keep our hands in there as we go down the aisle. Why, I have no clue. (A.J. says it's to keep us from flipping the bird at the designer who is a friend of the bride and attending the wedding.) I'll get to wear it again if a pirate ever asks me to a retro seventies disco when it's ten below zero outside. Or if Macy's ever needs an orange float in the Thanksgiving Day parade.

"Well, people will be looking at the bride."

"Yeah, but they'll be laughing at the bridesmaids." I hear the car horn outside and know the girls are here to pick me up. "Okay, you've got my cell if you need anything."

"Don't worry, Miss Shaw, the kittens are in good hands."

I crack open the door, hoping none of the neighbors will see me but as luck would have it the weather is spectacular and everyone is outside on this beautiful Saturday afternoon. I quickly rush for the car. The guy who lives across the street spots me, starts to laugh, pulls out his cell phone and points it at me to take a photo.

I practically dive into the back seat before he has a chance.

Rory is behind the wheel with Tish riding shotgun while A.J. is next to me. "Drive! Now!"

Rory turns around. "What, you don't want the neighbors to see you dressed like the Sunkist blimp?"

"Just go!"

She turns back, puts the car in gear and drives off. "Count your blessings. At least you're not the only one wearing this."

"Yeah, but I'll be the only one with a photo that goes viral."

After a ceremony during which all the people in the church, including the priest, tried their best not to laugh during what is now referred to as "the procession of tangerines", we all make it to the reception, where thankfully there is an open bar. Of course the bartender can't help himself and starts laughing as I approach since this outfit just cries out for something sarcastic. He grabs the orange juice and vodka, quickly makes me a Screwdriver. "The perfect accessory for your . . . dress," he says, as he hands me the drink.

"Very funny." But at this point I just need alcohol, so I keep it. I feel a hand on my shoulder and turn around to find Rory with my blind date.

It's all I can do to keep my jaw from dropping, as the guy is even more handsome than his photo. About six-three, short dark hair, deep-set dark eyes, a classic anchorman's square jaw, and filling out an expensive dark gray suit like a model.

"Madison, this is Rob."

He extends his hand. "Great to meet you, Madison."

I shake it as I can't help but stare at this Greek god. "Uh, yeah, you too. Thanks so much for bailing me out today."

"My pleasure. I feel like I already know you since I watch your network. You look very different in person."

"I would imagine since we all just got here from the citrus queen pageant. The talent competition knocked me out."

He laughs. "I didn't mean the dress. You look more . . . real."

"Well, they do pile on the makeup at the network."

Rory lightly touches my arm. "I'll leave you two to get acquainted."

"Thanks again, Rory."

"Yes," says Rob. "Thank you." He gestures toward a table. "Shall we?"

It's very late and I'm slightly buzzed as Rob drives me home. Thankfully he has ignored my hideous outfit and we are really hitting it off. He's a fabulous dancer and a gentleman, with his hands not going anywhere they weren't supposed to be. Even during the Bunny Hop.

I can't help but think how much has changed in just a week all because I inherited a box of kittens. How much I've changed.

And how quickly I am putting Jeremy in the rear-view mirror to the point I can't even see him.

Pretty easy with a guy like Rob as my escort.

I point at my house as he turns onto my street. "I know it's late, but would you like a nightcap or some coffee?"

"Sure, that'd be great."

I look at my watch and see it's just after midnight. "Well, it's past twelve. I guess I didn't have to turn into a pumpkin since I already look like one."

He laughs as he pulls into my driveway. "So, you ever gonna wear that thing again?"

"If I'm the grand marshal of a Halloween parade. The minute we get inside I'm getting out of this dress." He gets out of the car, walks around to my side and opens the door for me. "Thank you, kind sir." I lead him to the front door just as Kelly opens it.

Her eyes widen as she checks out my date. "Did you have a good time?"

"Yeah. Rob, this is Kelly. She lives down the street and was my sitter tonight. So, were the little guys okay?"

"I was just about to feed them again."

"I'll take care of it, Kelly."

Rob's face immediately tightens and he puts up his hands. "Whoa, you never said you had kids."

"I don't. C'mon in, I'll show you." I quickly pay Kelly and thank her. She leaves and I lead Rob over to the box of kittens, beaming like a proud parent. "Aren't they cute?"

"You hired a babysitter for a litter of kittens?"

"They're orphans. The mother cat died. So they have to be bottle fed every few hours."

"You're kidding."

"Nope." The tortoiseshell starts meowing, so I pick it up. "This one's my favorite. Feel how incredibly soft the fur is."

He actually backs up a step and puts up his hands again. "Uh, that's okay."

"What, you don't like cats?"

"Not a big animal lover. They're as needy as children."

Oh, shit. Is he another Jeremy?

I hold the kitten out toward him. "C'mon, he won't bite."

The kitten looks at him and hisses.

Well, so much for that. I pull the kitten back. "Tell you what, Rob, I'll let you feed one and maybe you'll change your mind."

He wrinkles his nose. "Can't you do that later?"

"No, they're hungry now. They're on a feeding schedule. It won't take long. Half as long if you help me."

"I thought when you said you wanted to get out of that dress . . . well, you know . . ." He gives me a seductive look.

"I meant I was gonna change into something normal."

He moves forward and takes my shoulders. "Well, regardless of what you meant—"

Anndddd . . . cue the red flag. "No. For God's sake, Rob, we just met."

The kitten lets out a guttural growl.

I back away. "Rob, just so we're clear, I invited you in so we could have a drink and talk some more."

"I think we had enough conversation at the wedding. Look, Madison, we're both adults—"

"Apparently one of us isn't. Get. Out." (I'm getting good at this, huh?)

"Seriously?"

I point at the door.

He glares at me, shakes his head, says nothing, turns around and leaves.

Just like that.

The phone immediately rings. Rory. I answer the call as I move to the window and pull back the drapes to see her looking at me from across the street. "What?"

"I've heard of a quickie but that's ridiculous. What happened?"

"He hates cats and kids and is apparently as selfish as Jeremy.

When I said I wanted to get out of this dress he thought that meant I wasn't going to put on something else."

"Oh. Geez, I thought he was a decent guy. Sorry about that."

"Hey, you couldn't know. At least I had fun at the wedding."

"How are the fur babies?"

"Fine. Oh, get this, the tortoiseshell hissed and growled at him."

"Hmmm. Very perceptive cat. And protective of you."

"That's twice the little guys have saved me."

"They're just repaying you, Freckles."

"I guess. Well, it's feeding time, so I have to go." We say our goodbyes and I set about filling up the bottles with formula, then start feeding the tortoiseshell. "Thanks again, kitty."

Chapter Three

It's my first day back at work and I cannot wait to get home. The live shot kept me at my job longer than normal, and I'm already imposing on Rory enough asking her to take care of the kittens during the day. But what surprises me is how much I missed my fur babies, especially the tortoiseshell. That kitten has a ton of personality. (I called Rory four times today to check on them, and she called me a helicopter cat parent.) Anyway, I'm speeding through the neighborhood. I slow down for a stop sign and take a quick look in both directions before rolling through it. I'll see the kittens in a minute.

The flashing lights and the short blast of a siren breaks my train of thought. I look in the rear-view mirror and see the police car right behind me. "Oh, hell. Not now." I pull into my driveway as the cop stops in front of my house. I open the door and hear the voice over the loudspeaker.

"Please remain in the car."

I roll my eyes and get back in, reminding myself to be polite and keep my hands in plain sight, then roll down the window as I see the officer approaching in the side mirror. I look up as he reaches the car, not really able to see his face as he's backlit by the streetlight and is just a silhouette. "Sorry, officer, I was getting out of the car because I actually live here."

"How convenient. License and registration please."

I pull the license from my purse and registration from the glove compartment, then hand them to the cop. He shines a flashlight at them. "Huh, you really do live here."

"I'd have to be kinda stupid to lie to a cop."

He laughs. "Happens ten times every day, Miss."

Okay, have to try my best to get out of this. I put on my innocent little girl face (referred to by my friends as my Strawberry Shortcake look), dipping my head and looking up at him through my eyelashes. "So, did I do something wrong, officer?"

"You were well over the speed limit and you blew through a stop sign. What's your hurry?"

"Trying to get home to take care of four orphaned kittens. My best friend has been stuck at the house bottle feeding them."

He shakes his head. "Well, that's a new one on me. Speeding to take care of cats."

"I'm not kidding."

"Seriously, Miss . . ." he looks at the license again. ". . . Shaw, you couldn't come up with something better than that?" He pulls out a ticket book and clicks his pen.

"Well, since we're at my house, why don't you come in and take a look? And if I'm lying you can write me the biggest, most expensive ticket you can think of. But if I'm not, maybe you'll cut me some slack."

"Fair enough. Can't wait to see this." He opens the door for me and I get out. Still can't see his face. "Oh, you're the TV reporter."

"Yeah."

"Thought the name sounded familiar. Anyway, let's see exhibit A."

I lead him up the stairs and into my home. Rory is on the couch, busy bottle feeding one of the kittens. "Rory, thank you so much. So sorry I'm late."

Rory looks up and sees the cop behind me. "What'd you do, get a police escort?"

"No, my lead foot got me in trouble." I turn to face the cop and get a good look at his face for the first time.

Damn.

The guy is beyond cute. Tall, mid-thirties, maybe six-one, thick black hair and olive green eyes. A face with a five o'clock shadow that's all angles and planes. A uniform that shows off a lean, muscled physique. His Italian features confirmed by his name plate. *Officer N. Marino.*

He looks right past me at the kittens. "Well, I'll be damned. You really were racing home for a bunch of orphans."

I fold my arms and flash a big smile. "And the defense rests."

"Point taken. Sorry I doubted you." He crouches down next to the box. "Where'd you get them?"

I tell him the story. "So, anyway, they're not ready to adopt out yet and Rory takes care of them while I'm at work."

He nods as he gently strokes the head of a kitten, which rewards him with a purr. "Very nice of you both." He stands up and puts his ticket book back in his pocket. "Well, since you win the monthly award for the most ridiculous but honest excuse given to a cop and you're doing a good deed, I'll let you off with a warning."

"Thank you, Officer. I'll drive safely in the future." Another dose of Strawberry Shortcake.

He locks eyes with me, sending a bit of electricity through my body as he extends his hand. "Nick Marino."

I shake hands. "Madison Shaw. And this is my best friend, Rory Callahan."

"Nice to meet you both."

He doesn't look at Rory but keeps his gaze on me, adding a soft smile. Finally he lets go of my hand.

Rory finishes feeding the kitten, burps it, puts it back in the box and stands up. "Well, they're all fed. I'll get going." She grabs my forearm as she leans over to whisper in my ear. "Very cute cop. And he already has his own handcuffs."

"Rory!" I begin to blush as the officer looks down and laughs. Apparently her whisper carried a bit.

Rory heads for the door. "Anyway, thanks, Officer Marino, for giving my friend a break."

"My pleasure," he says, as she leaves and closes the door behind her.

I shake my head as I roll my eyes. "You'll have to excuse her. She has a dirty mind."

He flashes a devilish grin. "Fortunately, that's not breaking any laws. If it were I'd have to arrest the whole city."

"Would you like some coffee, Officer? It'll just take a minute."

"Thank you, but I've already had my break and I need to get back on patrol."

Damn. "Cold soda for the road?"

"Sure."

I head into the kitchen and open the fridge. "Cream or root beer?"

"Cream."

I pulled out a can and hand it to him. "Here ya go."

"Oooh, Doctor Brown's. The young lady has the good stuff."

"Only the best for New York's finest."

"Thanks, Miss Shaw."

"Madison."

"Right, Madison." He starts to head for the door and I follow. He turns to face me, then shakes his finger at me like a teacher. "Now remember, young lady, no more speeding or running stop signs. Who would take care of those kittens if you got into an accident?"

I playfully put out my lower lip in a pout. "Yes, Officer. I promise to be a good girl. You won't have to pull me over again." *Though I wouldn't mind.*

He reaches into his pocket and hands me a card. "Here's my card if you ever need anything."

"Such as?"

He shrugs. "You know. Ne'er-do-wells harassing you. Jars you can't open. Cat up a tree."

"I thought that last thing was the fire department's jurisdiction."

"Normally it is, but I'm a cat whisperer. I can talk one down if necessary."

"Good to know. And now that you mention it, I do often have a problem with opening jars."

"I'm a Jedi Master at that. Seriously, it's a really nice thing you're doing for those kittens."

"Thanks. At first I thought it would be a burden, but now I really miss the little guys when I'm at work. Hence the lead foot."

"Well, I know they appreciate the care you're giving them. Cats are very perceptive creatures. They can sense when someone has a good heart. Anyway, gotta go and thanks for the soda."

"Thanks for cutting me a break, Officer."

"Nick."

"Right. Nick."

"Well, have a good night."

"Be careful out there."

He gives me an old fashioned tip of the hat, then heads out the door. I watch him get into his patrol car, see him shoot me a little smile before he drives away.

Rory is right.

Very cute cop.

And a cat person.

The phone rings the second I close the front door. Rory. Who was no doubt spying on me from her house again. I pull back the drapes and see my best friend through the window as I answer the call. "What?"

"Well?"

"Well, what?"

"Extremely hot cop alert. You could get your own personal

Magic Mike sequel going with that one. I detected some definite chemistry."

"Your radar is spot on. He gave me his card and told me to call if I needed anything. Like someone to open jars. Real cute."

"Ah, he's interested."

"So why didn't he ask me out?"

"He couldn't. Yet."

"I don't understand."

"He just let you out of a ticket and it would look like he traded a date with you for that. Either that or he probably figured a girl on national television already has someone."

"Yeah, I guess that makes sense."

"But trust me, he will. I saw that look he had."

"He doesn't have my phone number."

"He knows where you live, sweetie. And he's a cop, he could easily look it up."

"True."

"And you have his number. If I were you, I'd start lining up those jars you can't open."

I've just about made it through my first week at work but I've been doing something I've never done during my entire career.

Watching the clock.

Generally reporters don't have time to do that since our days are so busy, but now I look forward to getting home and seeing my furry friends.

It's four-thirty and thankfully I don't have a live shot tonight so I'll be home at a decent hour unless some breaking news keeps me here. Politicians are famous for their Friday afternoon document dumps, so I'm hoping that isn't the case today. Besides, I'm clandestinely working on finding the smoking gun on a United States Senator who the CEO refers to as "Madison's white whale." I keep my research under the radar since I have been told in no uncertain terms to back off. I've always wondered if the Senator has photos of the CEO naked with a goat because everyone in the news business knows the guy is the poster child for dirty politicians. But I'm handcuffed since corporate won't let me expend the time or newsroom resources digging up dirt on the guy. The other reason is that countless reporters have tried to go full Ahab on the guy over the years and come up empty. The Senator is really smart and has the unlimited resources to cover his tracks.

Or make them go away. Which is the scary part.

When I see my boss heading in my direction, I quickly shove my notes in a drawer and smile at him.

Barry Post, my short, bald forty year old News Director, arrives at my desk and leans his bulky frame on the edge. "Your story in the can already?"

Dammit, a document dump. He needs a reporter to go out on something. "Yeah. Why?"

He's wearing a bit of a smile. "Need to run something by you in my office." He cocks his head in that direction and gets up, so I follow him. Barry closes the door behind me as I take a seat in front of his desk. "I just got some bad news."

"What, you sick or something?"

"No, I'm fine. It's Fred."

Our senior political reporter who covers the President's re-election campaign. "What happened?"

"He fell down the stairs getting off Air Force One and broke his ankle. Compound fracture. You know, the kind where the bone sticks through—"

"Yeah, I get it. Ugh." My face tightens as I try not to picture the accident. "Poor guy."

"Anyway, he'll be laid up for several months, and I need someone to fill in for him. Madison, I know this has always been your dream assignment."

My eyes widen as I can't help but smile. "Seriously? You want me to—"

"Yeah. Cover the President's campaign till Fred's back on his feet. Of course that means being on the road for weeks at a time."

Suddenly it hits me.

The kittens.

My face drops a bit and he notices. "I thought you'd be doing cartwheels, Madison."

"I, uh . . . well, I have some personal obligations. I would, uh, have to make some arrangements."

"Something with your family? Everyone okay?"

Hell, I can't tell the guy I might blow off the plum assignment of a career to take care of a bunch of kittens. "Yeah, it's . . . well, it's personal."

"I hope *you're* okay, Madison."

"Yeah, I'm fine. Listen, Barry, can I let you know on Monday?"

"Sure. But I can't wait any longer. I need a yes or no first thing Monday morning, and if it's a no I have to give the assignment to Jennifer."

He just made the decision even harder.

Chapter Four

It's Friday night and I'm waiting for Kelly so I can go out and have a drink with my friends.

I need their input on this very difficult decision I have to make. Actually, the most difficult career decision I've ever made.

The doorbell rings as I'm staring at the ball of fur asleep in the box. When I get up and open the door I don't find my cat sitter, but my next door neighbor the veterinarian. "Hi Jeff, I didn't know you were back. How was your vacation?"

"Wonderful. How was the Hamptons? I hear it's spectacular."

"Didn't go. Long story. I don't wanna tell it and trust me, you don't wanna hear it."

"Oh. Anyway, I just got back and I thought I'd see where the kittens ended up. So, since you didn't take them with you on your trip did you find a shelter to take them?"

"Nope. They're still here. I never bothered to look for a shelter. C'mon in and check 'em out."

He moves inside, crouches down next to the box and starts to examine the kittens. "They look very well fed. And clean. You're doing a really good job with them. I'm impressed. If you ever want a job as my assistant, let me know."

"I cannot take all the credit. Rory runs kitten day care for me while I'm at work."

"Now that's a true friend." He reaches into the box and pulls out a kitten. "Let me give them a quick check. This one looks good." He picks up each one and nods. "They look fine, Madison. Bring 'em by the clinic next week and I'll give them a thorough exam. No charge."

"That would be nice. Thank you."

He stands up and smiles. "I must say, I never expected this from you."

"I never expected this from me either. But I got attached to them really quick."

"And they can get attached to you. When you get kittens that young, they can imprint on you."

"Huh?"

"Imprinting. That means they think you're their mother."

I stir my drink, not really looking at it but deep in thought.

Presidential campaign.

Leaving kittens who think I'm their mother. Would it break their little hearts?

Don't answer that.

"Earth to Madison . . ."

I look up and see my three friends staring at me. "I'm sorry. I've never been in a position where I have absolutely no idea what to do. It's the assignment every reporter dreams about, and it should be a no-brainer. But . . . damn, I just don't know."

Rory reaches over and pats my hand. "Whatever you decide, we'll support you. You know that."

A.J. sips her drink. "You leanin' one way or the other?"

"It changes every five minutes. Of course it doesn't help that if I turn it down the queen bitch of the newsroom will get the assignment. And she would find a way to rub it in my face every day till the election."

"Don't even take that into consideration," says Tish. "I know you, and I know you want someone else to make this decision for you. That ain't happenin'. This one you've got to figure out for yourself."

"I know. At least I've got till Monday morning. Dammit! Why does this have to happen now?"

"Because sometimes life gets in the way of our plans." Like I said, Tish is the most logical. "Perfect timing is a rare thing."

A waiter interrupts the conversation as he slides a drink in front of me. "From the man at the end of the bar, near the door."

I look up and see a short, bald guy with a goatee in a leather jacket and a spider web tattoo on his neck. Totally out of place in a classy bar like this one. He shoots me a smile while chewing on a toothpick. Not remotely my type. I shake my head. "Not now." I hand the drink back to the waiter. "Tell him thank you but I have a boyfriend."

"Sure thing." He heads back to the bar as I turn to my friends. "Didn't need the kittens to eliminate that one."

Rory laughs. "A man is the last thing you need tonight. Neither is a ride on a Harley."

"I dunno," says A.J. "It might clear her head."

"The man or a ride?"

"Both, with or without the motorcycle."

Just as she says that, the drink reappears in front of me, hand delivered by the guy. "I bought you a drink, least you could do is take it."

I look up at him and lean back since the guy smells like an ashtray. "Look, I'm not available, so send it to some other girl."

"C'mon, Red, lighten up."

"I *said* I'm not interested." I slide the drink away without looking at him.

A.J. glares at the guy and turns on the accent. "Get lawst, buddy."

"Hey, I wasn't talkin' to you."

"I'm counting my blessings."

I feel his hand on my shoulder and whip my head toward him. "Get your hands off me."

And then I see another hand grab the guy's shirt collar and pull him away.

Officer Marino.

"You're bothering these young ladies," he says, now holding the guy's arm behind his back. The cop is not in uniform, but dressed head to toe in black. "Did you not hear her say she wasn't interested?"

The guy winces. "I was just talkin' to her."

"Bull. I heard the woman ask you to leave her alone." He turns to me. "Do you want to have a drink with this guy?"

"Hell no."

He looks at my friends. "Do any of you want a drink with this guy?"

"No!" A chorus from the girls.

The cop turns back to him. "Now, here's a life skill for you to learn that applies to women. No means no. What part of *no* do you not understand, the N or the O?"

I can't help but laugh at the line.

"Now apologize to the young ladies."

"Sorry."

"That didn't sound terribly sincere."

"I'm sorry I bothered you."

"Good. Now we're gonna take a little walk outside and I'm going to give you directions to the dive across town where I'm sure you'll fit right in." The cop turns and shoves the guy toward the door, following him out.

"Cute bouncer," says A.J., watching him the whole way.

Rory smiles. "He's a cop."

Tish turns to her. "What, you know the guy?"

She nods and points at me. "The other night he pulled Freckles over in front of her house 'cause she was speeding to get home

42

to the kittens but he didn't believe her story. So she invited him in to prove her case and he let her off with a warning after he saw the kittens. Of course, she gave him the Strawberry Shortcake look."

Tish rolls her eyes. "Her trump card."

"Hey, give me a break," I say, stealing a quick look at the door. He still hasn't returned. "He's really nice."

"Damn, a hot cop," says A.J. "So invite him over to play *stop and frisk*. I'd jump on that if I were you."

"You'd jump on anything," says Rory.

A.J. waves her hand like she's shooing a fly. "Pffft."

"Anyway," says Rory, "they had this big eye contact thing going and when he left he gave her his card, told her to call him if she needed anything. He's definitely interested."

I hear the door open and see Officer Marino come back inside and head toward our table. I slide my chair over to make room for him. "Thank you, kind sir. Appreciate the rescue from, as you put it, one of those ne'er-do-wells harassing me."

"Not a problem."

I pull an empty chair over from the next table and pat the seat. "Please, join us. I'm buying."

"Sorry, I'm working. Hope that guy didn't ruin your evening."

"Thanks to you he didn't." I hear one of my friends clear her throat. "Oh, I'm being rude. Officer Marino, you already know Rory. That's Tish and A.J."

He nods at them. "Pleasure. We'll if you guys are okay, I'd better get back to my duties."

"So, you moonlight here?"

"Yeah, pick up some extra bucks. Saving up for a house. Well, see you around the neighborhood."

"Sure. Thanks again."

He starts to leave, then stops and turns back to me. "Oh, by the way, how are the kittens?"

"They're doing fine. Fat and happy."

He gives me a smile. "Good. Most people would have just dumped them at a shelter. It's great that you didn't abandon those little guys."

Annddd . . . cue the guilt.

He heads back toward the bar while I turn back to my friends.

Rory locks eyes with me. "So . . . that clear things up a bit for ya?"

Kelly looks up from her textbook as I get home. "Have a nice time?"

"Yeah. Any problems?"

"Nope. They're fed and cleaned up. All asleep but one."

Suddenly I pick up the pace toward the box. "Something wrong?"

Kelly smiles. "Nah. I think your favorite is waiting up for you."

I look at the box and see three kittens curled up together in a ball while the tortoiseshell sits in front of them. It starts to meow the moment it sees me and paws at the air, wanting to be picked up. "You okay, little guy?" I crouch down and pick up the kitten, resting it on my chest. It keeps talking, then begins to purr.

"I think he just missed you. He's quiet when you're not here."

"He does demand more attention than the others."

"I don't think that's it. He's not that way with me. I think the tortoiseshell is a one-person cat, and you're his person."

I'm on my third cup of coffee at my usual corner table in A.J.'s family deli. The Saturday morning rush finally ends and she moves out from behind the counter to join me, sliding an Italian pastry in front of me as she sits with her own cup of java. "You get any sleep last night?"

I shake my head. "Hell no. Couldn't stop thinking about my big decision. Kittens versus Air Force One."

"So the wheels are still spinnin'?"

"Yeah."

"What direction are they going?"

"Can we talk about something else?"

"Okay. What's the story on the hot cop?"

"Rory already told you."

"So, you gonna call him?"

"Huh?"

"I thought he gave you his card?"

"Yeah." I reach in my purse and hand it to her.

She looks at it and rolls her eyes. "Marino. It figures."

"What?"

"You guys get all the good *paisans*."

"What do you mean, *you guys*?"

"You Irish girls. Italian men can't resist you. They see the red hair and the freckles and it's game over for the rest of us. You're like their damn kryptonite."

"Oh, stop it. You have men beating down your door."

"All named Smith and Jones. I can't ever find a good guy with a vowel at the end of his last name. So, you gonna call this cop, or what? You obviously like him."

"You know I don't call men."

"Oh, I'm sorry. Did we miss the Sadie Hawkins dance? For God's sake, it's not nineteen-fifty. You can ask a guy out."

"I wouldn't even know how to do that."

"You pick up the phone and say, *Hey, I think you're smoking hot and wanna jump your bones*."

"Very funny. Seriously, I've never asked a guy out for a date. I'm not sure I could do it. It's a little scary for me."

"Let me get this straight. You're a network reporter, you take no prisoners with major politicians, you go on live television in front of millions of people, and you're afraid to pick up the phone and call a guy?"

"The microphone and camera give me license to do all those things on TV. Without it . . . well . . . it's just me."

"Okay, so here's what you do. Use a back door method of getting a date. You call the guy and tell him you want to thank him for saving you at the bar by cooking him dinner."

"That might chase him away. You know I can burn a salad."

"I'll give you some simple recipes. Or how about this . . . I can simply box up some cannolis and you can drop by the police station to thank him personally. The precinct is right down the street from your house."

I shake my head not wanting to deal with this right now. "I'll think about it."

"Yeah, right. Coward." She starts clucking like a chicken.

I shove the pastry in my mouth, take a big bite and talk through the crumbs. "Leave me alone."

"Of course, if you take the Air Force One thing, you can't ask him out. He thinks a lot of you because you're taking care of those kittens. How would it look if you ditched them?"

"I think *ditched* is a rather strong term."

"You like *abandoned* better?"

"I don't believe this is happening. I'm considering turning down the dream job of a lifetime because of a bunch of cats and a guy who *might* like me. And I'm actually conflicted about it."

She flashes a big smile. "Yep. And I must tell you, this is fun to watch."

"I'm glad you find my current situation so amusing."

The bell above the door rings announcing a customer. A little blonde girl carrying a bunch of papers who is trailed by her mother moves toward our table. "Excuse me . . . I need some help."

A.J. turns to the girl, who is maybe eight years old. "What can I do for you, sweetie?"

She hands each of us a sheet of paper. "Would it be okay if I put this in your window?"

What's on the paper tugs at my heart.

46

LOST CAT

Our beloved cat, Snowflake, got out of the house and is missing. She's an indoor cat and not used to taking care of herself. She's all white with one blue eye and one green eye, is wearing a red collar and answers to her name. She is very friendly. If you see her please call.

Below that is a photo of the girl hugging the cat.

A.J. smiles at her. "Sure, honey, put it right on the front door."

"Thank you."

The mom thanks A.J. as the girl moves to the glass door and tapes the flyer on the inside. I can't stop looking at the picture. "Poor kid, lost her pet."

"Poor cat," says A.J. "Not sure how long an indoor cat can survive outside."

"Hopefully one of your customers will see her."

As previously mentioned Tish is my most logical friend and the one whose advice I seek when I'm stuck. (Though I didn't take it regarding Jeremy.) We're both dateless tonight while A.J. and Rory are out, so we're sharing a bottle of wine and binge watching *Justified* on Netflix. Watching Timothy Olyphant waste a bunch of dumb rednecks is an enjoyable pastime of ours. (Okay, even if he didn't shoot anyone we'd watch. *Mea culpa.*)

A soft meow makes me hit the pause button as I see the kittens are up, with their spokesman the tortoiseshell announcing the arrival of feeding time. I look at the clock and see they're right on schedule. "I think they can tell time."

Tish laughs. "Their stomachs can. You want help?"

"Sure." I bring the box into the kitchen and prepare the bottles as Tish takes a seat. "Honestly, I don't know how people with babies do this for a couple of years. This is wearing me out. I have new respect for working moms. And moms in general."

"Well, this is a good experience if you ever become a real mom, though that is a helluva lot harder. I remember helping my mom take care of my little sister." She picks up a kitten and starts to stroke its fur. "Speaking of which, did you ever talk about having children with Jeremy?"

"Why are you bringing up he-who-must-not-be-named?"

"Just curious. Since your date at the wedding made it clear he didn't like kids. I was just wondering since you were talking about marrying the guy. It's an obvious subject for a couple to discuss."

"Now that I think about it, Jeremy never really talked about it much. Then again neither did I. Our careers were pretty much dominating our lives." I hand her a bottle while I sit and grab the tortoiseshell. Tish starts feeding her kitten while I do the same.

"And now?"

"You're starting, aren't you?"

"What?"

"Doing your lawyer thing where you ask a question when you already know the answer. I know all your tricks."

"So you admit you've changed."

"What, am I on the witness stand here? Stop cross-examining me. But yes, I've changed."

"Isn't it true that despite the lack of sleep you are enjoying taking care of these kittens?"

I don't respond and look away.

"The witness is directed to answer the question. And may I remind her that she's under oath."

I shake my head and look back at her. "Fine. I like having them depend on me. And the way this one looks right into my heart . . ."

The kitten meows. I swear the furry little thing understands English.

Tish laughs. "I think we've just heard from the jury. You have been found guilty of caring."

48

"So, you ever gonna give me your opinion on what I should do?"

"Asked and answered last night."

"C'mon, Tish. I need help here."

"Okay, fine. Sidebar. Let me ask you this. What's the best story you ever did as a reporter?"

"That's easy. The series I did on the veterans' facility on Long Island that was run down."

"Why do you consider that one your best?"

"Because it changed lives. The government got embarrassed and fixed the place up, the vets got the care they needed and the people who were embezzling funds are still in jail. And I felt really good after all that happened knowing I was responsible. I still have all the letters from veterans thanking me."

"So, basically, would you agree that as a reporter the most important stories you do are the ones that make the world a better place?"

"Right. And I had to do a lot of old school journalism on that one. A ton of legwork and digging. I like investigative stuff. It's like putting a really difficult puzzle together and you're missing some pieces, but you can find them if you work hard."

"And if you follow the President around on his campaign for a few months, will that take any investigative work?"

"Probably not. You're part of a pool of reporters and just report what he does, get the best sound bites and do nightly live shots. I would ask strong questions, but the guy is a master at filibustering so you never get a straight answer. The odds of getting anything but his memorized talking points are slim."

"Will your work on that assignment make the world a better place?"

I don't answer as I look at the kitten.

"And will it make *you* a better person?"

I look up at her, my eyes a little wet. "I can see why you rarely lose a case." I finish feeding the kitten, burp it, then pick up another

49

one. "Tish, you know the worst thing about this decision?"

"No. What?"

"No matter what I choose, I'm going to feel bad about it. And always wonder if I did the right thing."

"Something tells me you won't."

I finally get up around ten on Sunday morning, feeling like crap after too much wine and too little sleep. The middle of the night kitten feedings are catching up with me, but that will be over soon when they can feed themselves.

And of course, I still haven't resolved my big dilemma.

A.J. made it worse throwing the cop into the mix.

Tish hit me with logic like a damn Vulcan on Star Trek.

Rory? She just gives me a look that tells me which way I should go.

A few weeks ago my life was simple. Decisions were easy. Black and white.

Now I've added gray and tortoiseshell and stripes into the equation.

I stagger into the kitchen to prepare the bottles for the kittens when I see something that makes me wide awake.

The box of kittens is empty.

They're gone!

"What the hell?"

My eyes widen as try to replay the events of the evening. I fed them at two in the morning and put them back in the box.

Didn't I?

A loud meow distracts me and I whip my head toward the noise.

And see the tortoiseshell halfway up the dining room curtains. "Oh, for God's sake. There you are. Where are your friends?"

The doorbell rings as the tortoiseshell continues talking, as if to say, "Hey, look at me, I can climb!" I head to the door, shuffling my feet so as not to step on a kitten along the way.

It's Rory, carrying a grocery bag of food for Sunday brunch. "Watch where you walk!"

She studies my face. "Huh?"

"The kittens got out of the box and I don't know where they are." The tortoiseshell meows and I cock my head in his direction. "Well, I know where one is."

"Oooh, I love what you've done with the curtains." Rory comes in and we start looking for the kittens. She finds one under the couch while the other two are busy playing on a chair with a hair scrunchy.

The tortoiseshell protests as I pull him off the curtains. "Okay, I need a bigger cardboard box."

Rory rolls her eyes as she holds two of the kittens. "Uh, you do know that cats can climb trees, right?"

"What's that got to do with anything?"

"They'll just climb out of a bigger box. They have claws."

"Oh, right."

"They're obviously bored and tired of being cooped up. They want to play and explore. Cats have that curiosity thing hardwired into them. You're gonna have to let them out."

"Well I can't have them running around the house getting underfoot. I might accidentally step on one. And I can't have them climbing up the curtains."

"Put 'em in that spare room. All you've got in there is exercise equipment. It's a warm, sunny room and they can run around and play. But make a bed for them so they can snuggle."

"So now the kittens are getting their own room."

Rory nods and shoots me a smile. "They're like the camel asking to stick its nose under the tent. Pretty soon you'll be asking *them* for space."

Chapter Five

Befitting my mood, it's raining heavily as I drive home on Monday evening.

Below the speed limit. (Not a good thing to do in New York if you don't want the bird flipped at you.)

My emotional roller coaster has sucked the life out of me. And my lead foot. I've become like those zombies I see in Grand Central about to go home on the train, one of the commuting undead.

The moment I gave my boss my decision, I began to second guess myself.

Back and forth all day.

I did the right thing.

Or did I?

I pull into my driveway and trudge up the steps, head down. Inside I find Rory working on her laptop. She looks up and studies my face. "Uh-oh. I know that look."

I shake my head as I attempt to hang up my raincoat, but I miss the hook and it falls to the floor.

I roll my eyes and leave it there.

She gets up and moves toward me. "Well? What did you decide?" She grabs my raincoat off the floor and hangs it up.

"I'm not on Air Force One, am I?"

She flashes a wide smile, then gives me a hug. "I'm proud of you."

"Are you still proud of me if I tell you I've been wondering if I made the wrong decision all day?"

She breaks the embrace and leans back. "Yep. You can replay it all you want. Bottom line, you did the right thing. Freckles, you've got nothing to prove. You've already reached the top of the food chain in your career. Covering the guy in the White House for several months cannot be that appealing."

"I guess. Y'know, funny thing I discovered about my chosen profession today that I never noticed before. People will eat their young for a promotion. Right after I told my boss I was turning down the assignment he threw it open to anyone who wanted to toss his hat in the ring."

"I thought he was gonna give it to that woman you hate?"

"Perhaps the higher-ups realized she's a brainless bimbo. Anyway, you should have heard my cohorts bad-mouthing one another all day, trying to get the assignment."

"So who got it?"

"They hadn't decided when I left."

"Ah, so you're thinking it's not too late to change your mind."

"Actually, I'm not. I'm thinking that the people in the news business need souls."

"Well, you're okay in that department, Freckles. Yours is beautiful."

A loud meow from behind distracts me. "Aren't the kittens in the spare room?"

Rory looks past me and points. "That's not one of your kittens."

I turn and see a soaking wet cat in the window, shivering and crying. "Awww. Poor thing got stuck in the rain." I move to the window and open it. The cat dashes in and immediately shakes, sending a spray of water everywhere. But it's still shivering. I grab a towel from the bathroom and kneel down to begin drying it off. "Talk about a drowned rat. Okay, kitty, you can stay here till the rain stops."

And then it hits me.

White cat with one blue eye and one green eye.

And a red collar.

"Rory, I know this cat!"

"Huh?"

"She's been lost. Belongs to a little girl I met at A.J.'s deli." I quickly run to the kitchen and grab the flyer I'd put on the bulletin board, then head back to the living room and hand it to Rory, who has taken over cat drying duties. "Her name is Snowflake."

The cat meows and looks up at me when I say her name.

Rory looks at the flyer. "Well, one little girl is gonna be real happy."

I grab my phone and call the number on the flyer. It goes to voicemail so I leave a message. "Nobody's home."

"The cat is probably hungry."

"I don't have any adult cat food. I've got a can of salmon. Think she'd eat that?"

"Geez, Freckles, I dunno if cats like fish."

Palm slap. "Duh."

Three hours later Snowflake is dry and curled up at my feet as the doorbell rings. I answer the door and find the little girl and her parents wearing big smiles. The girl yells "Snowflake!" and runs past me. The cat immediately perks up, runs to the girl and jumps in her arms, then starts licking her. The girl hugs her tight.

I feel my eyes well up a bit as I usher her parents inside.

"Thank you so much," says her mother, the spitting image of her daughter. "By the way, I'm Joanne and he's Jonathan. My daughter has been devastated since the cat went missing. How did you find her?"

"I saw her in the window when it was raining, so I brought

54

her in. Then I realized she was the lost cat on the flyer. I was in the deli when you guys came by."

"Really nice of you," says her dad, a tall, sandy-haired man around thirty who looks like a young Robert Redford. He smiles as he watches the girl and the cat.

"Looks like your daughter and Snowflake have a special bond."

The guy turns back to me. "Oh, I'm not her dad. I'm her uncle. Joanne's brother."

The woman drops her voice a bit. "My ex is out of the picture."

"Oh, sorry."

"Don't be. Samantha and I are doing fine. And Jonathan is a big help."

I hear the tortoiseshell crying from the spare room.

The little girl looks at the door. "Oh, you have a cat too?"

"Right now I have four little kittens. You wanna see them?"

"Yeah!"

I lead everyone to the spare room where I find the tortoiseshell sitting up in front of the other three, as it's feeding time. The little girl kneels down and begins petting them. "Where's the mother cat?" she asks.

"Well, unfortunately she went to cat heaven."

"Oh no."

I tell them the story of finding the kittens. "Anyway, I'm taking her place until they're old enough to feed themselves. Would you like to help me bottle feed them?"

The little girl turns to her mother. "Can I, mom? Please?"

"Sure, honey."

I go to the kitchen and return with the bottles of formula. I sit on the floor next to Samantha and show her how it's done. "Okay, now, hold your kitten very gently and put the bottle in front of it. It knows what to do."

The child follows my instructions and beams as the kitten latches onto the bottle and begins draining it.

Her mother pulls out a cell phone. "Oh, this is too cute. I have to get a picture and some video of this." She crouches down and aims the phone.

"You take care of them all by yourself?" asks Jonathan.

"I live alone, but my best friend lives across the street and helps out when I'm at work."

"Oh. So you're single."

"Yeah."

A few minutes later we're done and we get Snowflake into a pet carrier. Joanne shakes my hand. "Again, can't thank you enough."

"Not a problem. And seeing your daughter with that cat is quite the reward."

The uncle locks eyes with me, sending a shiver through my body as he takes my hand. "Uh, I hope this isn't too forward. I'd ask for your phone number but we already have it. Mind if I call it again?"

I can't help but smile. "Sure. That would be fine."

I wouldn't mind saying "uncle" to this guy.

Two days later . . .

"You've gone viral!"

I rub the sleep out of my eyes as I try to focus on the phone. The clock reads five-thirty in the morning. "Rory, what are you, a friggin' rooster? Why the hell are you calling me at this hour?"

"Because you've gone viral!"

"About what?"

"That lost cat. The little girl's mom posted pictures and video of you showing the kid how to bottle feed kittens, and she wrote a post about it. It's all over social media. I'm sending you the link."

"Oh, shit."

Now I'm awake.

"Freckles, it's cute as hell. Call me back after you've watched it."

I end the call, throw back the covers, jump out of bed, grab my laptop and power it up. I click on the link in Rory's email and the screen fills with video of me and the little girl bottle feeding the kittens.

Below the video is the counter.

More than seven hundred thousand hits.

And below that is the post from the mom.

You won't believe who found our lost cat . . . famous network TV reporter Madison Shaw! She took my daughter's beloved pet in out of the rain and got in touch with us after seeing one of the many flyers we posted around town. When we arrived to pick up Snowflake we discovered Ms. Shaw was taking care of four orphaned kittens she'd found while on a story. So she showed Samantha how to bottle feed them. My daughter is so happy thanks to this wonderful woman, who is obviously a saint in her own right as she gets up in the middle of the night, every night, to feed these precious orphaned fur babies. Thank you, Madison Shaw, for giving my daughter her pet back and for letting her feed your kittens which she enjoyed immensely. It was like Christmas morning, only better! God bless you!

And below that are a bunch of photos. All what we would call "warm and fuzzy" in television news.

I grab the phone and call Rory back. "Okay, I watched it."

"I just saw it on your network's morning show!"

"Dear God . . ."

"What? I thought you'd get a kick out of it."

"Do you know what this does to my reputation as a hard news reporter?"

"Yeah, it shows you're human."

"And beyond that, it tells my boss why I turned down Air Force One."

I dread walking into the newsroom because I have no idea how my boss will react. Will he be ticked off? Not care? Think I don't consider my job a top priority?

The newsroom suddenly goes quiet as I enter. No one makes eye contact or says good morning, but I can tell they're all stifling laughs as I hear a few snorts and giggles.

And then I see it.

My desk, covered with more of that cat lady starter kit.

A giant bag of cat treats, a catnip mouse, scratching post, a whole bunch of cat toys, a cat condo, a case of canned tuna. And a big box wrapped in Hello Kitty wrapping paper.

Fine, I'll play along. "Okay, okay, very funny."

The newsroom erupts in laughter.

"Open your present!" shouts a reporter from across the room.

I tear the paper from the box and open it, then pull out a multi-colored crocheted monstrosity that would be best described as something an old lady would put on the back of a couch. "Oh, very nice."

A photographer points at the box. "There's more in there."

I reach inside and find a big box of DVDs. "Ah, the complete collection of *Murder She Wrote*. That's it? No Depends in here? Polident for my false teeth?"

"Keep looking."

I rummage through the tissue paper and find a gold, sparky halo, which I promptly put on my head. "So, I've been canonized."

Everyone applauds as I see my boss heading toward me, wearing a big smile. "Can I see you a minute in my office?"

Uh-oh. "Sure, Barry." I follow him into his office and take a seat opposite his desk.

He's still smiling as he sits. "I must say, of all the people in this newsroom, I never expected—"

"What, that I have a heart?"

"I wasn't going to say that. You just never struck me as the type to do something like this. You're one of the most career oriented people I've ever known. I was blown away seeing you bottle feeding a bunch of kittens."

"Well, I have recently discovered that there's more to life than a career."

"Never thought I'd hear you say that either. So I gotta ask . . . is this the reason you turned down the President's gig?"

"Will you be mad if I say yes? Or think less of me as a reporter?"

"Of course not. I'll actually be impressed."

"Then yes."

"Well, I'm impressed that you would do such a thing."

"I have second thoughts about it every day."

"Don't. You just became the most popular reporter on this network. Madison, you can't buy promotion like you're getting off that social media post. Even people who hate the media now see you as a human being with a big heart."

"I didn't do it for the publicity."

"I know that. But the cat's out of the bag now. Literally and figuratively." He grabs a few slips of paper from his desk and hands them to me. "Oh, the morning show wants you and the kittens as guests."

"Huh?"

"And the CEO insists you do it."

As I drive home, it is clear that my life will never be the same. Requests for interviews didn't stop so I didn't get a damn bit of work done today, but management didn't care because I'm now some sort of role model who can improve the media's approval rating, which has been, as my boss says, lower than whale shit.

Meanwhile, my new status as "network cat lady" has been cemented forever. The local no-kill animal shelter called and asked if I would be part of their fundraiser. Sure, no problem. A national pet rescue organization wants me to do a public service announcement. Okay, I'll do it. The switchboard at the network lit up with offers wanting to adopt the kittens. Grumpy Cat is now one of my Twitter followers. I got an email from Morris the Cat. Signed with a paw print.

Then there were the comments on social media, which were about ninety-nine percent positive. Of course, some men couldn't resist trying to be clever and/or sleazy. "I'd like to be nursed by Madison Shaw."

And the story leaked (I'm looking at you, newsroom diva Jennifer) that I had blown off the assignment covering a presidential campaign to take care of the kittens. Which, incredibly, resulted in the President of the United States actually making a comment about it during a news conference. "Ms. Shaw has literally confirmed that I am not a warm, fuzzy guy. Guess I need to work on my people skills with the media. And perhaps the Oval Office needs a cat."

That last line resulted in cat people overloading the White House switchboard with calls demanding the Commander-in-Chief adopt a shelter cat.

Which he did by the end of the day. The ensuing photo-op showed him signing a bill in the Oval Office while a huge ginger cat slept on the corner of his desk.

And *that* went viral. Probably beat the hell out of a campaign commercial.

I see a big overnight delivery truck parked in front of my house as I turn onto my street. Two men with hand trucks are wheeling boxes into my house as Rory holds the door open. I quickly get out of my car and head up the stairs, running into a delivery guy who's on the way down. "What's all this stuff?"

"Deliveries."

"I can see that. I didn't order anything."

"I just drive the truck, lady. Everything's got your address on it. Hence, I am delivering it to you. And don't even think about saying *return to sender* after we hauled everything into your house."

He heads back to the truck as I move into the house. The living room is cluttered with boxes stacked to the ceiling. Rory is signing a clipboard for the delivery guy. "What the hell is all this?"

She smiles at me as she hands the delivery guy the clipboard and he takes off. "Free cat supplies."

"From who?"

"Companies that make stuff for cats. You've got a year's supply of food for four cats, three hundred pounds of kitty litter, a collection of toys, cat beds, cat houses, cat books, brushes, collars, flea medication, treats—"

"Whoa, wait a minute. Did you say *three hundred pounds* of kitty litter?"

"That's what the delivery guy told me. It was on his manifest. But at least it's in manageable twenty-five pound bags."

"But three hundred pounds? Do they think I own a friggin' tiger?"

"Hey, don't complain. It's all free."

"Rory, I can't even see my couch. This place looks like a warehouse. Where the hell am I gonna put all this stuff?"

"Donate some of it to the shelter. I'm sure they'll be thrilled."

"Good idea."

"So how was your day?"

"Wall to wall cats. They didn't even send me out on a story today. Just got a ton of calls about the kittens. I'm management's favorite person right now."

"I'm sure. Well, I gotta run. Just fed the fur babies so you can relax a bit."

"Actually, I can't. And you're not going anywhere. Gotta straighten up this place. The network is doing a live shot from here tomorrow morning."

Chapter Six

At six in the morning the kittens are still asleep, I'm bleary-eyed sitting on the floor next to them, Rory is being her perky morning self and the photographer is standing by with his camera pointed at me. Our "hit time" (the time we go live) is five minutes after six, when the morning team is done with the "real news" and can move on to what is known as the "kicker": an uplifting, funny, or heartwarming story.

In this case, "warm and fuzzy" is literal.

(And after that, as is typical of morning shows these days that are targeted to women, about three hours of discussion on purses, shoes and child care tips. Hard hitting stuff that makes men turn off the TV and listen to sports talk radio.)

Rory, who is camera shy, is sitting out of the shot in case the kittens start running all over the place. I've got my bottles of formula lined up, as the network wants viewers to see the feeding process.

Of course as luck would have it, the photographer is the same one who was working with me when we found the kittens. He keeps shaking his head in amazement as he double-checks his equipment. "I never would have expected this from you, Network. Getting up in the middle of the night to feed kittens."

"So, in other words, you didn't consider me to be a human being before."

"Let's just say you have blown up the reputation you used to have. Which, I might add, is a very good thing. I might actually take more time lighting you in the future."

"So, you gonna stop calling me Network now?"

"Sorry, you're stuck with that one. Unless you wanna be called Catwoman?"

"No way. I refuse to wear a black spandex suit."

Rory reaches over and pats my hand. "But you'd look good in it. And it would be an appropriate choice for Halloween."

"And now I know I'll never hear the end of this."

The photographer looks at his watch. "We're two minutes out."

I'm frankly still amazed at the attention this is getting considering all the important stuff going on in the world. I mean, compared to moms with real babies who get up in the middle of the night and provide round the clock care, what I'm doing is nothing. But it has somehow struck a nerve with the country, and cat videos do rule the internet. As my boss put it, "You're someone in a glamorous job with never a hair out of place who seems to have life by the tail, and yet you're doing something incredibly kind and out of character for a hard-nosed network reporter. Completely different from the image you project on the air. It's a perfect storm of unselfishness."

I don't see it that way, but whatever. If it will create more awareness for homeless pets and raise a few bucks for shelters, I'm happy to be the poster child for a while.

As for the hair never being out of place, that reputation is about to be blown up as well. I'm wearing the roll-out-of-bed summer collection. Hair by eggbeater. No makeup. Sweatpants and a New York Giants t-shirt. The freckles will make their debut. Screw *gravitas*.

I'm the real me these days.

I hear the commercial ending in my ear piece and get a "stand by" from the photographer. I look at the monitor that's been set up with the sound off and see the unfamiliar view of the network morning show set. It's unfamiliar because I'm never up this early and hate morning shows anyway as the perky attitude of the female anchors would give me a cavity. (Which is why Rory usually stays out of my way in the early morning hours. I think she was a morning show host in a previous life.) The network's morning anchors, Kayla and Sherman, fill the screen as I hear them talk about "an amazing story" involving one of the network's own reporters.

"Let's go live to Staten Island," says Kayla, "where we check in with political reporter Madison Shaw, who is standing by with the four new members of her household. Good morning, Madison, thanks for getting up early to join us."

"Not a problem, guys, it's feeding time anyway." I take a quick glance at the monitor and see myself sitting next to the kittens, curled up in a ball. The tortoiseshell is waking up.

"Your story has gone viral," says Sherman. "So tell us how you came to be a foster parent to four orphaned kittens."

"Well, viewers of our evening news might remember a story I did a while ago on the demolition of a stadium. While we were touring the place before they blew it up, the foreman heard these kittens crying and found them in an office. The mother cat had died. So I put them in a box and tried to give them to the foreman, but he was tied up at the project. It was Friday night and there were no animal shelters open. So I took them home and luckily a very nice veterinarian lives next door and showed me how to take care of them."

"So, originally you didn't intend to keep them?" asks Kayla.

"No, so people need to stop calling me a saint. But I couldn't just leave these helpless little guys and within a day I grew attached to them." The tortoiseshell meows. "Ah, it's feeding time, and I'd better not be late." I pick up the kitten and hold it in front of the camera as it continues to meow. "This one's my favorite, and he's always up first. He's not gonna shut up until he gets his bottle." I pick up one of the bottles of formula and hold it in front of the kitten. It latches on immediately with its paws and begins draining it. I hear both anchors say, "Awwww."

"That is absolutely adorable," says Kayla. "So how often do you have to feed them?"

"Every few hours. So while I'm gone during the day my best friend Rory who lives across the street takes care of them. Kitty day care without the expense or car seats. She's literally been a lifesaver to these kittens."

"Has this been hard for you?" asks Sherman.

"Well, I'm single and don't have any experience with children, so getting up in the middle of the night takes some getting used to. I have new respect for all parents out there. What I'm doing pales in comparison to real child care. But it's not forever, since they'll be old enough to feed themselves pretty soon. Though since cats are nocturnal, they might want me to play with them in the middle of the night anyway, so sleep is not necessarily an option."

"The network has been deluged with calls wanting to adopt them," says Kayla. "Have you already found their *furever homes*?"

Oooh, I like that term. "Well, I'm keeping this one and three of my friends are each adopting one. But there are plenty of animals at your local shelter that desperately need a home, so I would encourage those people wanting to adopt to go and save a pet's life."

"There's more to this story than meets the eye," says Kayla, "as it came out yesterday that you had turned down the assignment to cover the Presidential campaign to stay home and take care of the kittens. Was that a tough decision for you?"

"Absolutely. That was a dream assignment as it would be for anyone who covers politics, but when it was offered to me I'd become attached to the kittens and couldn't bear to leave them for weeks at a time. And this little one has become very attached to me as well. The vet says kittens this young can imprint on humans. Basically they think I'm their mother."

"That's a wonderful story," says Kayla. "So, since you're keeping that one, does it have a name yet?"

"I don't even know if it's a boy or a girl. And I'm told you have to wait for a cat's personality to reveal itself before you give it a name."

Sherman nods. "I've heard that too. Now, Madison, did the fact that you grew up as a foster child weigh into your decision?"

My fists are tight and teeth clenched as I fight to hold in my emotions until the photographer heads out the door.

The minute he does, the dam breaks and the tears flow.

Rory quickly moves toward me and gives me a strong hug. "Go ahead, Freckles, let it out."

I hang on for dear life, the demon that is the memory of a mostly horrible childhood dancing in my head. "How the hell did they find out?"

"I don't know, sweetie." She leans back, breaks the embrace and leads me to the couch. We sit and she takes my hands, giving me a soulful look. "It doesn't change who you are. But I know it's something that still haunts you and pushes your buttons. You need to focus on what you've become, what you've accomplished. The obstacles you've overcome. The friends who love you now. You're the sister I never had."

"And none of it would be possible if you hadn't befriended me in high school." I give her another hug, the harsh memories starting to subside.

I'm laser locked on my news director's office, eyes filled with fire. I power-walk inside, shut the door and stand next to him, stretching to my full height so that I look down my nose at him.

He looks up at me, then backs up a bit. "Uh-oh. I know that look."

I follow him, going full Amazon warrior on the guy, folding my arms as I tower over him. "I cannot believe you broadcast the fact that I'm a foster child to the entire world."

"I didn't think you'd have a problem with it. It sort of explains why you did what you did."

"And what you're not saying is that it makes for a better story. You know, I didn't take those kittens in just for the purposes of promoting this network. I didn't want any credit for doing it. Maybe you remember that Bible passage about charitable acts and the right hand not knowing what the left hand is doing. And by the way, how the hell did *you* know I was a foster kid?"

"Remember when you were an intern here and one of the anchors was considering adopting a child? I overheard you telling him your story and encouraging him to do it."

The memory comes back. "Oh. I forgot about that. But still—"

"You need to return this call." He grabs a couple of pink message slips from his desk, in an attempt to divert my anger. "Catholic Charities called. They have a ton of kids that need homes and were hoping you might be a spokesperson."

He locks eyes with me as his words instantly drain my anger, the thought of homeless kids killing my argument. "Sure. I'll be happy to help them out."

"And a United States Senator called asking if you'd testify in Congress. They've got hearings coming up about funding some new program for children who need homes. Basically it would provide free college for any child that is actually permanently adopted. And, you know, that would encourage people to, you know . . ."

I slowly nod as I look at the name of a prominent politician on the slip. "Yeah, no problem. I know about this bill they're trying to pass. It would do a lot of good."

"Madison, I understand you're upset with your story getting out and I do apologize for not checking with you first. But right now you're a role model, whether you like it or not. Your story shows how someone who grew up under tough circumstances can make it to the top and use your position to influence people in a good way. Do you remember what I asked you during your job interview? About why you wanted to be a reporter? Most people say they always wanted to be on TV or they were inspired by some great journalist. Do you remember your answer?"

"Yeah. I said I wanted to tell great stories and along the way make the world a better place."

"Well, here's your chance. The only difference is that *you're* the great story."

Chapter Seven

Generally on Saturdays I'm so fried from work I spend the morning and afternoon recharging before doing something with my friends (or, before Jeremy was exiled to the Hamptons, something with him.) But today's schedule is jam packed, thanks to the kittens. Later this morning I'm taking them for their first full checkup at the vet's clinic. This afternoon I'm part of a fundraiser for the local shelter.

And tonight, the uncle of the girl with the lost cat is taking me out.

But I have an hour to kill before Jeff the veterinarian opens his office, so I'm unpacking the box of cat toys to give the little guys some exercise. I take a few items that look like fun into the spare room, where I find the kittens already running about. I toss a catnip mouse in their direction and two of them immediately pounce. Then I jiggle a wand that looks like a fishing rod with a stuffed fish on the end over the other two. The tabby jumps to get it and misses, while the tortoiseshell simply gets up on his hind legs and swats at it. The tabby gets distracted by the mouse and turns his attention to it, so I hold the stuffed fish over the tortoiseshell. Again, he doesn't jump, so I lower the wand to let him catch the thing.

I bring out a few more toys and toss them on the floor. The kittens are now in a frenzy, high on catnip as they race around chasing things.

And then the tortoiseshell runs face first into a piece of exercise equipment. I immediately pick him up and hold him close. "Poor little guy. Watch where you're going." He meows and seems unfazed, so I put him back down. He joins the chase with his siblings, and once again runs face first into the leg of a chair. I pick him up again, but he seems okay.

Still, I sense something is wrong and I want Jeff to check it out.

Jeff shines a light into the eyes of the tortoiseshell. "I can tell you why he's running into things. This kitten is blind in one eye. So it has no depth perception and can't judge where things are."

"Oh no." I reach out for the kitten.

He nods as he hands it to me. "And one of his back legs is deformed. That's why he's not jumping. Because he can't."

"A cat that can't jump or see?" I hug the kitten close. "Poor thing."

"That's a *special needs* cat you have there. But otherwise it's healthy. And it obviously likes you."

"Can you restore his vision and fix his leg?"

"I'll have a specialist look at his eye, but I don't think so. Nothing can be done about the leg. He needs to be an indoor cat, and can live a normal life, but there are some things you can do to make it easier. Don't move furniture around, as eventually he will create his own pathways. And you can't take him outside unless he's on a harness."

"Huh? Are you saying that I can walk a cat?"

He laughs. "Yeah. If you want really strange looks from your neighbors, go for a walk with a cat on a leash. So, you still want to keep this one? The others are perfectly healthy."

"Yeah, this one's mine. Oh, is he a boy cat or a girl cat?"

Jeff lifts up the kitten's tail and takes a look. "He's a guy. And that means later this year I'll have to do something to him that will seriously piss him off."

"What?"

He makes a scissor motion with two fingers. "Snip, snip."

My jaw drops as I pull into the parking lot of the shelter.

There's a long line of people with cats from the front door and around the block.

All, apparently, to get a picture of me with their kitty.

I agreed to spend an hour doing this for the shelter, which is taking ten dollar donations for each photo, but it looks like I'll be here awhile.

The manager of the shelter greats me as I get out of my car. "Miss Shaw, I'm Ginny. We spoke on the phone. Thank you so much for helping us today."

"Not a problem. And please, call me Madison."

She's a petite blonde, maybe forty, wearing a red polo shirt and jeans. "We're all set up and ready to go. But I don't think we'll be able to get to everyone in an hour."

"Don't worry about it, I'll stay as long as there are people who want a picture. I'm sure you can use every dollar you can get."

She opens the door to the shelter. "You really are a saint."

"Oh, stop it." She leads me past a bunch of cages, all filled with cats. "Wow, you got a lot of cats that need homes."

"Hopefully we'll adopt some out today with you here."

She leads me into the lobby where a photographer is set up, his camera pointed at a chair. "So this is like getting a photo with Santa."

"Basically." I take a seat as she opens the door.

Cat people pour in.

Four hours later we're done. I have been licked, hissed at, pawed and clawed, but enough about last night at a bar. (Sorry, couldn't

71

resist.) I have cat hair from dozens of different felines covering me. Most of the cats were friendly, but a few (I'm looking it you, neurotic Siamese with the rhinestone collar) were obviously those one-person cats and I was not their person. Many of the owners donated more than the required ten bucks. To say my ego has been built up is putting it mildly. When one person after another tells you how wonderful you are, well, it's a nice way to start the weekend.

But the best part, I saw people adopting cats.

Ginny closes the door as I get up from the chair. She takes my hands. "Hear that?"

I listen but all is quiet. "I don't hear anything."

"That's because every single cat was adopted."

"Seriously?"

"Even found a home for that fat thirteen year old ginger cat. Every cage is empty. Which is more important than the ton of money we took in today. And all because of you."

She smiles and I feel my eyes well up a bit. "Happy to help. Next time you need a fundraiser, just give me a call."

As first dates go, Jonathan is okay.

While the chemistry isn't off the charts, he seems to be a decent guy, though I carried the conversation during dinner since he wanted to know everything about television news, which is an occupational hazard for those of us making a living in the public eye. Fortunately the movie we saw afterwards gave me a chance to stop talking. He's nothing to write home about yet, but I'm reminded of past relationships that started out just okay and then blossomed. So a second date is doable.

As for the physical part, Jonathan is definitely doable, as A.J. would say. Though not tonight. I made it a point not to say "I can't wait to get out of this dress" when I brought him in for coffee.

Kelly has already fed the kittens and just took off, so I head into the kitchen to make some java. Jonathan is in the living room playing with the kittens.

At least the guy likes animals.

"Madison, you need any help in there?"

I finish loading the coffee machine. "I'm good. This isn't rocket science. Coffee will be ready in a few minutes."

"You stupid cat!"

I quickly move to the living room and see him holding the tortoiseshell at arm's length. "What happened?"

"This damn kitten clawed my cashmere sweater! Look, there's a thread pulled out!"

Oh, this isn't good, and I'm not talking about the sweater.

Annddd . . . cue the red flag. "It's not ruined. I can pull the thread back in from the other side. Take it off and I'll fix it for you."

He glares at the tortoiseshell. "Damn cat!" He reaches back with one hand and swings it toward the kitten.

I manage to grab his wrist before he hits it. "What the hell? You don't hit animals! It's just a little kitten."

"Your kitten needs to learn a lesson. If you don't teach it when it misbehaves—"

I grab the kitten, which is now shaking from all the yelling, and pull it close to my chest. "Get! Out!"

"Hey, don't get all bent out of shape—"

"And I suppose you'd have no qualms about hitting a woman if *she* misbehaves. Get out, now!"

He gets up and shakes his head. "A two hundred dollar sweater, ruined."

"Send me the friggin' bill. And if you paid two bills for that ugly thing, you got taken."

He storms toward the door, slamming it on the way out.

Between the yelling and the door slam the poor tortoiseshell is still shaking. I gently stroke his head, soften my tone. "It's okay, little guy, he's gone. You're safe. No one can hurt you when I'm around."

The phone rings. (Guess who.) I answer, still holding the kitten. "Rory, do you have a State Department drone maintaining surveillance on me, or what?"

"What was wrong with that one?"

"He was just okay until the tortoiseshell pulled a thread out of his sweater and he was about to hit it."

"Yikes. Well, that speaks volumes."

"I seem to be ending every date these days with *Get! Out!*"

"At least you're not wasting time with any of these guys. Is the kitten okay?"

"Yeah, I stopped him before he hit it. But the poor thing is scared to death and his little heart is beating a mile a minute."

"Well, give him lots of attention. He *is* the one you're keeping."

"Yep. And you just reminded of something. I need to hit an office supply store tomorrow morning for some cat stuff."

"What does a cat have to do with office supplies?"

"I need a ton of bubble wrap and rubber bands. Plus some chalk."

Chapter Eight

Tish shakes her head as she looks around the house. "Okay, give me a hint. Why do you have the legs of every piece of furniture covered in bubble wrap?"

"Because the kitten I'm keeping is blind in one eye and keeps running into things. He has no depth perception. So now he won't get hurt."

"Ah. And all the curtains are doubled in half over the rods for the same reason?"

"He cannot jump due to a deformed leg. Hence, he likes to climb. He would ruin the curtains."

"Yes, they look so good this way."

I proudly point to a cat condo given to me by the newsroom staff. "I sprinkled a little catnip on that to encourage him to climb there. And it worked." I smile and nod.

"Last question . . . why are your floors covered with chalk marks?"

"So I put the furniture back in the same place after I vacuum. Since he can't see properly he gets around by developing pathways, and moving things would throw him off."

"I see. What time does his chef arrive?"

"Oh, stop it. I'm just trying to help the little guy."

"Are we allowed to have our Sunday brunch in the dining room?"

"Of course."

She studies my face. "You don't see this as a little bit obsessive?"

"Not at all."

A.J. arrives, stops in the doorway and furrows her brow. "You get robbed or something?"

"No. Why?"

"Generally chalk marks on the ground in my neighborhood means somebody got whacked."

The brunch discussion turns to the annual Fourth of July party on Wednesday, which is held at Tish's house on the water. Food, fun and fireworks, always an enjoyable time.

And once again, I am a third wheel.

A.J. shares the menu of the food she's bringing, then turns to me and hits me with her Jewish mother accent, which she does quite well. "So, you want I should bring a nice guy for you?"

"Not your cousin!" says Rory.

"Nah. I got someone else in mind."

I shake my head. "To be honest, I think I need a break from men."

Tish rolls her eyes. "That's how it starts. She's beginning to turn."

"Excuse me?"

"Into a cat lady."

"Oh, leave me alone. Just because I take a few steps to make things easier for a special needs kitten."

"Just yankin' your chain," says Tish. "So, what's the deal? Now you think it's too soon after he-who-must-not-be-named?"

"Nah, it's not a rebound thing. But the final words the last three men heard in this house were *get out*. My luck with guys hasn't been the best lately."

Rory and I arrive at Tish's house, already filled with people (mostly lawyer types) and food, as A.J. has put out a huge spread. We make our way to the back deck, where a grill is already going.

Tended to by a chiseled, shirtless hunk in a bathing suit.

My eyes widen and mouth hangs open as I take Rory's arm. "Damn. *Who* is *that*?"

"No idea. Must be one of Tish's friends. But I definitely want more than one hot dog today if he's the cook."

I'm staring at the guy as Tish comes up to me and grabs my arm. "If your jaw drops any more, it'll hit the floor."

I turn to her. "Very funny. So who's the hunky grill master?"

She leans over and whispers. "Remember the guy I mentioned who rented the office next to me? The nameless one with the great ass?"

Rory nods, as she can't stop staring either. "The rest of him ain't so bad either."

I glance back at him. "Tish, I told you not to try and fix me up."

"Hey, he's nice, he's new in town, doesn't know anybody and would have spent the holiday alone. Name's Mark. C'mon, I'll introduce you guys."

I try not to smile but am unsuccessful. "Well, if you insist."

"Well, don't let me twist your arm."

Tish leads us over to the guy who is focused on flipping burgers. "Mark, I want you to meet two of my best friends. Rory and Madison."

He smiles at us, bringing deep dimples into play. "Nice to meet you both."

I stare up at yet another Greek god, who must be six foot four and chiseled out of granite. Short, light brown hair and ice blue eyes. "Uh, hi."

Tish grabs Rory's arm. "Rory, I need your help in the kitchen."

Rory, a foot shorter, is staring straight ahead, eye level with the guy's ripped chest, looking like she wants to devour him. "Huh?"

"Kitchen. Now. Madison, maybe you could help Mark out on the grill."

"Yeah. Sure." Tish and Rory head back to the house (with Rory's head on a swivel), leaving me with the man from Mount Olympus. "So, Tish tells me you're new in town and don't know anybody."

"Yes, I've only been here a few weeks. But now I know you." His smile makes my heart flutter. He sips a beer, then turns his attention to the grill for a moment. "Of course, I already know you from TV. And those kittens you rescued."

"Y'know, thirteen years in journalism and I'm more well-known for bottle feeding cats than any story I ever broke."

"It speaks volumes about your character."

"Thank you. So, where are you from?"

"Florida. So I'm told I'd better enjoy the summer while it lasts. Not sure if I'll be able to keep warm this winter."

I'm sure you won't have a problem finding a woman to help with that.

Mark spreads a blanket on the ground as the sun dips below the horizon. The fireworks will begin any minute.

Though I've been feeling fireworks with this guy all day. Probably because I've never been around a guy with such a perfect body. (I know, I'm acting like a man. Thinking with the wrong head.)

He actually found a relatively quiet spot in the waterfront park, away from the crowds. He places his six pack of beer on the sand and then I realize we've forgotten something. "Oh, no. We left the chairs back at Tish's place."

He sits on the blanket, then pats the spot directly in front of him. "I'll be your chair." He shoots me a smile I cannot resist. "C'mon, get comfortable."

I'm already too comfortable with this guy, but I'm not complaining. He's smart, interesting, and has a great sense of humor. We've spent most of the day together and I feel safe with him. I sit on the blanket in front of him and lean back, molding myself to his body.

He wraps his arms gently around my waist. "Comfortable?"

"Very."

He opens a beer. "Want one?"

"Nah, I had my limit during dinner."

He takes a long swig. "Perfect weather for fireworks, huh?"

"Yeah. It's been a really nice day. I'm glad you came, Mark."

"You made it a nice day."

A Sousa march fills the air, telling us the fireworks are about to start. "Here we go." The first ones explode, reflecting off the water as the crowd oohs and ahs. "I've loved fireworks since I was a little girl."

"Hey, who doesn't? I've never seen them on the water. This is spectacular."

I rub one hand over his thick forearm. He pulls me a little closer. "This is nice, Mark."

"You know, the fireworks make your hair look like it's shooting sparks. It's beautiful."

I turn my head to look at him. Our eyes lock and lips meet as the fireworks between us continue.

We head back to the parking lot half an hour after the fireworks show ended. We decided to wait for traffic to thin out.

Okay, so you don't believe that lame excuse.

Of course, I didn't see much of the show.

I couldn't resist him or the situation. The gorgeous nice guy, sea breeze caressing my body, perfect temperatures and reflections from the fireworks were simply too much. I spent an hour basically kissing the guy. Luckily with everyone watching the light show no one noticed a couple making out. Then the park cleared out and we picked up where we left off.

Rory texted me, telling me she was going home and assuming I had a ride.

So we're headed back to his car. Mark has one arm around my shoulders while he carries the empty six pack of bottles with the other.

And then it hits me.

He's downed six beers in an hour and a half. And I see a bunch of cops directing traffic out of the park. "Hey, how about I drive?"

"What for?"

"I haven't been drinking and you have."

He shrugs. "It's not a big deal for a guy my size. I'm fine."

"You sure?"

"Relax, Madison. I'll get you home in one piece. Do I look drunk to you?"

I'm slightly apprehensive but he actually seems sober. Still, as a rookie reporter in a small town I covered enough car wrecks to know that driving drunk or even buzzed is not a good idea. But traffic is almost gone and we only have to drive a few blocks. Besides, I don't want to start an argument with a guy I really like. "You're not even buzzed?"

"Nope." We pass a recycling bin and he drops the empty bottles inside. He leads me to his car, a nice sedan, and opens the door for me. I get in and say a quick prayer, determined to make him drink coffee when we get back to my place. He gets behind the wheel, starts the car, backs up—

And bumps the car behind him, setting off an ear-splitting alarm.

"Dammit!" He pulls forward, puts the car in park, turns it off and gets out. I see him check the other car to see if there's any damage. He gets back in and smiles as the alarm stops. "I just bumped it. No problem."

And just as he starts the car I see one of the cops directing traffic walking quickly in our direction.

It's Officer Marino.

Dammit.

This is not good.

Mark shakes his head. "Oh, hell." He rolls down the window as the cop reaches the car. "No damage, officer. I just nudged it enough to set off the alarm."

The cop moves behind the car, checks the other vehicle, then comes back. "Yeah, it's okay." Then I notice him lean forward as he sniffs the air. "Been drinking, sir?"

"I had a beer during the fireworks."

The cop shines a light in his face as another officer heads in our direction. "Please step out of the vehicle."

"Officer, I'm fine."

"If that's the case then you'll be on your way in a minute." Mark steps out of the car as I see him handed a Breathalyzer. "Blow into the tube." He does so, then hands it to the cop, who shakes his head. "Point one-six. That's twice the legal limit. One beer, huh?"

"Must be something wrong with your machine."

"Take it up with the judge. I'm afraid I'll have to place you under arrest, sir. Is your companion sober to drive your car home?"

"I live in Manhattan. She lives here. If you can give her a ride home you can leave the car here and I'll pick it up tomorrow."

"Fine. I'll lock it." Officer Marino hands Mark, now a prisoner, off to his partner while he gets in the car to get the keys and lock it up.

And then he sees me. "Oh. It's you."

I nod as I look down. "Good evening, Officer Marino."

"Did you know he was drunk?"

"I thought he was fine. But I just met him at a cookout this afternoon. I don't really know him."

"Are you—"

"I had two glasses of wine about five hours ago. That's it. Honest. You can have me blow into the thing if you want."

"That won't be necessary. C'mon, let's get you home. I know where you live."

We both get out of the car and I'm thankful the place has mostly cleared out. The last thing I need is for someone to take a picture of me getting into a police car while my date for the evening is arrested. Officer Marino tosses Mark's keys to his partner, leads me to his police cruiser and holds the door for me.

I'm beyond embarrassed.

I see his partner look at me, then turn to him. "I'll do the paperwork, Nick. You get your, uh, *friend* home." He smiles and winks.

Marino slides behind the wheel, grabs the two-way radio and keys the microphone. "Unit ninety-nine is ten-ten."

"Copy that."

He starts the car and heads for the parking lot exit, passing Mark being loaded into another police car wearing handcuffs.

I turn to face him. "You probably don't think too much of me."

"If I didn't I wouldn't be driving you home." We come to a red light and he faces me. "But you're a reporter. You should know better than to get in a car with a drunk."

I nod. "You're absolutely right. I actually did offer to drive but he said he was okay. I could have walked home. It's only a few blocks."

"Well, lucky for you he hit the other car and set off the alarm."

"Lucky for me you seem to always be around to save me."

He smiles a bit as the light turns green. "That's my job."

"Somehow I don't think providing personal protection to redheads who make bad decisions is in your police department manual."

"Actually, it's chapter one. Damsels in distress. Last week I found one tied to the railroad tracks."

I can't help but laugh. "You're a good man, Marino."

"Considering that's coming from the country's most famous rescuer of cats, I'm honored."

"Yeah, that thing has taken on a life of its own. But a lot of good has come of it."

"I'm sure." He turns the corner and pulls up in front of my house, then turns off the car. "Home sweet home." He hops out, comes around to my side and opens the door for me.

"Thank you." I see Rory spying on me through the drapes from across the street and roll my eyes at her. We start walking up the steps. "Hey, Marino, can I ask you something?"

"First, I'd like to know why you keep calling me by my last name."

"It's a newsroom thing. We use last names."

"Okay. So, what did you want to ask me?"

"Was that your partner tonight?"

"Yeah."

"I noticed he looked at me and then gave you a wink. What's all that about?"

He looks down with a sheepish grin. "I, uh, might have mentioned that I've run into you a few times. You know, a celebrity sighting."

"Ah, I see. Can I ask you something else?"

"Sure."

"Code ten-ten means you're off duty, right?"

"How'd you know that?"

"Police scanner in every newsroom."

"Right, forgot about that."

"Anyway, since you're off the clock, would you like to—"

"*Attention all units! Officer down! Officer down! All available units respond!*"

He immediately heads down the stairs. "Gotta go!"

"Sure. Hope everything is okay."

He waves at me, gets in his car, cranks it and leaves skid marks as he races away, tires squealing.

"Curses, foiled again." I trudge up the stairs and head inside, pay Kelly, and grab my phone, waiting for the inevitable call from Rory. It rings the minute Kelly is out the door. "What?"

"What the hell happened with barbecue Thor?"

"He's spending the night drying out in the drunk tank."

"Huh?"

"When you drink six beers in ninety minutes, back into another

83

car and set off the alarm, the police come over to investigate. He was twice the legal limit."

"Damn. Now that I think about it, I did see him drink a lot this afternoon. Didn't you notice?"

"Yeah, but I didn't want to."

"So that's why Officer Goodbody drove you home."

"Yeah."

"And . . . why didn't you invite him in?"

"I was about to, but he got an emergency call. Officer down."

"That's never good."

"No. Hope everything turns out okay. Anyway, I think I'm gonna take the plunge and do it."

"Do what?"

"Ask him out. Officer Goodbody, as you call him."

Long pause. "Hang on a minute, I gotta check the Weather Channel."

"Why?"

"To see what time hell froze over."

Chapter Nine

By the next morning, I'm losing the resolve to follow through on my decision to ask a man out. Sounds good when you're talking to a girlfriend, very different when you start playing out the possible scenarios in your head. And of course, the worst scenario, the one every woman fears.

Rejection.

What if he turns me down?

The shoe is on the other foot.

Still, I need to take a shot. But how?

Madison Shaw date invite, take one:

"Uh, hi, Officer Marino? Yeah, this is Madison Shaw. You know, the girl who runs stop signs and hangs out with drunks. May I cook you a dinner you probably wouldn't feed to a dog?"

Take two:

"Hello, Nick? It's Madison, the obsessive pet owner. Look, in five years I'll be forty and qualify as a spinster with a house full of cats and probably start going to Celine Dion concerts unless I find a decent guy. Help me out, will ya?"

Take three:

"Officer Marino? If you let me play with your siren I'll let you put those handcuffs to good use."

Cut!!!

I'll get back to this later. Right now my boss has taken me off the street for the day. In the news business that means I'm not doing a story. Anyway, I'm not working today so I can travel to a production house and record some public service messages for a national pet rescue association. They wanted me to bring the kittens but I told them they were too young to haul 'em all the way to Manhattan for the entire day. When they're grown up a bit they can be spokes-cats. For now I'm told they have several well-behaved felines that will be my furry co-stars. But in reality we all know the cats are the stars and I'm simply a supporting character. Which is as it should be.

The facility is just a few blocks from the newsroom, so I hoof it there. Two people from the animal group meet me in the lobby, gushing over me like I'm the Mother Teresa of the cat world. They lead me back to the studio, where I find a set that looks like a typical living room. Cameras are set up while a lighting person checks things.

"Welcome, Miss Shaw."

I turn to follow the voice and find myself face to face with a very cute guy. "Hi there."

He sticks out his hand. "Jamison Rogers. This is my production house. We're really happy to have you for this project."

"My pleasure."

Oh, yeah.

I lock eyes with the guy for a moment, getting lost in his baby blues. He's about my height, slender with dark hair and has that boy-next-door thing going on. Probably one of those guys who looks thirty but is actually forty and will always have a boyish charm.

"Well, Miss Shaw—"

"Madison, please."

"Sure. Madison. I assume you already looked over the scripts but I can put them in the prompter if you like."

"They're only thirty seconds." I tap my head. "Got 'em memorized."

"Great." He places one hand lightly on my back and ushers

me across the room. "Let's get you made up then and we'll be ready to roll."

Two and a half hours later (and a few scratches from a temperamental Siamese . . . which I was told is redundant) we're done. All but one of the cats was wonderful and we did three versions of the public service announcements. My boss has given me the whole day for this but Jamison and his staff were incredibly organized, on the level of news people who have multiple deadlines every day. The video we shot looked great and hopefully the finished product will have the same quality.

I'm thanking the production crew and getting ready to leave when Jamison approaches me. "Madison, I must say, it's great to work with someone who came prepared. You nailed every take. It'll be hard to find the best ones because they're all so good. And the video of you playing with the cats is gold."

"Well, I must compliment you on your staff. Very professional and organized."

"Most of them worked in your business. As did I."

"Oh, really."

"Yep. You're looking at a former reporter who only got a few rungs up the ladder in news before I started doing this. But I picked up some very valuable skills. The best being time management. Nothing forces you to be organized more than a job in television news."

"No kidding. How long have you had this business?"

"Started it about twelve years ago."

"Well, you seem to be doing quite well for yourself now. You have a great facility with all the toys."

"Yeah, we do okay here. Listen, since we had booked the entire day for this and we knocked it out so quickly, you free for lunch?"

Of all the professions in the world, none like talking shop as much as television news people.

The topics are endless, but the ones at the top of the pyramid generally can fill hours:

—My boss is an idiot.

—Our anchor is a brainless beauty pageant queen. (Another redundancy.)

—Bias is killing the business and viewers hate us.

—Consultants are the devil's spawn who borrow your watch and then charge to tell you the time.

—Our cheap CEO throws nickels around like manhole covers.

And since I've got someone who worked in the business sitting across from me at lunch, small talk isn't necessary to get things going. Jamison may as well have left the business yesterday. The man is certainly up on things regarding the news media, well read on current events, and shows a great interest in my quest to take down the media's great white whale, corrupt Senator Joe Collier, AKA Teflon Joe, named because nothing ever sticks to him. Jamison has a personality that was made for on-camera work. (Or a fun date.) Why he's not on the network or in a major market is probably due to the one common denominator with those of us who did make it.

Pure luck.

Go to the smallest market with a TV station, and you'll find someone just as smart or smarter than someone at the network. And you can find plenty of people at any network who should be working as crash-test dummies.

In my case, a network executive driving across the country happened to be watching my station in his hotel room the night I broke a huge investigative story while working in a place I refer to as Upper Buttcrack, Arkansas. And when he found out I'd interned at the network, the brass ring was mine.

In Jamison's case, the stars didn't align so he bailed after eight years out of frustration and started what is now a successful production company. (And yes, I did the math, which makes him about forty.)

An hour after trading media stories, it's time to find out more about this guy. I take a bite of cheesecake as I begin my search for red flags. May as well get the big one out of the way. "So, I guess you like cats."

"I wouldn't have brought a bunch of 'em into my studio if I didn't. We've actually been doing those public service announcements *pro bono* for a while. Our business does so well I'd feel guilty if I didn't give something back."

"Ah, very nice of you."

"Not as nice as what you're doing for those kittens. Must be quite a lot of work."

"It's not that big of a deal."

"Turning down the Presidential campaign gig? Not sure I could have done it. To me that's a very big deal."

"Seemed like the right thing to do. At least I still get to hound Senator Collier in his campaign, not that I'll find anything on that sleazeball. Anyway, since you know what I do in my spare time, tell me what you do with yours?"

"I have a small sailboat I like to take out on weekends when the weather's nice. Really clears your head to get away from video and technology to commune with nature. I've always loved the water."

"That sounds great. Where do you sail?"

"I've got a little place on the Jersey shore. It's a bit of a commute but I couldn't spend my entire day in Manhattan. And half the time I can work from home anyway when I have writing or editing to do."

"And when it's too cold to take the boat out?"

"I build a fire and look at the ocean."

"Sounds wonderful."

He looks down a minute, takes a deep breath, then back at me. "I'm, uh, taking the boat out on Sunday. Weather's supposed to be perfect. I sure could use a first mate."

"Sounds like fun. But I've never been sailing. So, what might be the duties of a first mate?"

"Enjoy the sunshine and drink wine. Then have dinner with me on the patio as the sun sets."

"I think I can handle that."

Chapter Ten

I'm putting groceries away from my Saturday morning shopping when I hear the doorbell ring. I close the fridge and head for the door. "Coming!" I'm expecting a package of cat supplies but find a surprise instead.

A very pleasant surprise.

Officer Marino.

I hold out my wrists as if to be handcuffed. "Well, I guess you figured out my true identity. Damn witness protection program. I'll surrender peacefully if you don't do a perp walk for the media."

He laughs. "And good morning to you too."

"So to what do I owe this visit from one of New York's finest?"

"I'm selling tickets for a fundraiser to help the family of an officer who was killed in the line of duty two years ago. I figured a woman who would take care of orphaned kittens might be the kind to help out."

"Absolutely. Come on in." He's dressed casually, khakis and a white linen shirt that shows off buffed biceps. "I assume you're off duty today."

"Yep, I'm a Monday to Friday cop."

"So in that case you have time for that coffee you missed when you pulled me over."

He flashes a smile. "Sure thing. I'd love some."

"Actually you have three cups coming. One from the Fourth of July as well. And another for rescuing me at the bar." I lead him to the kitchen and point to the breakfast nook. "Have a seat and I'll get you a cup. How do you take it?"

"Light and sweet."

"Just like your women, huh? Sadly I'm neither."

"Y'know, you're funny as hell. How come I don't see that side of you on television?"

"Covering politics is a serious business. Though not nearly as serious as yours." I fix two cups of coffee and join him at the table. "So, you actually watch my network?"

"Yeah, I'm a political junkie and I love election coverage. Your stories are very objective, not biased like so many of your cohorts."

"Thank you. My journalism teacher always said to tell the viewers what you know, not what you think. No one will ever know how I vote."

"Very admirable. Oh, how are the kittens?"

I cock my head at them in a sun square where they're sleeping in a ball. "Still fat and happy. They're coming along really well. Do you have a cat?"

"I'd love one, but my apartment building doesn't allow pets."

"That's not right."

"But I plan to get one when I buy a house. Our family always had cats when I was growing up. I like their independent attitude. And they're smart as hell."

"So, what's the deal on the fundraiser?"

He pulls a stack of tickets from his pocket and removes a rubber band. "It's a dinner dance for Sergeant Tim Rockwell's family. Left behind a wife and two kids. Maybe you remember the story? He was sitting in the patrol car and a guy came up and shot him."

"Right, who could forget that one? Really sad. Did you know him well?"

He bites his lower lip and looks down. "He was my partner."

I realize he was a big part of that story, so I reach over and take his hands. "Oh my God, I'm so sorry. So you're the officer—"

"Right. I was in the donut shop getting coffee when it happened. Sarge usually got the coffee because his best friend owned the donut shop but he had pulled a muscle and was driving that day." He shook his head. "There but for the grace of God go I. I don't mind telling you I feel guilty about it every day. It should have been me."

"Don't say that."

"Well, I often wonder if the killer had shown up on a different day. It would have been me instead of him, and he'd be there for his wife and kids. I'm just a single guy with no one depending on me."

"That's not true. Look at all the people you help in your job. Like me. You can't beat yourself up about it. And at least you did take out the murderer. But hey, you're doing a good thing to help out his family. Focus on that." I lean over to a kitchen drawer and pull out my checkbook. "You said it's a dinner dance?"

"Yeah. The tickets are a hundred bucks apiece. We've got a great band and the food is being donated from Castelli's."

"That's worth the money right there. I'll take four. My friend Rory and her boyfriend love to dance." I start to write a check as he peels off four tickets. "Who do I make it out to?"

"Rockwell family fund." He sips his coffee as I write the check. "You know, you look so different from television. Or how you did when I pulled you over."

"Yeah, they try to turn me into a fashion model. Good luck with that. So now you see I'm a plain Jane."

"You're not remotely plain. I meant to say you look better in person. Why do they cover up your freckles?"

"The consultants said they don't have enough *gravitas.*

According to my boss, it would be like getting breaking news from the Little Mermaid. So our makeup person puts the pancake on with a trowel."

"I don't know why. You sure don't need it."

I can't help but smile. "You're very sweet."

"So, I guess you'll be double-dating with your best friend. You do that a lot?"

"It won't be a double date. I don't have a boyfriend. And I'm not currently seeing anyone."

"Really."

I look up and hand him the check. "Yeah, really. I'm a free agent."

"So the guy on the Fourth of July—"

"Like I told you, friend of a friend I met at a cookout. I'm certainly not going to see him again."

"Ah. I was worried you might be upset that I put your boyfriend in jail. By the way, he had two DUIs in Florida. Judge will throw the book at him and take away his license."

"Damn. See, you probably saved lives keeping him off the road. And you saved me from someone who isn't responsible."

"Yeah, guess so."

"Anyway, since I don't have a boyfriend, maybe if your girl-friend isn't the jealous type you might take me for a spin on the dance floor."

"I don't have a girlfriend. And I'm not seeing anyone either."

"Really?"

"Yeah, really. A lot of women aren't big on dating cops. High risk profession and we get a lot of bad press."

"I hope you know that none of that bad press comes from me. I really respect what you guys do. I wouldn't be here if two cops hadn't saved my life."

"Really? What happened?"

"Long story, I'll tell you some other time." I study his face for a moment, the sincerity in his eyes. The bravado I'd lost about asking a guy out is back a bit since I'm going sailing with Jamison tomorrow. So if he turns me down, it won't hurt as bad with another good guy on my dance card. I've never really played the field, but . . .

What the hell.

Alert the Weather Channel. Tell Satan it's about to get real friggin' cold down there.

My heart starts pounding a bit as I take a deep breath. (Damn, if guys go through this every time they hit on a woman, I'm amazed most aren't dead from heart attacks.) "So, anyway, uh . . . the, uh . . . I was . . ."

"Yeah?"

Dammit, girl just spit it out. "Well . . . since I'll be a third wheel with Rory and her boyfriend, and you don't have a jealous girlfriend, perhaps you'd like to be my escort? And should you do me this huge favor, I'd be inclined to cook you dinner tonight in return."

He leans back with his coffee. "That has to be the cleverest approach to ask a guy out I've ever seen."

"I'm not asking you out. You're helping out a woman who doesn't want to be alone on the dance floor and I'm making dinner to thank you. Plus I already owe you for making me drive safely, saving me at the bar, getting me home on the Fourth of July . . ."

"Okay, whatever you wanna call it. But I'd be happy to be your . . . escort . . . to the dance. And I would love to have dinner with you tonight. Should be done selling tickets to people I know by four."

"Good. Dinner is at seven."

"Looking forward to it. You wanna catch a movie after?"

I cock my head toward the kittens. "I haven't arranged for a sitter and I know my usual girl is visiting a college today. They still have to be bottle fed every few hours."

"No problem. I'll pick up a movie."

"That's fine."

"I guess you'd like a romantic comedy?"

"Hell no. Get something with a lot of explosions where the good guys win."

He starts to laugh. "Can't believe I'm saying this, but I'm really glad you ran that stop sign."

"I hope it won't ruin your reputation showing up at the affair with a felon. Or one who associates with them."

"Very funny." He starts to fold the check. "Hey, this is for *five* hundred. The tickets are a hundred apiece and you bought four."

"It's for a good cause. Besides, lately I've started to realize I'm blessed. I mean, hell, I tell stories for a living and you're out there risking your life to protect me. Anyway, time I started giving back a lot more. Keep the change."

"Very generous of you." He puts it in his pocket. "Well, I better get back to selling some tickets."

"Right. We can talk more tonight."

"See you then."

The minute he leaves I'm on the phone to A.J. "I need help. Now."

"What happened?"

"I asked the cop out on a date."

"Holy shit! Oh my gawd, I just saw pigs fly by my window."

"Very funny. Anyway, I need your assistance."

"What, you want me to come along and hold your hand?"

"No, I invited him over for dinner."

"I hope you mean you invited him *out* to dinner."

"No. Here. My house. I'm making dinner."

"*Madonne.* You'd better put the phone number for poison control on the fridge. You tryin' to chase him away on the first date?"

"Fine, I admit I'm a disaster in the kitchen."

"So you call an Italian."

"Hey, some stereotypes are based on fact. But I don't have a

96

sitter for the kittens tonight so I had no choice. Can you come over and help me cook something great?"

"Sure. This is a DEFCON ONE dating emergency. On my way."

My hands are getting tired as I roll the mixture into meatballs. "I thought the only thing in meatballs is, ya know, meat."

A.J. sips her wine as she directs me. "Typical non-Italian assumption. Most people try to make meatballs with ground beef and nothing else. You're basically eating hamburgers and ketchup. You gotta have the ground pork in there. The pork gives the flavor to the meatballs and the sauce."

"Interesting. And all the other ingredients?"

"You need the eggs and breadcrumbs to soften them up. The garlic, parsley, salt, pepper and other stuff gives it a kick."

"We really need to start this early?"

"The sauce has to simmer for four hours, minimum. It's a slow process. That's why most people make a ton of meatballs and sauce, then freeze a bunch of containers. If you're gonna tie up the kitchen for a whole day, you might as well. Too much trouble and time to make a small amount."

"Yeah, looks that way." I finish rolling the meatballs. "Okay, now what?"

She points at a frying pan. "Now we lightly fry them in olive oil on a low heat, just enough to hold them together. Then you toss 'em in the pot and the heat from the sauce cooks them the rest of the way. That's how you get nice soft meatballs. And the sauce picks up the flavor."

"From the pork."

"Among other things."

I start putting the meatballs in the olive oil. "I just realized, I didn't write anything down. And we didn't measure anything."

"After a while you just know how much spice to use. As for the meat, it's always two pounds of beef to one pound pork. Season to taste. If you like things spicy, go wild. If not, tone it down."

"I love your sauce, A.J."

"Then you go wild. Italians aren't shy with spices."

I finish putting the first round of meatballs in the oil. "Starting to smell good in here."

"I'll bring you some provolones from the deli and you can hang them from the ceiling if you really wanna impress this guy."

"I think this will be enough." I keep an eye on the meatballs.

"So, what made you do it?"

"What?"

"Ask a guy out. I never thought you had the guts."

"I met another nice guy yesterday who is taking me sailing tomorrow. I figured I had nothing to lose."

"*You're* playing the field? Hold on, let me call the network."

"Hey, what I've been doing hasn't been working. Besides, I keep running into the cop. It's almost like the universe wants us to be together. He seems like a nice old fashioned guy. Protective of women. Honorable profession."

"Dangerous profession."

I nod. "Yeah, I know. Anyway, I haven't had much luck with fix-ups or guys asking me out until yesterday, so I figured I'm on a roll. Also figured it was time I did the choosing."

I'm rather overdressed for dinner at home, in a royal blue dress and heels, but if dinner isn't perfect I at least want to look as good as possible.

And maybe that will distract him from the fact I'm nervous as hell.

This must be how guys feel. It's obviously different when you're doing the asking.

The sauce is done and tastes delicious. Meatballs are just like A.J.'s. I've got fresh pasta ready to cook and some nice garlic bread ready to go in the oven. Honestly, there's no way he'll be disappointed in the food.

And yet I still feel like a virgin on prom night.

The doorbell rings and makes me jump. I try my best to exhale some tension without success. (Shoulda hit the wine earlier.) I force a smile as I head to the door and open it.

He's overdressed for dinner at home as well, in a nice dark sport coat and tie. "Right on time, Marino."

He's carrying a bottle of wine and a box from a bakery as he enters. "Wow, it smells good in here. Like my mom's house."

"I assumed you like Italian food."

"Not too much of a stretch, huh?" He heads for the kitchen, takes a look in the pot. "Damn, that looks good."

"I confess I had help from a *paisan*."

"Ah. You need any help now?"

I hand him a corkscrew and a couple of glasses. "You can take care of the wine and I'll get the pasta going." I turn on the oven to heat the garlic bread already inside and start boiling the water. I hear the pop of the wine bottle and turn to see him pouring two glasses. He hands one to me and I hold it up to him. "To New York's finest."

He clinks my glass. "To damsels in distress who need us. Especially those worth saving." He locks eyes with me and all my tension disappears.

Maybe I really am on a roll.

I watch him lean back and pat his stomach. "Damn, that was good. Madison, I'm impressed."

"Like I said, I had help from A.J. Otherwise you might be eating cat food. But thank you."

And then I hear the meow.

I toss my napkin on the table. "And now some other guys need dinner."

"Right. You still bottle feeding them?"

"Yep. Wanna help?"

"Sure."

I move to the kitchen, prepare the bottles and hand two to

him. "Grab a seat on the couch and I'll bring them out." I head to the spare room, grab two kittens, and take them back to the living room. I hand him the tabby while I sit down with the tortoiseshell. "Okay, just hold a bottle up in front of the kitten and it knows what to do." I demonstrate with my kitten, then watch as he follows suit.

He flashes a wide smile. "I can see why the video went viral. This is really cute. How much longer till they can feed themselves?"

"Not much. So, you like cats?"

"Yeah. I know that sounds out of character for a cop, not to be a dog person, but I like the fact that they're independent. I like women who are the same way as well." He points at my kitten. "So, that one's your favorite?"

"How did you know?"

"You're feeding him first. As you did on TV."

"Yes, he's my favorite. And I'm keeping him."

"He got a name?"

"Not yet." The tortoiseshell finishes his bottle. I burp him and put him in my lap. "Want to see more of his personality before I name him."

"Ah. Hey, you ever read that thing about how to name a cat?"

"There's a guide book on that?"

"No, it's from that book of poems . . . they based the musical *Cats* on it."

"I'll have to give it a look." I hear a meow and see that the tortoiseshell has climbed over onto his lap. "Well, you little turncoat. Here I say I'm keeping you and you run away."

"Like I said, I'm a cat whisperer." The tortoiseshell curls up, looks at me and meows, then starts purring.

He approves of the officer.

"Well, I guess you are."

He looks out at the room. "By the way, not to be nosy or anything . . . did you by any chance have a grandmother like mine with a plastic covered couch?"

"Huh?"

He points at the legs of a chair. "What's with all the bubble wrap? You just buy this furniture?"

"Well, the one I'm keeping is blind in one eye and kept bumping into stuff since he has no depth perception."

He looks down at the tortoiseshell. "This one's blind? Poor little guy."

"He can see with one eye, but the vet says he'll develop pathways eventually as long as I don't move the furniture. Anyway, he can't jump either, since one of his back legs is deformed."

"So you've basically cat-proofed the house."

"Yep. Now he can play with his friends and when he bumps into stuff he doesn't get hurt."

"You're really amazing, you know that?"

With the kittens fed and put to bed, I sit next to the first man I've ever asked out as the movie starts, handing him a glass of wine. Between the two glasses I've already had and the fact that he makes me feel perfectly safe, my anxiety is gone. His earthy cologne distracts me from the movie.

So, what's the protocol when a woman asks a man for a date? Is the woman required to make the first move since the roles are reversed?

What the hell, I'm on a roll. Give him a hint.

I slide closer, resting my head on his shoulder. He puts his free arm around me. "You comfortable, Madison?"

"Yeah. You?"

"Very. This is certainly a nice way to repay me for doing that . . . *favor* for you."

I turn and smile at him. "Glad you're enjoying yourself."

"I'm trying to think of ways to do more favors."

"I do have those jars that need opening."

"Line 'em up."

"Later, Mister." I grab the remote, pause the movie, then turn back to him. We lock eyes.

"Giving up on the movie already?"

I nod. "The opening credits weren't terribly interesting."

"I agree." He begins to stroke my hair. "Damn, you've got great eyes. They're like emeralds."

"You gonna kiss me, Officer, or do I have to call 911 and report a romance emergency?"

"That won't be necessary. Unit ninety-ninety is ten-ten."

"Copy that."

He takes my head in his hands and gives me a long, soft kiss.

Two hours later (the movie was on "pause" for so long the DVD player shut itself off) he looks at his watch. "I hate to say this, but I need to get going."

"It's only ten."

"I've got an early flight tomorrow morning."

Now in the annals of dating, telling a woman you have an early flight, appointment, or crack of dawn workplace starting time is a classic way for a man to leave. Usually, though, it's after sex. My face drops a bit.

Then I remember Tish's trick to find out if the guy is telling the truth. "You want a ride to the airport?"

His face lights up. "Seriously? Wow, that would be really nice of you."

Well, that's the answer I was hoping for but not expecting. (Of course, now I actually have to get up early and drive the guy to the airport. Truth serum does have its down side.) "So, where are you going?"

"Arlington, Virginia. My Chief is sending me there for special training. I want to eventually become a detective. I've been spending some of my free time investigating cold cases and actually solved a few. The powers that be took notice so they're sending me."

"Wow, that's terrific. How long will you be gone?'

"A month."

My face tightens. "A month?"

"Yeah, but I'll be back the day before the dance. Not exactly the best timing considering how much I enjoyed this evening."

"I'll be here when you get back, Officer. I'm not a flight risk."

Chapter Eleven

As I drive Nick Marino to LaGuardia Airport this morning, I can predict with reasonable certainty that this conversation will take place during Sunday brunch:

A.J.: "Lemme get this straight. She had a great date with the cop last night, is driving him to the airport, and then is going straight to Jersey to go sailing with another guy?"

Rory: "The woman feels like she's cheating if she has lunch with two different guys during the same month. Her guilt will be off the charts."

Tish: "I'd pay good money to see the look on her face if the cop hugs her at the airport and she heads off to see the other guy. She'll feel like a cheap bimbo. Probably stop at a church and go to confession as a pre-emptive strike."

Nick pulls his plane ticket from his pocket. "I can't tell you how much I appreciate this, Madison. But you really didn't have to get up early for me."

Uh, I was gonna get up early anyway to . . . demon, be gone! Out, guilt spirit! "Hey, you've done plenty for me. It's not a big deal. Besides, the thought of you on that awful airport shuttle . . . well, I couldn't live with myself."

"Still very nice of you, Madison."

I pull up to the curb at the departures lane and turn off the car. We both get out and head for the trunk. Luckily the airport is very strict about how long you can park there, as a long goodbye would make the guilt monster even worse. I pop the trunk and he grabs his suitcase. "Well, have a good trip and come back ready to be the next Sherlock Holmes."

He smiles and shuts the trunk for me. "See you in a month. But talk soon." He leans forward and gives me a big hug, then heads for the door.

What a surprise. I feel guilty as hell.

It is a little known but seriously cool way to get from Manhattan to the Jersey shore.

Basically, it's a water taxi. Actually it's bigger than a checker cab, as it's a boat that will hold about a hundred people.

Beats the hell out of the Jersey Turnpike or a train.

After dumping my car in the network parking lot I boarded the boat for the one-hour ride to Jamison's place in a town called Monmouth Beach. He was right, the weather is spectacular while looking at the water is incredibly relaxing. And for someone who has rarely been on a boat I'm spending pretty much the whole day on the Atlantic Ocean.

The floating taxi pulls up to the dock and I see him waiting on the pier, looking for all the world like he belongs on a sailboat with JFK. Tousled hair, khaki shorts, a white linen shirt with the sleeves rolled up, Ray-Ban sunglasses, and docksiders with no socks. I give him a wave and he waves back, flashing that cute boyish smile.

Okay, the guilt is gone.

I'm a big girl. I can have two first dates in twenty-four hours. It's not cheating. On either one.

It's just one date.

Yeah, let's go with that.

He greets me with a smile as he takes my beach bag. "Enjoy the ride?"

"Seriously, that's your commute every day?"

"Yep. Well, on the days I go into the city."

"Damn, you've got everything figured out about working in Manhattan, don't you?"

"I grew up here. By the end of the day you'll see why I came back and never want to leave. You might not want to leave either."

He leads me down the pier to the parking lot and over to a gleaming candy apple red Mercedes convertible. "Nice ride."

He shrugs as he tosses my bag in the back seat and opens the door for me. "It gets me from point A to point B."

"Yeah, right."

He pulls out of the parking lot and within minutes we're riding along next to the Atlantic Ocean, the sun warm on my face while the salt air whips through my hair. Hard to believe I'm an hour out of Manhattan, as it's like another world here. New Jersey gets a bad rap, but it has some spectacularly beautiful areas, and this is one of them. The street across the road from the ocean is lined with gorgeous mansions. It's pretty obvious this is a well-heeled town.

He pulls into the parking lot of a marina. "Okay, first mate, ready to work?"

"It's a tough job, but somebody's gotta do it. But remember, I've never done this."

He gets out and opens the trunk while I grab my beach bag, filled with a hat, a change of clothes in case I get wet and SPF 1000 sunblock, which will keep you from getting burned on the planet Mercury. Redheads are very sensitive to sun and we have to be careful. He pulls out a very large picnic basket with a bottle of wine sticking out the top, and cocks his head toward the water. "All aboard, young lady."

I look for a small sailboat as we walk down the pier. There are no small ones. There are no medium sized sailboats either. He stops in front of a beautiful vintage wooden sailboat that has to be forty feet long. "*This* is your small sailboat?"

"Gets me from point A to point B." He holds my hand as I climb aboard, noticing the name painted on the back.

Miss Right.

"So, who's the boat named after?"

He hops onto the boat. "No one."

"Was that the name of the boat when you bought it?"

"No, it had a horrible name. *Mid-Life Crisis*."

"So who's *Miss Right*?"

"Don't know yet. Still searching for her. When I find her she gets the keys to this thing." He puts the basket down and points to the middle of the boat. "You can change down there."

I'm wearing white linen pants and a green cotton top. "Change into what?"

"Oh, I'm sorry. I guess I didn't tell you the first mate is required to wear a string bikini."

"Nice try, Mister. Too bad I don't own one."

"Just kidding, Madison. Though it is a waste of a pretty redhead. Anyway, why don't you open the wine and I'll get us underway."

I give him a salute. "Aye, Aye, captain. That's something I know how to do. I've had lots of practice with wine bottles."

A half hour later a gentle breeze is taking us slowly along the calm water. The sun and temperature are perfect. Jamison sits next to me and opens the picnic basket. "Ready for lunch?"

"Always. So, what's on the menu?"

He pulls out a few plastic containers. "Nothing fancy. Lobster salad. Cheese and crackers. A few other goodies."

"Right, nothing fancy."

He dishes out the lobster salad onto a couple of plates. "I'm really glad you came, Madison. It's more fun sailing when you have company."

"Hey, thank you for inviting me. This is a treat."

"So this is really your first time on a sailboat?"

107

"Yep. But this is not what I expected. You buy this thing from the Kennedys?"

He laughed a bit. "I like vintage stuff. Boats were made a lot better years ago. Now everything is plastic and falls apart. This boat doesn't have the modern amenities, but who cares? The whole point of sailing is to enjoy the water. And I really missed this when I was stuck in jobs working in places like Kansas and Wyoming. Big part of the reason I quit the news business."

"Well, looks like you made the right decision. You're obviously doing very well with your production company."

"I do okay."

"Yeah, right." I take a bite of the lobster salad. It's so good I have to close my eyes and savor it. "Damn, that's awesome."

"Well, I didn't make it. I will be cooking dinner though."

"I'm almost afraid to ask what's on that menu if you consider this to be nothing fancy."

"Actually, just steaks on the grill. I'm not a great cook."

"Well, neither am I, so that sounds fine. I'm a pretty simple girl at heart. I think you never really change from the way you grew up. Of course, I rarely had steak when I was a kid."

He nods and gives me a soulful look. "Yeah, I saw that interview you did on the morning show. Must have been tough. Not exactly a normal childhood."

The memory makes me cringe a bit.

He notices. "Sorry, Madison. Didn't mean to bring it up. I'm sure it's not an experience you want to re-live."

"That's okay. Actually, it did some good. I'll be doing some promotional work for Child Social Services to help raise adoption awareness. Try to find some good homes for kids."

"You have a good heart, Madison."

"I'm no saint. If you'd met me a month ago, you'd be sailing with a different girl. Actually, you wouldn't have invited me."

"I find that hard to believe."

"Oh, believe it. You know those people in every newsroom who will steamroll anyone to get ahead? That was me. I think I left footprints on some backs climbing up the ladder."

"Seriously? I can't picture you like that."

"Yep, that was me. Honestly, Jamison, I had lost my soul. My ambition stole it and I forgot where I came from."

"So what changed you?"

"The kittens. Hard to believe, huh?"

"Obviously they brought out the real you."

"I'm still in shock. It feels like this is my true personality. I went from bitter foster kid to driven reporter to . . . well, I'm not sure yet."

"I am. You're a good person."

"If that's the case, I'm a work in progress. But I like what I see in the mirror lately."

We're heading to his home after a wonderful day of sailing. I feel invigorated after being on the water, breathing the salt air, just relaxing and enjoying nature. The beautiful beach homes are capturing my attention. "All these houses are gorgeous."

"Yeah, and many of them have been here a long time. Most of them even survived Hurricane Sandy."

"Like you said, Jamison, older stuff was well built." I point toward a spectacular home up ahead. "I love that one with the tile roof. You don't see those too often in this part of the world."

He pulls into the driveway. "I was hoping you'd like it."

"No way. This is yours?"

He nods with a big smile. "Welcome to my humble abode."

"This is your *little place on the shore*?"

"It's a roof over my head."

"Damn, Jamison. How in the world do you ever leave this lifestyle and get to work?"

He gets out of the car, comes around and opens the door for

me. "When it's weather like this, I call in sick. But I can do that since I own the place."

I lean back on the teak bench next to Jamison as the sunset lights up the wispy clouds with reds and oranges. "I have really enjoyed the day, young man. Can't thank you enough. Everything was wonderful. The trip on the water taxi, sailing, lunch, dinner, sitting here looking at the ocean. It's been perfect."

"It would be perfect if we were looking at the Pacific Ocean. We're stuck with the sunrise here. Gotta go west for the sunsets."

"Sky is still gorgeous." I turn to face him. "Hey, after the sun goes down, know what I'd like to see?"

"What?"

"Some of the stories you did as a reporter."

His face tightens. "Uh, I really didn't keep any."

"Seriously? C'mon, don't be shy. I won't rip your stories apart. Every reporter keeps old resume tapes of their greatest hits. "

He shakes his head. "Not this one. My reporting career was so frustrating I choose not to remember it, like it was a different life. I threw everything away when I left the business."

"That's kinda sad, Jamison."

"Well, when you get stuck in the middle of nowhere for years and can't get out, that's not a memory you want to re-live."

"Yeah, I guess I can understand that. But I'll bet you were good with that great personality."

"Thank you, but you're ten times the reporter I ever was. I really wasn't cut out to work in journalism even though I'm a news junkie. I'd rather hear about the stories you're working on. And I'm much better at what I do now."

I look around the property. "Yeah, considering all this, I'd say you made a good decision. Long as you're happy and don't miss the business."

"Honestly, I don't give it a second thought." He looks at his watch. "Oh, almost forgot. You have a decision to make."

Uh-oh. What's this? "About what?"

"The last water taxi leaves in forty minutes. I can send you back on that or drive you home."

Whew. Thought he was going to hit me with something serious. "I'll take the taxi. You know how bad Sunday night traffic is going back to the city, especially during the summer. And you've done enough today."

"You sure? I don't mind."

"You'll be in the car for four hours. Besides, I'm sure the view of the Statue of Liberty from the water is spectacular with the thing all lit up."

"It is. Well, then, we need to get going in about ten minutes. And there's one other decision."

"What's that?"

"Can I see you again?"

"Seriously, Jamison? You have to ask?" I lean over, take his head in my hands, and give him a soft kiss. "You can take that as a yes."

I'm enjoying the view, sitting on one of the outside benches on the water taxi as it passes Miss Liberty illuminated in all her glory, when my cell phone beeps. It's been such a back-to-nature technology-free day I haven't checked the thing since this morning. I pull it out and see I've got a text that is several hours old.

Made it to Virginia okay. Thanks again for the ride to the airport. Can't wait to see you again. Talk soon . . .

-Nick

Annddd . . . cue the dancing guilt demon.

My next thought is that I need a hug from my kittens.

Chapter Twelve

The newsroom is buzzing as usual with tales of weekend adventures as I arrive on Monday morning. Thankfully there are no cat supplies on my desk.

But my boss is leaning against it with a smile.

I toss my purse on the desk as I face him. "Okay, Barry, you've got that look like you've got a story I'm going to love."

"You'll like what I'm about to tell you more than any assignment I could possibly give you."

"The network fired the consultants?"

He rolls his eyes. "Be serious, Madison. Hell hasn't frozen over. But it's almost as good, at least from your point of view."

"Well, don't keep me in suspense. Waddaya got for me?"

"It came out of your live shot with the kittens on the morning show. Corporate noticed that the response has been overwhelming and hasn't stopped."

"Yeah, I know. People love the kittens and the bottle feeding video."

He shakes his head. "Not that. It was the way you looked."

Now it's my turn for the eye roll. "Oh, shit. So let me guess . . . corporate got emails from people about the fact my hair wasn't done and I looked like I rolled out of bed. Probably because I did."

He shakes his head. "Just the opposite. Viewers loved the fact that you looked so natural." He hands me a bunch of papers. "Check out some of the emails."

I take the papers and begin to read.

"*Madison Shaw is so naturally cute! Why doesn't she look that way all the time?*"

"*Stop trying to make Madison look plastic on the evening news. Love the natural look.*"

"*No offense, Miss Shaw, but I love that you look like the rest of us at six in the morning.*"

"*She's a real person who wears sweatpants? Who knew?*"

"*Lovin' me some freckles! Don't ever cover them up again!*"

I look back at Barry. "You gotta be kidding. People like me as a frump?"

"You're not remotely frumpy. I didn't print out the ones from men who . . . well, you can read them later if you want a good laugh. Or an ego boost."

"Fine, so people like me natural. *I* like me natural."

"Well, now corporate wants you that way all the time."

"Rolled out of bed in sweatpants with my hair looking like I stuck my finger in a light socket?"

"No. Without makeup. And from now on you do your own hair. In other words, the way you look right now is fine for high-def."

I point at my face. "This is actually okay."

"Yeah."

"For network television."

"Yep."

My eyes widen as does my smile. "I don't have to get plastered with pancake anymore?"

"Nope. You're not wearing makeup now, right?"

"Correct. Not a bit."

"As far as I'm concerned, you are camera ready, young lady. And don't touch a hair on your head."

"So does that also mean the Little Mermaid can still do hard political stories and maintain credibility?"

"You bet. Your job description doesn't change. You're still my top political reporter."

"Woo-hoo!" My scream of joy makes everyone in the newsroom turn to me. "Hey everyone, I don't have to wear makeup anymore!" I open my desk drawer, take out the makeup kit I use in the field, and execute a perfect basketball jump shot sending it into the waste basket. Jennifer the diva practically tramples people as she dives for it, then pulls it out of the trash, beaming like she's caught the bride's bouquet.

Barry then hands me another sheet of paper. "Glad I made your day. Now here's your assignment."

I look at it and see a political investigative story. My favorite. In this case, the ultimate.

One I've been begging to do for years.

One that every political in reporter in America has failed to break.

The Great White Whale.

Another huge smile. "Are you kidding me?"

"The new CEO hates the guy. Told me personally to turn you loose. His exact words were, '*Give Madison carte blanche on this. I want that sonofabitch out of office and in jail.*'"

"You're not yankin' my chain, are you, Barry?"

"Nope. Knock yourself out. You need time off the street, photogs for stakeouts, you got it. But since you know the guy's reputation, please watch your back. The game he plays is beyond hardball."

"He doesn't scare me."

"That's one reason you're getting the story."

I arrive home from work Monday evening to find Rory and Jeff the veterinarian chatting in the living room, each holding a kitten. My pulse spikes. "Oh my God, what happened?"

Jeff smiles. "Nothing, Madison."

I rush to check the tortoiseshell sitting in Rory's lap. I take him from her, hold him up and look at him. "So they're okay?"

"Relax, they're fine. I came over to help you start weaning them off the bottle. I think it's time to teach them how to drink from a dish."

Big smile. "Seriously? No more bottles?"

Rory shakes her head. "You're so easily thrilled these days. I can only imagine how excited you'll be cleaning the litter box."

"Hey, you're not the one getting up at two in the morning."

Jeff stands up with his kitten. "You still have to get up and give them their formula. They can't exactly use a can opener and you can't leave the stuff out all night."

"Oh. Right."

"And you have to make sure each one gets the right amount of food. C'mon, class is in session." Jeff leads us into the kitchen and I see he already has a saucer, a spoon and some formula on the table. He sits down with the tabby while Rory and I watch him pour some of the formula into the saucer. "Okay, we need to teach the kitten to make the connection that the formula is in the saucer." He dips his finger into the formula and holds it to the kitten's mouth. The tabby eagerly licks it off. "Now we put a little in a spoon." He holds the formula filled spoon in front of the kitten and it starts to drink. "Okay, let's see if he can figure it out." He puts the kitten on the table next to the saucer and it quickly starts drinking like a normal cat.

"Wow, he picked that up fast," says Rory. "Okay, Freckles, your turn."

I follow the procedure with the tortoiseshell, holding my finger in front of him. He doesn't do anything but purr. "C'mon, little fella." Still nothing.

"Be patient," says Jeff. "He's curious like any cat and wants to learn. He'll figure it out. Instinct will kick in."

Finally the kitten sniffs my finger and starts to lick the formula.

115

After that he licks the spoon clean and quickly makes the connection, joining the tabby already lapping formula from the saucer. I'm beaming like a proud parent. "I taught my kitten to eat!"

Rory laughs. "Like I said, Doc, she's easily excited."

Tish and A.J. arrive a half hour later for dinner, which will feature leftovers from Saturday night since we made a ton of meatballs and sauce. I was told earlier that an emergency meeting was being convened due to the fact that, a) I had missed Sunday brunch; and b) I was dating two men at the same time for the first time in my life and had two different dates within twenty-four hours. My friends are concerned I have gone off the rails due to the fear of becoming the crazy cat lady spinster of the neighborhood. And that my only friend would be the curmudgeon down the street who sits on his porch waiting desperately to yell "get off my lawn" at kids like Clint Eastwood in *Gran Torino*, but not being successful since children don't play outside anymore.

And, of course, they know I'm dealing with guilt. In spades. Though I'm not sure "coveting" two single guys at the same time is against the rules. I'd check with my priest, but it would be too embarrassing and he thinks I'm a nice girl.

Tish, being the lawyer, officially brings the meeting to order as we begin dinner. "Okay, explain yourself."

"Regarding . . ."

"The witness is directed to answer the question."

"Fine. I wanted to learn how to cook. How do you like my meatballs?"

A.J. shakes her head. "Stop being evasive. You know damn well why we're here."

I twirl some pasta onto my fork. "Why, because after a string of bad dates and a boyfriend you wanted to wish into the cornfield, I happen to meet two nice guys at the same time?"

"Because this isn't like you, Freckles," says Rory. She points at her plate. "Neither is this. Damn, this sauce is terrific."

"Thank you, but it's A.J.'s recipe. As for the guys, it's not like I'm sleeping with multiple partners, which you know I would never do. I just had two very enjoyable first dates on the same weekend."

Tish nods. "I see. You do know we need to vet both of them."

"You've already met the cop."

"Yeah, for thirty seconds," says A.J.

Rory is focused on her dinner. "He's okay with me. I wanna know about the other guy. You should have already prepared a dossier for us. Since we do, after all, now have veto power."

"Veto power? When the hell did this happen?"

"We voted on it when you weren't here Saturday night."

I roll my eyes. "Okay, here's the deal. His name is Jamison Rogers and he owns a production house where we shot those public service announcements for cats the other day. We have a lot in common since he used to be a TV reporter. He has a beautiful home on the Jersey Shore and took me sailing. He has this gorgeous boat named *Miss Right* since that's who he's looking for."

A.J. laughs. "Most guys are looking for *Miss Right Now*."

"Oh, stop it. He was a perfect gentleman. Didn't make a move. Actually, I had to make the first move."

Rory drops her fork and looks up at me. "Excuse me. Something in this sauce is making me hallucinate. What the hell did you put in this?"

"Oh, stop it."

A.J. rests one hand on my forearm. "This is not you, honey. Why did you of all people make the first move?"

"Because I did it the night before with the cop and it worked."

"Whoa!" A chorus from my friends as their hands go up and the eating stops.

"What?"

A.J. turns to me. "You jumped the cop's bones? I was kidding."

"I didn't *jump his bones*. I told him to kiss me."

117

Rory studies my face. "And what possessed you to do this?"

"Duh-uh. Cute guy with his arm around me and I wanted to be kissed."

Rory turns to A.J. and Tish. "I think what we have here is a *Freaky Friday* scenario."

"I agree," says Tish.

Now *I* stop eating. "What the hell are you talking about?"

"Look," says Tish. "Since you got out of college you have been a kick-ass reporter who's not afraid of a damn thing and a single woman terrified of hitting on a man. Since those kittens came into your life, the roles have reversed, just like the personalities switching bodies in the movie. You gave up the dream assignment of the Presidential campaign and now you're taking the initiative with men. It's *Freaky Friday*, the multiple personality edition."

"I agree," says A.J. "Her professional and personal personalities have switched."

"Damn," says Rory. "If we let this continue she might turn into a cougar."

I stop for a moment and consider what they've said. "Y'know, what you guys are saying actually makes sense. I'm not afraid of men anymore and my career has become secondary. What the hell happened to me?"

"Meow," says Rory, wearing the appropriate Cheshire cat grin as she points at one of the kittens.

Tish starts eating again. "Anyway, back to the two men on your dance card. We need a post-mortem."

"Fine. Cooked dinner for the cop Saturday night, and he was impressed, so thank you A.J. for your help. Since I couldn't get a sitter for the kittens we didn't go out and he brought a movie. He helped me feed them and then we moved on to the movie."

"How was he with the cats?" asks A.J.

"He likes cats. Oh, my favorite crawled in his lap and purred. A very good sign."

"Okay," says Tish. "So, then you watched a movie."

I look down at my plate. "Uh, not exactly."

Rory reaches over, takes my chin and tilts it up. "What do you mean, *not exactly*? Was it a bad movie?"

"We, uh, didn't get past the opening credits before I asked him to kiss me. And then, we uh . . ." I look down again. "We made out for about two hours."

"Whoa!" Another chorus.

"And then about ten o'clock he says he has to get going because he has an early flight. I figured this was totally bogus and he was using that as an excuse in order to leave. So I used Tish's trick to see if he was lying by offering him a ride to the airport. Turned out he actually had an early flight to Washington as he's going to Arlington, Virginia for special training. So I ended up driving him to the airport Sunday morning."

Tish starts laughing. "And after two hours of making out the night before, what sort of goodbye did you have at the airport?"

"He gave me a big hug."

She nods. "And then you felt guilty on your way to Jersey."

"Big time. Anyway, I took the water taxi and Jamison was waiting for me with this Mercedes convertible. He took me to what he had called a little sailboat, which looks like something from one of those Kennedy home movies. Spectacular. Then he took me to his gorgeous home on the ocean and cooked dinner for me. As since he was really shy about asking me for a second date, I simply answered by kissing him."

Rory rests her head on her chin. "Hmmm. Interesting."

"I wasn't finished. On the boat ride home I got a text from the cop thanking me for the ride and saying he can't wait to see me again."

A.J. grabs her wine. "Guilt city."

"Big time again."

"So who do you like better?" asks Tish.

"Too early to tell. Both are gentlemen, both interesting guys. But very different. Time will tell."

119

"So you're going to juggle these two guys," says Rory.

"I'm not juggling anything. But after a bunch of bad relationships it's a nice problem to have. Though I realize I have to be careful." I turn to A.J. "So I need your advice."

She leans back a bit, eyes wide. "What are you lookin' at me for?"

Tish rolls her eyes. "Oh, please."

A.J. turns to her. "What?"

"Seriously, A.J.? Have you forgotten you once got two proposals of marriage in the same week? From two different men?"

"Yeah, but I liked the third guy I was dating better."

I frantically wave my hands. "Okay, enough. I'm in need of help here, guys. I don't know what to do. I like two guys and one is gone for a month. If I only date Jamison for a month he'll have an advantage over Nick."

Tish puts up her palms. "Hey, love isn't fair, sweetie."

"I know, but my journalism fairness made the jump in your *Freaky Friday* scenario. If I'm going to compare them, I can't do it if I see one four weeks in a row while the other is out of town. It might be *out of sight, out of mind.*"

"Or it might be *absence makes the heart grow fonder,*" says Rory.

"You're not helping."

We go back to eating. No one says anything for a minute or so.

Then Tish stops. "I've got it. Okay, here's what you do."

Chapter Thirteen

I've got a few hours to kill on the train from New York to Washington, D.C. as I head to the Capitol on this Friday to testify in front of Congress on a new adoption program. I'm not sure why it's called "testifying" since that implies I'm involved in some sort of crime or lawsuit. But there's an oath involved and a hand on a Bible, so it's the only choice. I'm not wild about doing this, as it will dredge up bad memories (which kept me up all night) but if it will save even one kid from being shuttled around it's worth it. My friends all offered to come along, but somehow this is something I need to do alone. Besides, if they were here I'd break down after testifying in the hallway in front of all the cameras, and if I'm going to appear to be the poster child for this, I have to put up a strong front.

Too bad I couldn't bring a kitten. The purring from those little guys relaxes me more than a bottle of wine. I read somewhere that a purring cat can actually lower your blood pressure. If that's true, everyone in Washington should have a kitty. Of course the President has been "using" his cat in photo ops and the thing now has an Instagram account. Trying to cultivate the "cat people" vote, I suppose. Anything is fair in politics. This has, of course, resulted in some of the other candidates featuring their pets in campaign commercials.

And as if I don't have enough stuff bouncing around in my head, there's the matter of the two guys on my aforementioned dance card. That "nice problem to have" had better resolve itself eventually, since I have no desire to resolve it myself. Hopefully one of the guys will rise to the top. Though maybe neither one will. I've only been on one date with each, after all. But something feels different this time. Like I'm ready for the real thing.

Tish, meanwhile, came up with the solution to the problem of the cop being away for a month as she reminded me of this trip and the fact he's training in Arlington, which is next door to the nation's capital. So after I'm done with Congress we're going to meet for dinner before I take the train home tomorrow. By the time I go out with him at that charity dinner in a few weeks, I will have been on three dates with each man. Assuming the relationships don't implode after the second date.

The shoe is on the other foot as I run the gauntlet of media people on my way to the hearing which starts in five minutes, telling them I'll be happy to answer their questions after I'm done. I'm about to enter the room when a skinny teenage girl with stringy blonde hair lightly takes my arm.

"Excuse me, Miss Shaw?"

"Yes?"

"I'm a foster kid and I just wanted to personally say thank you for coming here to speak on our behalf. It really means a lot."

"Thank you, I appreciate that." I note the sadness in her expression. "You in a bad situation?"

She nods, her blue eyes filled with hurt. "Yeah." She rolls up her sleeve and I see a series of bruises. "I was hoping you might have some advice for me about what to do. I'm sixteen and I'm stuck for two more years. I don't think I'll make it."

Not good.

And I can't walk away.

I grab a pad from my purse and hand it to her. "Write down

your name, address and phone number and I'll have someone take care of it."

"You'd do that for me?"

"Hey, we gotta stick together."

She writes her contact info on the pad and hands it back to me. I see she came all the way from Newark. "Thank you for caring."

"Not a problem." I hand her a business card. "You need anything else, call me. Call collect if you have to."

Her eyes well up. She moves forward and gives me a strong hug, hanging on longer than normal. Which is, of course, captured by the cameras.

My heart pounds as I sit down after taking the oath. I'm about to tell my life story in front of millions of people.

Julianne Flint, the fortyish United States Senator from Florida who asked me to testify, puts on a pair of wire-rimmed bifocals, brushes her brunette hair back and nods at me. "Miss Shaw, first, we'd like to thank you for coming today. I'm sure some of what will be discussed might be unpleasant for you, but your perspective will be instrumental in getting passage for this bill."

"Thank you, Senator, but I'm no different than any other foster child."

"But your experience is different than most, as you have risen to the top of a very high profile profession. If you wouldn't mind, can you give us an overview of your personal experiences, as I understand your childhood was spent in six foster homes."

I note my fists are clenched, so I put my hands in my lap. I tell my story, what it was like to grow up with six different families. How some cared and some didn't. What it was like in school when classmates found out your background. The room is silent with the exception of my voice and the auto-winders of cameras. After about ten minutes with my mouth now dry as a bone, I'm done.

The Senator slowly nods. "Thank you for sharing that, Miss Shaw. I'd like to ask you about the makeup of your various foster parents. What they were like, how they treated you. If you actually considered them parents in the traditional sense."

"Well, I'd classify four of them as basically in it for the money. The State would give them a certain amount which was supposed to be earmarked for each child, but very often little of that money ended up being used that way. To them it was a career and taking care of us was a job, not parenting. Two of my families were wonderful, people who sincerely wanted children and in both cases probably spent a lot more than the State provided."

"And yet you were still moved around?"

"Yes. The first good parents I had were both killed in a car wreck, so I was moved immediately. The other nice people simply felt they were getting too old to take care of children, and got out of the program. I still keep in touch with them. But look, I don't want to disparage all foster parents. I know other people who grew up in foster homes that were terrific and had a good experience. And there are plenty of couples who take in children because they genuinely want to parent them."

"So, mind telling us how you turned out so normal?"

I need to lighten things up a bit, for my sake and to break the tension in the room. "Senator, anyone who works in television news isn't remotely normal." Everyone laughs and I relax a bit. "But the guiding force in my life has been my best friend, Rory Callahan. She actually took me under her wing in high school and her parents moved me in with them when I turned eighteen. I am also blessed to have two other very close friends, and I consider them all family. Many times your friends are your family when you're a foster child." I'm thankful at this moment that they're not here, as the mere sight of them would make me tear up.

"What's your opinion of the new program we're proposing, offering free college tuition to a child provided the adoptive parents raise the child till eighteen? Without those monthly State checks along the way. Do you think this will work and be an improvement from what we have now?"

"I think it's a great idea. You wouldn't get the people who simply took a child in for the money. You'd get people who honestly wanted to raise a child. And I'll tell you this . . . to spend eighteen years in the same house with the same parents would be a dream come true for any kid in the system. Adoption is a lifetime commitment."

The Senator smiles at me and leans back in her chair. "Thank you, Miss Shaw. I yield to the Senator from New Mexico. Oh, I almost forgot . . . how are the kittens?"

I can't help but smile. "They're great. And adopting a pet is a lifetime commitment as well. So the President had better not get rid of that cat after the election."

An hour later I'm done after taking questions from five Senators. I greet the waiting media horde in the hallway and answer ten more minutes of questions. And when I'm done I smile and thank everyone.

The media packs up and starts to leave while I head down the hall to the ladies room. Thankfully it is empty.

I go into a stall. The emotions I've held inside explode and I throw up.

My last stop in DC is the office of a Congressman from Long Island who has tipped me off to a bunch of good stuff over the years. Brad Dexter is known as a scrupulously honest politician who made his bones as an FBI agent, then became a household name when he blew the whistle on some illegal stuff going on in the Justice Department. He resigned and used his notoriety to win election to the House of Representatives. It didn't hurt that the forty-eight year old legislator possessed classic good looks; his tall, solid stature and steel jaw making him seem like the poster child for law enforcement.

He greets me with a smile and extends a hand as I enter his office. "Madison, good to see you again."

"How you doing, Congressman?"

"Oh, stop with the formalities, will you?" He takes a seat behind his desk as I sit in front, studying me with his gray eyes. "More importantly, are you doing okay? I could tell you weren't terribly comfortable during that hearing."

"It was painful, I will admit. But it will help a lot of kids. If the bill passes, that is."

"It will raise awareness whether it passes or not. I will tell you it has a lot of support in the House and I've been lobbying for it."

"Thank you. Speaking of kids . . . you got any good contacts in Newark?"

"I'm good friends with a Congresswoman from that district. And I know a couple of agents in the FBI field office there. Why?"

"Need a favor." I hand him the slip of paper with the teenager's name and address. "I met this girl in the hallway before my testimony. Foster kid with a lot of bruises who says she needs help. She needs to get into a good home."

He nods as he looks at the paper. "Consider it done. What else you need?"

"Well, you're not gonna believe this. As you may have heard, our old network CEO has reached room temperature and his replacement wants me to take down Senator Collier."

His eyes widen. "Seriously? Your network is going after Teflon Joe?"

"Yep. And as you know, many have tried but no one has ever found the smoking gun that could put him away. I could sure use your help since you have access I don't."

"Well, this makes my day. I hate that sonofabitch. Whatever you need, I'll get. Any idea where you want to start looking?"

I pull a manila envelope out of my briefcase. "Right here. As

Deep Throat said in *All the President's Men*, 'Just follow the money'.

Seeing my friends and the kittens cheers me up. Of course it's via a video chat with the gals, who are having a slumber party at my house while taking care of the fur babies.

"We're really proud of you," says Rory, sitting on the floor between A.J. and Tish while the kittens run around. "I know what you did was hard."

"You have no idea."

"You okay?" asks Tish.

I shrug. "Just wrung out. I want to put the whole thing behind me."

"Well, what time is your cop picking you up?" asks A.J.

"In a few minutes. But to be honest, I don't even feel like going out."

"You need to," says Rory. "Oh, say hello to your favorite." She holds the tortoiseshell up to the camera.

I wave at the kitten. "Hey, little fella!"

He meows and puts one paw up to the camera. "See, he knows his special person," says Rory.

The hotel room phone rings. "Hang on a minute." I answer and am told Nick is in the lobby. "Send him up, please." I hang up and turn back to the video chat. "Okay, he's here. Gotta go."

"Try to relax," says Tish. We all wave and end the chat.

I take a quick look in the mirror and can see I look fried. It will be all I can do to force a smile and be cheerful tonight. Because right now I look like the death stare girl in high school.

I'm beginning to think meeting Nick like this was a bad idea. Just what the guy needs is a night with a depressed woman.

Too late now.

A knock on the door tells me he's arrived. I take a deep breath as I open it and find him dressed in a suit, giving me a comforting look. "Hey, Marino, c'mon in."

He moves into the room, saying nothing as he studies my face, then opens his arms wide.

He knows.

I move into his arms and hug him tight while he gently strokes my hair. My eyes well up as I rest my head on his shoulder.

We don't say a word for about two minutes.

Finally I compose myself and lean back as his hands slide down to my waist. "How did you know exactly what I needed?"

"I've been a cop a long time. You learn to read body language. I watched you on TV today. Listen, if you don't want to go out—"

"No, I'm feeling better now. Just seeing you cheers me up."

"Just another part of my job, ma'am." He lets go and looks around the room. "Damn, nice suite. Your network pay for this?"

"Nope, they had booked me a regular room. But the hotel manager is a cat person and upgraded me."

Nick offers a slight smile as I sip my wine in the restaurant. "You're a brave woman."

"Oh, please, what I did was nothing compared to your job. You'd take a bullet for a complete stranger."

"Bravery is more than physical, Madison. What you did today . . . I can't even imagine what you went through as a child. Anyway, I'm really glad I didn't have to wait a month to see you."

"Yeah, I guess the logistics worked out in that department. So, enough about me, tell me about that special training you're going through. Is it like an episode of CSI?"

"In some ways. It's about half in the classroom and half in the field. I'm learning a lot. Some different ways to approach investigations, how to consider other points of view. And how there are sometimes more than two sides to a story, but I'm sure you know that from the news business. We're each given a fictional case to solve during the week and I'm supposed to work on it this weekend."

"Sounds fascinating. The network just put me on a big investigative story. Maybe when you get home we can share strategies. I'd love to know how cops work a case."

"Hey, we could be like the partners in *Castle*. The detective and the writer. Except we're the officer and the reporter."

"Yeah, really. Would make a good buddy cop movie."

We're interrupted by a nicely dressed couple around thirty. The woman clears her throat. "Excuse me, Miss Shaw?"

I look up and smile at her. "Hi."

"Sorry to interrupt your dinner, but I wanted you to know my husband and I have been on the fence about adopting. Until we saw your testimony today."

The man smiles at me. "We're going to do it. Just wanted to thank you for helping us with our decision."

I can't stop my eyes from welling up. "You're welcome. And thank you for saving a life."

The couple leaves and I grab my napkin to wipe my eyes.

"Madison, you okay?"

I smile at Nick. "I am now."

We take a slow stroll back to my hotel, his arm around my shoulders, pulling me close. My arm tight around his waist.

I feel safe. Like the man would take a bullet for me.

Probably because he wouldn't hesitate to do so.

The doorman at the hotel tips his cap as he holds the door for us.

Nick lets go as we head to the elevator and takes my hands. "I'm glad we could get together, Madison, and hope I've cheered you up a little. So I'll see you in a few weeks."

I shake my head. "I'm not ready to say goodnight yet." I don't want to be alone. "Can you stay with me a little while?"

"Sure." He puts his arm back around me as I lean my head on his shoulder. We stay that way as we ride up on the elevator and walk to my room. I put the key in the door. "You up for a movie? They've got Netflix here."

"Okay, Madison. Whatever you want."

We head inside and find a small basket of fruit and bottle of wine on the table with a card reading *compliments of the hotel*. "Hey, want a nightcap? Neither of us is driving."

"Sure. I'll pour the wine and you find a movie."

I sit on the love seat facing the TV, grab the remote and start searching the new releases, quickly finding something I want to watch. He pops the bottle of wine, pours two glasses and sits next to me. "Hey, Madison, you know what?"

"What?"

"I'll bet you would like to watch the movie this time."

I can't help but smile as I take in his soulful look. I turn to the television set and lean on his chest. His arm goes around my shoulders.

And this time we actually watch the movie.

I don't know how, but the man knows exactly what I need.

Chapter Fourteen

Since I had to spend Saturday traveling back to New York and I was emotionally drained, my boss gave me what he termed a "pre-emptive mental health day" because he assumed I was gonna call in sick on Monday. (He was right.) Which meant I could give Rory the day off from cat sitting. They're all eating from a bowl now and don't need someone to be there 24/7, as they amuse themselves wreaking havoc in my spare room and the adjoining bathroom. The tabby has discovered the joys of playing with toilet paper, as he jumped up onto the roll and then went into the eternal climb as it spun around, covering the floor with paper. Why they can't play with the countless toys they have is beyond me, but I'm told cats often like the packaging better than what's inside, which I've found to be true since the tuxedo kitten likes to play stealth cat and hide in an empty box, then jump out at me when I enter the room. I had to take away the ball that beeps and lights up, since my nocturnal friends decided to play a game of hockey around three in the morning. Of course I'm sure they sleep while I'm at work. One of our photographers wants to set up a Go-Pro camera in the room to see what they do when people aren't around. Good idea that should make for a fun story.

I decided to use my Monday off to shop a bit after feeding

the kittens and meet Tish for lunch, since she has a trial here on the island and couldn't make our usual Sunday brunch yesterday. She's already seated in the restaurant when I arrive. She gets up and gives me a strong hug. "You doin' okay, kiddo?"

I nod as I put my shopping bag on an empty chair next to me and we both sit. "Better. Felt like I'd run an emotional marathon on Friday. But dinner with Officer Goodbody really helped."

"Ah, so my idea paid dividends."

"Yeah, he was just what I needed."

"So how far did you go this time?"

"Here's the thing . . . we didn't *go* anywhere if you're referring to anything physical. He gave me a big hug when he picked me up and took me to dinner, then we went back to the hotel and he held me while we watched a movie. Didn't make a move. The guy seemed to know I simply wanted to be held and nothing else. How many men would do that? I actually had to kiss *him* goodnight."

"Wow. Impressive. So he's in the lead."

"Right now, but he's had two dates to Jamison's one. We'll see where things stand when they're even. Still, the cop is very impressive. I do worry about getting serious with him, though."

"Why?"

"You know. Such a dangerous profession. I've done a bunch of stories on police funerals. I mean, if you're married to a cop everything could be gone in an instant. Imagine being a widow at our age. I'm sure spouses worry every day that their husband or wife won't come home."

"And if you're married to someone in another profession who gets hit by a bus, same result. Madison, you can't worry about stuff like that. If the guy turns out to be your soul mate, you consider his profession and live every day to the fullest. You wouldn't take him for granted like so many married couples do with their spouses."

I slowly nod. "Excellent point. Actually you should live that way every day. Oh, and I told him I was also seeing someone else and he shrugged it off with a great answer."

"And that was . . ."

"I don't own you. I'm just happy to spend time with you."

"Yeah, that's perfect." Tish points at my shopping bag. "So I assume you bought yourself something nice? You certainly deserve it."

I grab the bag and reach inside, then pull out four small ceramic bowls and set them on the table. "Check it out. The one with stripes is for the tabby, the black and white one for the tuxedo cat, the multi-colored one for the tortoiseshell and the solid color for the Russian blue." I beam, proud of my purchases.

"Seriously, Madison? You actually went shopping on your day off and bought color-coordinated bowls for cats?"

"Yeah, so it will be easier to make sure each kitten gets the right amount of food."

"And you really think the kittens will say, *Hmmm . . . I'm still hungry, but I'd better not touch anything in the striped bowl. That one's not mine.*"

"Oh, give me a break. Besides, when you adopt your kitten you get the matching bowl."

"You sound like someone at Bed Bath & Beyond selling dinnerware. Am I supposed to register at Bloomingdales for a kitten shower?"

I start to put the bowls back in the bag. "Leave me alone. I enjoy spoiling the little guys."

"You sure you're going to be able to give up three of the kittens?"

"Yes, I'm sure. One cat will be fine for me."

"That's how it starts."

"Will you stop with the cat lady stuff?"

"Sorry, it's too much fun yankin' your chain. I guess I'm still amazed at the wonderful change in you since you found them."

"Y'know, Tish, so am I."

We head out of the restaurant an hour later as Tish has to get back to her trial and the kittens are due to be fed soon. My phone rings and I see that it's a print reporter I know from New Jersey. "Tish, let me take this. I'll see you later."

"Sure, kiddo." She heads off toward the courthouse as I take the call. "Brian, how are you?"

"Fine, Madison. Hey, wondering if you can help me out if you've got a few minutes."

"I'm actually off today. What's up?"

"Newark FBI just busted a couple of foster parents and arrested them for child abuse. Apparently they beat the six kids they had on a regular basis."

"That's horrible. Hope they throw the book at them. So why do you need my help? You need a quote about the foster care program?"

"I was told you were the person who tipped off the feds."

"Huh? I don't know any agents in Newark."

"I meant to say you tipped off a Congressman who dropped a dime on the FBI. Something about a teenage girl you met when you were in Washington on Friday. So what's the story?"

THE DOMINO EFFECT OF
MADISON SHAW'S KITTENS
By Brian Schell

In a political climate which has paralyzed Washington for the past several years, it took a set of dominoes to fall in order to actually get something positive done. And the first domino was toppled by a paw.

One of the top stories on Monday was the swift passage of what is known as the "college adoption bill" which will pick up the tuition tab for any child permanently adopted by parents who raise the child till the age of eighteen. The other big story, at least in this part of New Jersey, was the FBI raid on an abusive foster home in which six children had been beaten with regularity by their foster parents.

None of this happens if network reporter Madison Shaw doesn't find a litter of orphaned kittens while doing a story.

Unless you've been living under a rock the past few weeks, you know the tale (or should it be "tail"?) of how Shaw has been bottle feeding four kittens and getting up in the middle of the night to do so. While this would seem on the surface to be a basic "celebrity does a good deed" story, the amazing ripple effect of this simple act of kindness seems to have taken on a life of its own.

If Madison Shaw doesn't take in a neighbor's lost cat out of the rain, the story of her fostering kittens doesn't go viral. That led to a live TV interview in which it was revealed that she had grown up in foster homes. That led to a Senator from Florida inviting her to testify before Congress about an adoption bill. Which made an abused teenager drive to Washington from Newark to meet Miss Shaw. Which made the reporter ask a former FBI Agent turned Congressman to get the girl out of a bad situation. Which led to the raid on the foster home and six kids being saved.

None of this happens if she doesn't become a nursemaid to those kittens.

"Frankly, I don't think what I've done is that big of a deal," said Miss Shaw. "I'm taking care of some little animals for a few weeks and asked a politician I know to help a girl in need. But in a strange way good things have been happening since I took in those kittens. It's a bizarre domino effect. And I hope it keeps going."

Those dominoes led to the bill passing yesterday, with bi-partisan agreement that Miss Shaw's testimony had tipped the scales. Florida Senator Julianne Flint credits Shaw with getting her bill over the hump. "Her words were so raw and honest, so powerful. More than a few members of Congress *who were on the fence about the issue said they voted for it after hearing her personal story of triumph over adversity. There wasn't a dry eye in the room."*

The teenage girl who contacted Miss Shaw (her name has been withheld to protect her identity) had skipped school and borrowed a car to make the long drive to Washington. She told the FBI, "Madison Shaw saved our lives. We'll never be able to thank her enough."

And since cats are said to have nine lives, it seems these kittens are sharing some of theirs.

After a publicity-filled week in which I was the center of attention, I want to do something mindless and fun, and when Jamison called with two tickets to a Broadway comedy on Friday night, I jumped at the chance. Of course I was to going see him again anyway, so this will be a nice way to kick off the weekend. But since the show starts at eight and I have a live shot and won't be done till nearly seven, we're not going to have time for a sit-down dinner. I told him we can grab a Coke and a slice (pizza) which was just fine with me, so he agreed to pick me up in the lobby of the network.

I practically fly out of the newsroom after I'm done at a few minutes before seven and find him waiting in a great looking suit and tie in the lobby. I give him a quick hug. "Thanks for meeting me here. Long day."

"Not a problem." He ushers me toward the front door. "Do an interesting story today?"

"Started on one, which may never pan out. Investigating Senator Collier."

"Really? I thought you reporters had given up on trying to nail him."

"Most have, but not me. I know he's dirty, and I just got the go-ahead from our new CEO to start digging."

"Oh right. I read that you got a new corporate boss."

"Yeah, the last one was a friend of Collier but this one hates him. Anyway, I need to get my mind off that so let's grab a cab. I know a good pizza joint across the street from the theater."

"Oh, I got a car for tonight." He opens the door for me and gestures toward a waiting stretch limousine.

"Jamison, you hired a limo? Really, you didn't have to do that."

He chuckles a bit. "It's also our restaurant for tonight." The driver greets me and opens the door. I slide into the back of the limo (it's actually my first time riding in one) and my eyes widen at what I see. A couple of silver trays filled with decadent hors d'oeuvres, a bottle of champagne chilling in a bucket. Jamison gets in next to me as the driver closes the door. "I wasn't sure we'd have time for pizza."

"Good God, Jamison, you didn't have to go to all this trouble and expense."

He shrugs. "Not a big deal. Anyway, dinner is served." He pours the champagne as I fill a small plate with some goodies.

After running myself ragged on a story today, it's nice to have someone wait on you. I lean back in the leather seat which is soft as butter, sipping champagne and eating bacon-wrapped shrimp as the limo pulls into traffic.

Damn, I could get used to this.

Traffic is bad so we get there just in time. Jamison ushers me into the theater, shows the tickets to an usher who points us in the right direction. We apparently have really good orchestra seats. He puts his hand lightly on my back as we walk down the aisle toward our seats, about ten rows from the stage in the center. "Wow, great seats, Jamison. Glad we made it in time." Suddenly the crowd starts to applaud so I pick up the pace. "Apparently *just* in time." The applause grows louder but the lights do not dim and the curtain doesn't open. I look at my watch and see it's five minutes till the play begins. "What the hell are they clapping for?"

He shrugs. "Beats me."

The crowd is still clapping as we find our row. I take off my jacket and am about to sit down when I see everyone standing, looking at me. Still clapping.

"Madison, I think they're clapping for you."

Chapter Fifteen

I'm deep in thought as I slowly pick at my cheesecake in the upscale restaurant. The play and the laughs that went with it faded into the background as I tried to process getting a standing ovation before the show started. And then during the curtain calls, the star of the show spots me, points me out and the crowd applauds again.

Honestly, I don't get it. Is America that desperate for a simple good deed? Standing ovations should be reserved for veterans coming home from war, not people who take care of kittens.

"Earth to Madison?"

I look up at Jamison. "Sorry. Still can't believe what happened tonight."

"Well, it was deserved. I was proud to be your escort."

"You're sweet. But I still don't understand all the attention I'm getting. I mean, I'm used to being in the public eye as a reporter, but it's like people now see me as a human being."

"They see you for what you are, not what you do for a living. They're impressed by what you do when you're off the clock, and how you're using your fame for good."

"I guess so."

"And having been a reporter, I know that a lot of the general public sees media people as less than human."

"Very true. We're right down there with car salesmen on the trust factor. Anyway, I'm sure my fifteen minutes will end soon."

"I wouldn't count on it. That applies to people who weren't famous. You already checked that box. Most famous people don't do what you did."

"Lots of celebrities have charities."

"They simply donate money. Writing a check is easy. What you did before Congress was hard."

"I guess." I check my watch and see I need to get home soon.

"Tired, Madison?"

"Not at all. But I've only got my cat sitter for another hour."

"Well, let's run you home then."

"While I'd love a long ride in a limo, my car is at the network. By the way, didn't you already miss that last water taxi?"

"I have a little apartment here in the city for when I have to work late . . . or have a great date."

"That's convenient."

"Y'know . . . it's a shame to let all those goodies in the limo go to waste. Hey, how about this . . . I give you a ride to your place, you take care of the cats, then I'll run you back to the city to get your car. And we never did eat a real dinner. I don't know about you, but I'm still hungry."

"Sounds like a plan. Besides, you need to meet the fur babies."

I'm rather surprised to see Jamison get down on the floor in what has to be a thousand dollar suit to meet the kittens. "So, you like cats?"

"I like all animals. We had a cat and a dog growing up."

"What kind of cat?"

"A white cat with blue eyes." He grabs a toy, a fuzzy ball attached to a wand, and holds it above the tabby. The kitten jumps and grabs it. "So you're keeping one?"

I pick up the tortoiseshell. "Yeah. This one's my favorite."

"He's a pretty little cat."

The Russian blue runs over to him and rubs against his leg, shedding a bit against his dark trousers. "Oh, sorry about that."

He waves it away. "Cats seem to be attracted to colors different than their own. Our white cat loved shedding on my dark clothes. It comes right off with sticky tape. No big deal."

I want to see the tortoiseshell's reaction to him, so I put him on the floor. Jamison reaches out to pet him. The kitten crouches down a bit and backs up, then moves forward to sniff his hand. "He's checking you out."

"Nah, he knows I had shrimp tonight." The kitten moves forward and licks his finger, then rubs his head against Jamison's hand. He smiles and pets the kitten.

I smile at the scene. "He likes you."

Jamison holds the toy over his head. The kitten rolls on his back and swats at it.

A few hours later I say goodnight to Jamison, too tired to be run back to Manhattan to get my car. I'll take the Staten Island Ferry tomorrow morning and pick it up. Hey, right now I'm into boat rides, and that one's free. By the way, one thing you should know about me; when you grow up without a whole lot of money, you generally remain thrifty as an adult even though I make an excellent salary. It makes me cringe to see people spend five bucks for a cup of coffee when I can brew a whole pot for twenty-five cents.

So tonight was something I've never experienced.

This was a date unlike any other. A hit Broadway show, champagne and dining in the limo . . . quite the upgrade from the cab ride, Coke and a slice I was expecting. I've always avoided rich guys, and Jamison's obviously raking in the bucks from his business. I've not been out with anyone like him before. One can only imagine what his "little apartment" in Manhattan looks like. Probably some penthouse next to Donald Trump.

As before he was a perfect gentleman, taking things slow in the romance department, which is fine with me considering the other guy on the aforementioned dance card. I decided it was time to tell him I was seeing someone else, and he didn't have a problem with it. He played with the kittens, which is important these days, especially since the tortoiseshell seems to have a built-in bullshit detector. Love me, love my cat. Not sure I could deal with a guy who didn't care about animals anymore.

He invited me to his house next weekend for his annual beach party for his clients, so that will be my third date with him. And I'm bringing my friends so they can "vet" the guy. The following week Nick comes home, so it will be three dates with each after that and perhaps things will resolve themselves. Like the tortoiseshell made my decision about which kitten to choose.

Right now, though, they are dead even. Two very different guys.

Litter box training for the kittens today. I have discovered that "scoop" means something other than an exclusive news story.

Let's skip this part. File it under "too much information."

But before we head to the beach it's time to pair up the kittens with their humans. I bring all the kittens into the living room and put them on the floor. "Okay, everyone get down there with them."

"What are we doing?" asks Rory.

"Time for the kittens to choose their humans."

A.J. furrows her brow as she kneels down. "We don't have any say in this? What is this, the rose ceremony on *The Bachelor*?"

I shake my head. "Hey, the kitten knows who it belongs with." The Russian blue sniffs the air and immediately heads toward A.J., then starts licking her fingers. "Ah, you've been selected already."

"I've been slicing pastrami at the deli. It might want me for my food."

"Same as the guys you date," cracks Tish. "Obviously a smart kitten. Though I don't think you should feed it cold cuts."

The blue stops licking her fingers and crawls in her lap. A.J. starts to stroke its head. "Okay, kitty, even though you're prettier than me you've got a home. And you'll look good with my furniture."

I nod. "It's a very calm kitten. It will be a good influence you."

A.J. looks at me. "You sayin' I need to calm down?"

"Nah, just that opposites attract."

Rory and Tish get down on the floor between the tabby and the tuxedo cat. "You got a preference?" asks Tish.

Rory shrugs. "Like Freckles said, it's the cat's choice. And I'll be happy with either one. They're both sweet kittens. Though I do have a favorite."

Both kittens are looking at Tish. The tabby slowly starts walking in her direction, then gets passed by the tuxedo cat who runs toward her. It crawls on her lap and starts swatting at her necklace. Tish dangles it over the kitten's head. "It likes jewelry. Considering it looks like it's dressed formally and that describes my usual outfit, I think we go together."

Rory claps. "Yay! I wanted the little tiger anyway." The tabby turns and runs toward her. She picks it up and holds it to her chest.

I get back up off the floor. "Okay, the kittens have spoken." After weeks of keeping these babies alive, I'm so pleased they've found loving, furever homes. Who knows, maybe the kittens will be good luck for my friends too—I glance down at my tortoiseshell—mine certainly has been.

The girls enjoy the ride on the water taxi, eagerly awaiting their chance to check out the other guy in my life. Tish, in particular, is licking her lips like she does in the courtroom when she's ready to interrogate a witness. Next weekend they'll get a better look at Nick, as I bought more tickets to that dinner so they could evaluate him as well. After the disaster that was Jeremy, I'm really going to take the advice of my friends to heart this time.

A.J.'s eyes widen as the boat pulls up to the dock. "Wow. Gorgeous town. I didn't know places like this existed in Jersey."

"Looks like there's some serious old money here," says Rory. "And this guy has a house on the oceanfront?"

I nod and smile. "Yep. It's incredible. But you guys are not here to judge the architecture or his bank account. While I must admit his lifestyle is pretty damned attractive, the financial aspects are not important. I don't need a man to provide for me."

"Me neither," says Rory. "Though one to wait on me would be nice."

We start heading off the boat and I realize this is not exactly the kind of place to find a traditional taxi. "Oh, hell, I forgot to ask him for the number of a cab company." I pull out my cell to look for one when I see it.

A driver holding a sign with my last name on it standing next to a limo.

A.J. takes my arm. "Don't think we need a cab, honey."

The slim, gray-haired driver smiles as his face fills with recognition and he greets us with a British accent. "Ah, Miss Shaw and friends. Welcome to Monmouth Beach."

"Thank you."

"Your host is already entertaining guests, so he sent me to give you all a lift to his humble abode." He opens the door and we all climb in, finding a bottle of champagne and a tray of hors d'oeuvres.

Rory shakes her head, amazed at all this. "Damn, Freckles, how loaded *is* this guy?"

I shrug. "No clue. But obviously his video production company is doing very well."

Jamison's home is already filled with music, good food, salt air, and a few dozen people, many of whom would be described as "old money." (*Old money* defined: They made it the old-fashioned way. They inherited it.) The kind of people I've never really been comfortable around. I recognize a few of Manhattan's movers and shakers, and of course, everyone recognizes me, more so from the cats and the adoption testimony than from television news. Frankly, I'm surprised at the guest list, as Jamison doesn't seem like the type considering he struggled as a reporter making no money in the middle of nowhere. But I guess when you have his kind of money your friends change.

Then again, he said many of these people are clients.

Speaking of our host, he's outside on the deck next to the grill, while Tish stands beside him, arms folded. I can tell from her expression she's doing her lawyer thing, looking for any possible red flag. Not sure what's being grilled more, the steaks or Jamison.

I'm heading toward A.J. and Rory who are next to the bar which overlooks the ocean. They've already spent some time with Jamison, so I'm eager to get their take on the guy. "Well?"

Rory smiles. "Great party. I could look at this view forever."

"Not what I'm asking."

"Food's okay," says A.J. "I coulda done better."

"I'm sure. Again, not what I'm asking. What are your takeaways so far?"

Rory grabs a glass of champagne from the bar and hands it to me. "Just yankin' your chain, Freckles. He's okay."

"Just okay?"

"No, I mean I didn't pick up on any red flags. He's cute, he's smart, he's obviously loaded and thoughtful enough to send a limo to pick us up. You two look good together and you have a lot in common with the TV thing. Of course you also look good next to the cop."

I turn to A.J. "And?"

She shrugs. "He passes my test. And of course, you know what they say . . . just as easy to marry a rich man as a poor one."

"You know I don't care about that."

"I know. But damn, I could get used to coming home to this after making sandwiches all day."

A bony Botox blonde in her forties wearing a pink and green

145

outfit that screams Greenwich, Connecticut arrives at the bar and gently puts one hand on my forearm. "Miss Shaw, I wanted to meet you. Ainsley Farrington."

"Hi. And these are my friends Rory and A.J."

She nods at them and smiles, then turns back to me. "I wanted to say how much I admired your bravery in telling your story to Congress the other day. You made quite a difference."

"Thank you, but it wasn't really brave. I did what anyone else would do."

"Jamison said you were very modest. But as for your visit to Washington, I must admit I was surprised that you asked that particular Congressman for help regarding the young lady in the bad foster home."

"Why?"

"Well, you know . . . he's a Republican." (I think her face is tightened, but with Botox you never know.)

"What's that got to do with anything?"

"I assumed all you journalists were liberal."

"Well, you assumed wrong. And in reality, a true journalist is objective, not like so many reporters who offer their opinions. I know plenty of people in my business who are conservative. The reason the public assumes all media people are liberal is because the national news comes from liberal places like New York, Washington and Los Angeles."

"So . . . you're not a Democrat?"

"I don't tell anyone what my views are on religion, politics or social issues. My job is to tell people what I know, not what I think. I have good contacts in both political parties. And as for the Congressman, I've known him a long time, he's an honest guy who has tipped me off on some good stories over the years and he took care of the problem."

"Oh. Well, I guess that's okay."

"You seem to have a problem with the fact that a Republican did something good."

146

"I'm sure he had an ulterior motive. He did get a lot of publicity out of it and will use it for his campaign."

I stand up straight and look down at her. "Listen, Ainsley, since I believe a reporter should tell people what I know and not what I think, I'm going to excuse myself before I tell you what I think of you."

My jaw is clenched as I head to the kitchen to get some ice water. That little exchange has me pissed off and I don't need to let Jamison see me like this. Besides, that bag of bones might be one of his good friends. Had he not been around I might have really laid into the woman. I pour a glass of cold water and sip it as I lean against the kitchen island to calm down a bit.

A pretty brunette around my age smiles at me as she enters the kitchen. "Hi there."

"Hello."

"You're Jamison's new friend."

I extend my hand. "I'm Madison."

"Kelly."

"You one of his clients?"

"Nah. My husband is one of Jamison's old college buddies. So, I've heard a lot about you."

"Don't believe a word."

"Well, he seems very taken with you, Madison. We've always hoped he would find someone nice."

"We've only been out a few times. But we're off to a good start."

"Good to hear. You don't strike me as a golddigger like so many of the other women he's dated."

"I can imagine. Any woman would be taken with a place like this. And a guy who has built such a successful business."

She laughs a bit. "Yeah, right." Her cell rings and she pulls it from her pocket. "Excuse me. Nice talking to you, Madison."

Fortunately Jamison and I had some alone time as the party thinned out when the sun went down. A long stroll on the beach

147

gave us a chance to be romantic as the sunbathers had gone home.

But as I look out at the ocean while the water taxi pulls away from the dock, I'm still confused.

A.J. lightly takes my arm. "Dollar for your thoughts?"

"A dollar?"

"Inflation."

I shake my head. "Trying to sort things out. But I can't. And I'm soon going to reach the point that I have to make a decision. The candle can only burn on both ends for so long until you run out of wax and get burned."

Rory locks eyes with me. "You like him a lot, huh?"

"Yeah. I also like Nick a lot." I still haven't asked Tish for her opinion, so I turn to her. "So, counselor, ready to file a brief on Jamison?"

"I enjoyed talking with him. Smart and funny. I noticed he seemed comfortable with everyone, and he had a wide variety of guests. And he might be the most relaxed person I've ever met, like he doesn't have a care in the world. He's like a walking bottle of wine."

"Yeah, he has that carefree attitude. Wish I could be that way. So, no red flags?"

Tish shakes her head. "Nope. Sorry, I know that doesn't clear things up, but I like him and I think you two look good together. However, I think we'll all have a final verdict after next weekend."

"Suppose we end up with a hung jury?"

"Since you're the ultimate authority on this, you can always overturn the decision."

"Y'know, it was a lot easier deciding which kitten I wanted to keep."

Tish nods. "Speaking of which, what exactly made you want the tortoiseshell?"

"He has an incredible personality, the other kittens are fun as well. But it's the way the little guy looks at me, right into my

148

soul. Like we're connected somehow. I can't explain it because I've never had a pet before, but I feel like we belong together."

Rory pats my hand. "Maybe you'll get that same look and feeling from one of your guys."

Chapter Sixteen

It's a half hour before the girls and I head over to the benefit dinner dance, and as I look at the four kittens playing, something I said last week hits me.

Why I chose the tortoiseshell as my forever companion.

The look.

After several weeks of care, do the other kittens look at me in the same way?

Time to use a television tactic. Welcome to the world's first feline focus group. Need to find out my approval rating.

The tuxedo cat is closest, so I pick it up, hold it in front of my face and lock eyes with it.

It "smiles" at me but doesn't have that soulful gaze.

Next, the tabby.

It simply meows, wanting to get away and return to the game they're playing.

The Russian blue is next.

It gives me a lick on the nose, but the look is nothing special.

Finally, my favorite.

The tortoiseshell immediately purrs and gives me the look I've grown to love as it locks eyes with me. I start to put him down but he reaches out and latches on with tiny claws. He'd rather be with me than his cat friends.

The look changes, gets deeper, like he can't bear to be without me.

Will I get that from Nick tonight?

With all other things being equal, should I base my choice on a simple look?

My jaw drops a bit as we arrive at the outdoor venue which is often the site of wedding receptions, noted for its dance floor overlooking the ocean. I was expecting some sort of bare-bones affair thrown together by a bunch of cops. Instead, the place is tastefully decorated. Each table features a floral arrangement with several red, white and blue ribbons attached.

And at the front of the room, a large framed photo of the fallen hero and his family.

Nick is busy greeting guests across the room as we make our way to our table. He spots me and his face lights up. He moves quickly in my direction and greets me with a strong hug, practically lifting me off the floor. "Madison, so good to see you."

"You too. You remember my friends."

He nods as he smiles at them. "Rory, Tish and A.J. Right?"

"Impressive," says A.J. "Usually we get the blonde, the brunette and the Italian chick."

Nick laughs as he leads us to a large round table with twelve chairs. "You guys are all sitting with us."

"Us?"

"My current partner, his wife, a few others I thought you'd like." He pulls out a chair for each of us and we sit. Nick reaches for one of the ribbons on the flower arrangements. "Oh, we're all wearing ribbons for Sarge tonight, if you don't mind."

"Sure."

He pins the ribbon on my emerald green dress. "You look great, by the way."

151

I note his perfectly tailored dark gray suit. "So do you."

"Listen, I gotta greet some more people but I'll be back in a little while." He takes off as I turn back to my friends. "Well?"

Rory nods. "Off to a good start."

Nick was right about the people at our table; it's a wonderful collection of cops and spouses. I've been a little quiet while taking in all the fascinating stories of police work, and also note how supportive the spouses are of the chosen profession. Nick's partner, a big, muscular dark-haired guy named Steve with pale blue eyes, has been studying me all night. Not in a seductive way, but as a cop might look at a witness.

And after finishing a story, he changes the subject to me. "So, Madison, you think you can straighten out my partner?"

I look at Nick. "Does he need fixing?"

Steve's wife rolls her eyes. "You got about an hour?"

Everyone laughs as another wife looks at me. "Nice to have a member of the media here who actually supports cops. We usually get hammered."

"Hey, you guys put your life on the line every day and I respect the hell out of what you do. Especially considering what I do for a living. I just tell stories."

Nick takes my hand. "Speaking of stories, you mentioned that two cops once saved your life but you never told me how. Care to share that one?"

I'm never wild about this subject, but everyone is making me feel so comfortable. Rory gives me a nod, telling me to go ahead. "Well, sure. As you all probably know by now, I was raised in foster homes. But the only reason I'm sitting here today is because of two cops. Right after I was born I was left in a bathroom with a note from my mother saying she couldn't take care of me. Apparently I was a loud baby because two officers heard my screams, followed the noise and found me. They took me to social services and my name comes from the two cops, whose last names were Madison and Shaw. So that's one reason I have such great respect for what you guys do."

Nick leans forward. "That's incredible. So, did you ever try to find your birth mother?"

"I never knew the story until I was eighteen, and then I tracked down the two officers. But they said there were really very few clues as to how I ended up in that bathroom. The only witness was a man who had talked to a teenage girl with an Irish accent who was holding a baby, and then he saw the girl later without the baby. So I have no idea who my real birth parents are. That's a cold case I'd love to solve."

"So you'd like to meet your birth mother?" asks Steve's wife.

"Yeah. Well, I say that but if the opportunity ever presented itself, I might think differently. I mean, even though I've rehearsed the meeting a thousand times in my head, what would I actually say to a woman who abandoned me in a bathroom? Anyway, I do keep in touch with the two cops, who are like very special uncles to me. But thank goodness they weren't named Lipschitz and Shaw."

Everyone laughs at the line. Nick finishes his cheesecake and looks at his watch. "Okay, you guys have to excuse me. Time to thank everyone." He gets up and moves to the microphone, then begins to thank all those who had a part in putting on the fundraiser. He then pulls a check from his pocket and presents it to the widow, who tears up as she gives him a big hug.

I turn back to my table mates. "Nice of you guys to do this."

"Hey, we take care of our own," says Steve. "Nick has really taken the lead on this. And after he ended up with the worst duty any officer ever has."

"What's that?"

"Delivering the bad news," says Steve's wife, who takes her husband's hand. "Showing up at her house, telling her that her husband was dead." She bites her lower lip as her eyes well up.

"No police spouse ever wants to see the partner show up

alone on the doorstep," says Steve. "Because that only means one thing."

Nick is a fabulous dancer. We've been tearing up the floor for an hour and it's like we've been partners for years. I catch my breath after a fast song. "Marino, you should be on *Dancing with the Stars*."

"Yeah right."

"No, seriously, you're terrific."

"You're not so bad yourself. Tired yet, Madison?"

"Hell no. But I'm ready for a slow one. Besides, the deejay is only here for another half hour."

And then it starts to drizzle.

"Aw hell," he says. "We almost made it."

He starts to lead me from the floor but I pull him back. "What, you afraid of a little sprinkle?"

He laughs as the rest of the crowd heads under cover. "I'm game." He turns to the deejay. "Keep playing."

The disc jockey laughs. "Sure, I got something appropriate."

And then my favorite song in the whole world starts. Belinda Carlisle's *Summer Rain*.

"I love this song!" We say in unison. "Seriously, Nick?"

He wraps his arms around my waist and pulls me close and starts leading me around the dance floor. "It's a beautiful song. Most people like *Heaven is a Place on Earth* but I've always thought this was her best."

I rest my head on his shoulder as the rain falls and I take in the lyrics about a couple dancing in the rain before the soldier goes off to war.

The rain starts to fall harder and he leans back. "You're getting awfully wet."

I look up at him as my hair starts getting matted to my head. "I've got a dryer at home. So shut up and dance with me, officer. That's an order."

He continues leading me around the floor as the crowd applauds. And then he gives me a look that makes the rest of the world disappear.

I pull Nick's hot, dry shirt from the dryer and carry it to the living room where he is playing with the kittens. "Your shirt's done."

He stands up and reaches for it, but I pull it back. "What, you're not gonna give it back?"

I take in his amazing body. The man is seriously ripped. "I have not decided yet. I kinda like you with your shirt off." I toss the shirt on the couch, move toward him, wrap my arms around him and give him a long kiss, taking the opportunity to run my hands across his toned back muscles. Damn. "Now you know why I wanted to dance in the rain. Aren't I clever?"

"Too bad you weren't wearing a tee-shirt." We both laugh as I hand him his shirt and he puts it on. Nick takes a spot on the couch and I sit on his lap. He wraps one arm around me. "I'm so glad you came tonight, Madison."

"Thanks for inviting me. I had a great time. I mean, considering the circumstances."

"Well, life goes on. Might as well make the best of it and help people along the way." He laughs as one of the kittens leaps out at the other one in a sneak attack. "This is better than TV. I can see why cat videos rule the internet."

"Yeah, I almost feel bad about breaking them up soon, they have so much fun together." The tortoiseshell is having a ball, running around the living room. "But mine will have to settle for me as a playmate."

"Lucky bastard."

I playfully slap his arm. "Watch it, Mister."

"You give him a name yet?"

"Not yet. Waiting for inspiration to hit me. But like it says in that poem you told me to read, a cat knows its name. I just have to figure it out." The kitten runs into one of the many bubble-wrapped pieces of furniture and then his siblings with no ill effects. "With him it's like watching bumper cars."

"Hey, that'd be a cute name for him."

"What?"

"Bumper."

The kitten stops playing, turns to Nick and meows.

"I love that!" I lean toward the kitten. "Is that your name? Bumper?"

He meows again and paws at the air.

Nick laughs. "I think that's a yes."

"Okay. Bumper it is." I turn back to Nick. "Apparently cops are meant to name everything for me."

"Hey, another part of my job."

"You mean besides rescuing damsels in distress?"

"Yeah, though it does depend on the damsel."

"Ah. By the way, I cannot believe you love the same song I do."

"It's a beautiful song. Even though it's sad. Y'know, the woman never seeing her husband again after he goes off to war."

"Yeah, but that's what makes it special. I think every woman wants to feel that way about her husband. Of course, without the dying part. So, you like Belinda Carlisle."

"I do. I've always had this thing for redheads."

"You know, A.J. says that's true of Italian men. That you guys cannot resist the red hair and the freckles."

He nods as he runs his fingers through my hair. "Now that I think of it, a few of my cousins are married to redheads. There must be something to that."

The look, again.

"Are your cousins *happily* married?"

"Very. So the theory is sound. Y'know, Madison, I'm going to say something I shouldn't."

"I need better mouthwash?"

156

He laughed. "It never stops with you, does it?"

"Nah. Part of my charm. So what's on your mind?"

"Well, saying this will give you an advantage in our relationship, but, what the hell. I have to be honest."

"What?"

"I really missed you."

My eyes get misty and I take his head in my hands. "Tell you what, Marino. Let's call it even. I really missed you too."

Chapter Seventeen

"I can't take this anymore. I have to decide."

My friends study my face as we sit down to our usual Sunday brunch. Tish pats my hand. "Nothing resolved itself, huh kiddo?"

"Unfortunately, no. I like both of them a lot. I even did the thing where I drew a line down the middle of a pad to compare them. They came out even. They're so different but I could see myself with either one. But it's not fair to them to keep dating both. Because I'm getting attached to both, and that's not a good thing. For me or them."

"I agree," says Rory. "I saw how you look at them. You're in danger of falling for both."

"Honey, that ship has sailed." I lean back with my mimosa as A.J. dishes out the food. "Okay, I need to de-brief you guys on Nick. Waddaya think?"

Rory shrugs. "No red flags from me. I like him a lot. He's smart as hell and an old fashioned gentleman. Plus, being a cop he's a real-life superhero. He'd take a bullet for you and always protect you. So he's a great guy and seems like a good match."

"Better than Jamison?"

"Sorry, Freckles. Dead even. Both have their good points and

I could see you with either one. Neither has any bad features as far as I can tell. Had you been dating just one of them I would have told you to keep going."

I turn to A.J. "So, can you look at the Italian guy objectively?"

"Of course. But they're even with me as well. Jamison is cute and rich. Nick is hot and brave. Both are smart with good personalities that work well with yours. I also agree you'd be fine ending up with either one, though after three dates it's hard to know how things might work out long term. But Nick is hotter."

"You already said that," says Tish.

"Just emphasizing the point in case it's a tie on all counts except for appearance. Hot trumps rich in my mind. And she looks better with him."

The image of Nick with his shirt off whips through my mind. Now I need Tish's opinion. "Okay, counselor, your closing argument, please."

"Alas, it is every lawyer's worst nightmare. A hung jury."

"Poor choice of words when sex is involved," says A.J., wearing a wicked grin.

Tish rolls her eyes. "For once, get your mind out of the gutter."

"Hey, at least if she slept with both she'd know a little more. You don't want her to end up with a guy who's bad in bed, do ya?"

Tish shakes her head. "Anyway, since sex is *not* part of the equation, I have to agree with everyone. Both have a lot to offer though they're very different. And may I add both are much better than he-who-must-not-be-named. The fact that all three of us approve of both guys is a good sign that one of them might be your soul mate. So the final decision rests with the judge in this case. You."

"Damn. Y'know, Nick gave me the look last night."

"What look?" asks Rory.

"The one my kitten gives me."

Tish's face tightens. "You're going to make your choice because one guy looks at you like a cat?"

"Hey, you know what they say. Eyes are the windows of the soul. And Bumper went right to Nick, while he was a tad apprehensive about Jamison."

Rory laughs. "Well, this is a first. Kitten sorts out love triangle, film at eleven. Freckles, you realize this makes no sense, don't you?"

"Hey, Bumper has been spot-on about men all along. Regardless, I have to make my choice this week."

"Why this week?"

"Because they both asked me out for this weekend and I'm not going out with both. But the clock is ticking and I'm running out of time."

I arrive home Monday night to find Rory working on her laptop while three of the kittens are playing in the living room. Bumper is waiting for me in the window, so I pick him up. "Hi, honey, I'm home."

She looks up at me and studies my face. "So, you didn't do it."

"What?"

"Decide which guy you want and break up with the one who came in second."

"I had, uh, a very busy day."

"Oh, bull. You're procrastinating."

"Fine. I change my mind every five minutes. Dammit, Rory, what the hell do I do? I'm now seeing the down side to playing the field."

"Wish I had a crystal ball, Freckles. You sure you don't want to go on one more date with each?"

"I really don't think so. I'm getting too attached. And it's not fair to the guys."

"Then go with your gut, sweetie."

A knock on the door distracts me. "Must be that stuff I ordered for the cats." I open the door but do not find a delivery man.

Instead I'm looking into the pale, drawn face of Nick's partner Steve.

And then it hits me. What was said about Nick at the dance.

He ended up with the worst duty any officer ever has.

No police spouse ever wants to see the partner show up alone on the doorstep.

Because that only means one thing.

My hands fly up to my mouth as the blood drains from my face. "No. Dear God, no . . ."

"He's in surgery. Let's go."

Steve speeds through town toward the hospital with his siren blaring. I'm staring straight ahead, about to lose it. "What happened, Steve?"

"He walked in on a robbery in progress. Just went into a convenience store to get us a couple of sodas. There was a lot of gunfire. I dropped the robber but Nick took a few bullets when he jumped in front of a woman and her child. He saved them, but . . ."

"What are his chances?"

"I don't know. There was a lot of blood, Madison. He was unconscious when we loaded him into the ambulance. And then I came to get you."

"Thank you for thinking of me."

"I couldn't help it. You were all he talked about today."

I bite my lower lip as my eyes well up and the tears begin to flow. Steve notices and reaches over to take my hand. "Hey, don't worry, Nick's a tough guy. And I've never lost a partner in twenty years."

That doesn't make me feel any better.

Steve comes to a screeching halt in the hospital parking lot.

We both jump out of the car and run to the emergency room entrance. The waiting room is already filled with a sea of blue uniforms. I see Steve's wife get up and move toward him. "Anything?" he asks.

She shakes her head. "They're still working on him." She turns to me and gives me a strong hug. "Thanks for coming, Madison."

"Sure."

She takes my hand and leads me to a couple of empty chairs. I notice a set of worn rosary beads around her other hand as we sit down. "Now you see what it's like to be married to a cop."

I remember Tish's words. "That's why you live every day to the fullest."

"Yeah. How did you know?"

"A good friend told me that."

"Please don't let it scare you away, Madison. Nick's a very good man."

"I know. Is his family on the way?"

"He doesn't have anyone. Nick's an only child and his parents are dead."

So, again, I'm it.

The doors to the emergency room slide open and I see the police commissioner enter. He starts shaking hands with all the officers, then spots me and heads in my direction. We know each other as I've interviewed him a few times. I stand up to greet him. "Commissioner . . ."

"Miss Shaw, I'd like the media to wait outside, if you don't mind."

And then, in a flash, I see it in my mind's eye.

The look from Nick.

Right into my soul.

The look from the kittens after I brought them home.

You're all we've got. Please don't leave us.

Things resolve themselves.

Decide, Madison.

162

Right. Now.

Go with your gut.

The words come out.

"I'm not here as a reporter, Commissioner. I'm Nick's girl-friend."

Chapter Eighteen

Rory, A.J. and Tish arrive half an hour later and we share a group hug. We break the embrace and sit in the ridiculously uncomfortable orange plastic chairs as Rory takes my hand. "So what's the story?"

"No news so far. His partner said he got shot a few times. Lot of blood." I look down at the floor. "He saved a few people."

Tish locks eyes with me. "He'll pull through. I know it."

"I stopped by my church and lit a candle," says A.J.

"Thanks for coming down, guys." I see another member of the police force come into the waiting room. Steve talks to him awhile, then points to me. I note the captain's stripes on his uniform as he moves in my direction and I stand to meet him.

"Miss Shaw, I'm Bill Warren, Nick's captain. Appreciate the support tonight."

"Sure, Captain."

He takes my shoulders and locks eyes with me. "Your boyfriend's a tough guy. He'll make it." The commissioner comes over and pats him on the shoulder. "Excuse me." He turns to the commissioner and they walk to a corner of the room as I sit back down.

"Why did he say Nick was your boyfriend?" asks Rory.

"Because that's what I told the commissioner. I made my decision."

"Sweetie, you're emotional right now—"

"No, that's not it at all. Somehow it just came out. But it feels right."

"And you're sure about this?"

"Yeah. Very sure." I smile for the first time since I arrived here. "It's the way he looks at me, Rory. And I'm guessing I look at him in the same way."

"Long as you're sure."

"Besides, how could I leave him now?"

"I hope you're not letting the situation guilt you into this."

"No, Rory. It's a gut feeling, and you told me to go with my gut. I know he's the right choice."

And then the memory hits me. Nick and I dancing in the rain to Belinda Carlisle.

In the song, the soldier dies and the woman never sees him again.

Is the song coming true for me? Will I never see him again? Will my last memory be of our dance?

The tears begin to flow as the lyrics play in my head.

Four hours later a doctor emerges and pulls off his mask. Everyone gets up and moves toward him.

I study his face, but it holds no clue.

"He's out of danger," says the doctor. I breathe a sigh of relief as I steady myself against the wall.

The commissioner moves in front of the doctor. "So he's going to be okay?"

"We still have a lot of work to do, but he'll make it. However, one of the bullets did a lot of damage."

I step next to the commissioner. "What kind of damage?"

"There's a chance he may never walk again."

His words knock the air out of me.

"But it's way too early to tell. We'll know more in a few days."

"When can I see him?"

"We've got a couple more hours of surgery, then he'll be in intensive care. He'll probably regain consciousness sometime tomorrow afternoon. So I suggest you all go home and get some rest."

"I'll stay."

The doctor takes my hands. "He'll need a lot of support when he wakes up. But right now there's nothing you can do here. We'll let you know when you can see him."

Rory wraps an arm around my shoulders. "C'mon, Freckles. There are others who need you at home, you know."

Three of the kittens are asleep in a ball as I arrive home.

Of course Bumper is up, sitting facing the door. As if he knows.

I quickly kneel down and pick him up, clutching him close to my chest. "C'mere, Bumper. Your human needs you."

The kitten gives me the usual soulful look, then rests his head on my shoulder and begins to purr.

And I begin to cry.

The smell of bacon fills the air as I emerge from my bedroom shortly after eight-thirty. Rory spent the night in the guest room and being the morning person she is, already has breakfast going. She gives me a soft smile as I head toward the kitchen. "You sleep okay, Freckles?"

"Yeah. I think all the emotion caught up with me and I was out of gas."

"You going to work today?"

I shake my head. "Already called my boss and explained the situation. He said I can work from home for a few days doing research. Like I can concentrate on anything other than Nick right now."

"Actually, it might help to lose yourself in your work, especially the way you can focus on things." She points at a chair at the kitchen table. "I heard you rustling around so I made breakfast. Sit. You need to eat."

"What would I do without you, Rory?"

"You'd do this for me, so it's not up for discussion. I know you always have my back as well." She slides a plate of bacon and eggs in front of me along with a big glass of orange juice, then sits down next to me.

"Aren't you gonna eat?"

"Already did." She leans forward and studies my face. "So, you still good with your decision?"

"About choosing Nick? Absolutely. Why?"

"Like I said last night, you were emotional. And to be quite honest, I'm a little worried you've painted yourself into a corner. You're committed to the guy now."

"I know, and I'm fine with it."

"You sure you weren't thinking that he needed you, and that you couldn't possibly break up with him while he's fighting for his life?"

"I didn't have time to think of all the factors, Rory. Somehow I just knew it was the right thing to do. And if I'm committed to a guy who will never walk again, so be it. You know what they say, for better or worse. Guess I'm starting out with the worse. May as well get it out of the way early. It can only get better."

"Speaking of worse, you've got something else to make your day harder."

"What?"

"You've gotta break up with Jamison."

"Oh, hell, I completely forgot about him. And I can't do it over the phone, either. Not after he's been so good to me. And I just thought of something else."

"What?"

"I'm committed to do a bunch of public service announcements for several organizations and Jamison is producing them all. So it won't exactly be goodbye. I'm still gonna have to see him."

"That's not a very good idea, Freckles. Maybe he can have someone else on his staff take care of it. Anyway, you can't go to see Nick till this afternoon anyway, so why don't you go into the city and get it over with."

"I dunno—"

"The longer you put it off, the worse it will get."

I'm walking on eggshells as I enter Jamison's office. He looks up from his newspaper and smiles. "Hey, what a nice surprise."

You won't think that in about two minutes.

"Hi, Jamison."

He gets up and gives me a hug. "So to what do I owe this visit today?"

"Need to talk to you about something."

He studies my face. "Uh-oh. I can tell this isn't good."

I exhale as I sit in front of his desk. "Jamison, this has been the hardest decision I've ever had to make."

"I get the feeling I'm about to get the *you're a nice guy, but* speech."

I look down and don't say anything for a moment. "Jamison, I'm so sorry."

"Did I do something wrong?"

I look up at him. "No, not at all. Please let me explain and then if you want to tell me to get the hell out of your office you may do so."

He sits behind his desk and folds his hands. "That's not going to happen. But say what you need to say."

"As I told you, I have also been dating someone else. I met you at the same time I met him, and this is the first time in my life I have, so to speak, played the field. That said, I have discovered that while it is nice to go out with different men, it's not possible for someone like me to have serious relationships with more than one. I can't sleep with multiple partners, and I can't get attached to more than one guy. And that's what's happened recently. I find myself getting attached to both of you, and that's not good. And not fair to either of you."

"That's perfectly understandable, Madison. And I've been getting attached to you as well."

"Anyway . . . Jamison, this is so hard because you have treated me so well . . . but I reached the point where I simply could not keep going out with both of you. So I made a choice, and I'm not going to be able to see you anymore."

He slowly nods. "Well, naturally I'm very disappointed. But I can certainly understand your feelings since I've never played the field or slept around either. Is there something specific—"

"Just a gut feeling, Jamison. Honestly, had I met only you we'd still be going out. But I can't burn the candle at both ends. It's really been tearing me apart the past few days."

"Well, I can't be mad at you, Madison. I will ask you for one thing, though."

"What's that?"

"If things don't work out with this other guy, I hope I'll be the first call you make."

"Even after what I just did?"

"Madison, I can't hate you because of this. I think too much of you. If you had cheated on me or sneaked around or lied, I'd be upset, but you haven't. So if I have to settle for *right of first refusal*, so be it."

"Jamison, you're being incredibly understanding about this."

"Well, we also have to work together in the future. So I'd like to keep you as a friend. If that's okay with you. That is, if you still want me to shoot your commercials."

Rory said this isn't a good idea, but the guy is being so nice. "Sure, that will be fine."

"Okay then. Well, while I hope you'll change your mind in the future, I hope you'll be happy with whomever you choose because you deserve it. But nothing's final until you walk down the aisle, right?" We both get up and he puts his arm around my shoulders as he walks me to the door. "So, you got the day off?"

"Just off the street today."

"Ah, still going after your great white whale?"

"Yeah."

"Any luck?"

"Not yet."

"Well, don't feel bad if nothing turns up. You won't be the first reporter to hit dead ends on that guy. I remember doing a lot of stories like that."

"Gotta take a shot, Jamison."

We reach the front door and he kisses me on the cheek. "Glad I don't have to say goodbye. So, see you later."

After that unbelievably smooth breakup with Jamison I'm in the hospital waiting room along with Nick's partner Steve and a few other officers. His condition has improved since last night, though we found out his heart actually stopped for a while during surgery.

Clinically dead.

That little bit of news made my heart skip a beat.

And also confirmed I've made the right choice. Not sure I would have felt the same about never seeing Jamison again.

The door opens and everyone stands as the doctor moves into the room. "I have good news. Officer Marino is awake."

Everyone exhales tension as Steve pats me on the shoulder. "Thank God."

"I'll let two of you see him for about ten minutes, but then he really needs his rest."

Steve takes my hand. "C'mon. I know he'll want to see you."

"You wanna go first?"

"No. We'll go together."

We follow the doctor down a hallway, then through a door marked Intensive Care. We pass rows of beds, all filled with people hooked up to various tubes and beeping machines. The doctor pulls back a curtain and what I see knocks the air from my lungs.

Nick, pale as a ghost, eyes barely open, a bandage around his head. He sees me and struggles to smile as I move to one side of the bed while Steve goes to the other. I take Nick's hand and give it a squeeze. "Hey, Marino, how you doing?"

"Is this heaven?" His voice is soft, almost a whisper.

"No, it's Staten Island."

"Then why am I looking at a redheaded angel?"

Steve laughs. "Told you he wanted to see you." He takes Nick's other hand. "Glad to have you back, partner. You're obviously getting better."

"Did you get him, Steve?"

"He's taking a dirt nap. Saved the justice system a ton of money."

"That's good. Are that woman and the little girl okay?"

"Yep. You saved both of them. Are you in any pain?"

"A little. I think the anesthesia is wearing off."

"I'll go get the nurse."

Nick turns back to me. "Guess I can't take you out to dinner this weekend, huh?"

"Hey, don't think you can use this as an excuse to get out of a date. I hear the food in this hospital is pretty good. Though we can't eat by candlelight because you're on oxygen. We'd blow the place up."

"How'd you get in here, anyway? They usually only let family members in."

"Told them I was your girlfriend."

"But you're—"

"Not anymore. I'm all yours. That is, if you still want me."

He reaches up and touches my hair. "You know what they say about Italian guys. Can't resist red hair and freckles."

"So I see. And by the way, young man, I understand from your partner that you were talking about me all day."

"Damn, you're really getting the advantage in this relationship."

I see his eyes flickering and can tell he's fading. I run my hand over his cheek. "Still think we're even, Marino. But right now you

need your rest. I'll see if the doctor will let me come back later."
I lean over and give him a soft kiss.

"That's better than any medicine." His eyes lock with mine, then close as he falls asleep.

I see the doctor on the way out and head in his direction. "Doctor, you got a minute?"

"Sure. That was a quick visit."

"He fell asleep."

"He'll need a lot of rest. And a lot of physical therapy."

"Have you told him everything?"

He shakes his head. "Not yet. It's best if there's a family member or close friend in the room when I do that. Then again, I'm hopefully wrong about the possibility of him not walking again by the time we get a clearer picture."

"How long will he be here?"

"Hard to tell. Several days, at least."

"Okay. Thanks for saving him, doctor."

"Just part of my job."

"Funny, Nick says the same thing. When can I see him again?"

"Come back tomorrow morning."

Chapter Nineteen

The girls are here for a quiet dinner tonight, and of course the elephant in the room is my hasty decision at the hospital. I get the feeling they're concerned that when I take time to step back and look at it objectively, I might regret not taking more time to think.

They're worried.

I'm not.

Tish brings up the subject of Jamison. "Rory tells me you said goodbye to Jamison today."

"Uh, not exactly."

Rory stops eating. "Freckles, you can't string him along—"

"I'm not. I told him I'd made a choice and that I could not date him any longer. And then he did something I've never heard of a guy doing. He said he wanted to be friends."

A.J.'s face tightens. "Huh? What guy does that? Every time I've had to break up with a guy he's furious."

Tish starts to laugh. "That's because he knows his endless supply of free cannolis is gone."

A.J. wrinkles her nose at Tish. "Smartass. But seriously, what guy does that? And why do you want to be friends with him? He's nice, but that kind of thing never works."

"Because I still have to work with him. He's producing all

those public service announcements. Anyway, he took it real well, didn't get mad or say he never wanted to see me again. He actually told me that if it doesn't work out I should give him a call."

Tish slowly nods. "Ah. This is a *second chance* scenario."

"Huh?"

"He's being the mature one, just in case it really *doesn't* work out. So that you really *will* give him a call if that happens. He likes you a lot to do that, Madison. If he didn't he would have told you he never wanted to see you again like most guys when they get dumped. He still has hope."

I shake my head and toss my napkin on the table. "Aw, shit."

"And the candle continues to burn at both ends," says Rory.

Tish shakes her head. "Nah, look at her. She's got it bad for Nick. Something tells me she won't even give the second chance option a thought."

Some color has returned to his face and he's wide awake as I head toward Nick's bed in his new private room. "You look better today, Marino."

"Yesterday was a blur. I remember you being here but that's it. I slept all day."

I sit on the edge of the bed, lean forward and give him a kiss. "Well, you needed it. We nearly lost you, you know."

He nods. "Yeah, the doctor told me. But at least I got to meet Elvis and found out who killed JFK."

"You really are feeling better, aren't you?"

"A little. I'm on some pretty strong meds. But I'm still very low power."

A staffer comes by with a cart and brings in a breakfast tray. I take it from him and put it on the table next to the bed. "Think you can eat something?"

"I could eat a lot of something. What's on the menu?"

I peel back the foil and see scrambled eggs, toast and orange juice and pivot the table so it is over the bed. "Standard hospital

174

breakfast. Maybe A.J. can sneak some contraband in here for ya in a few days."

"That would be nice." He reaches for a fork and tries to get some eggs, but his hand is shaking and he puts it down. "Damn, I'm so weak."

"I'll get it." I take the fork, scoop up some eggs and feed him. "Well, this is familiar."

"See, those cats were good practice."

"Don't get used to it."

"But you know, I would have guessed the first time you served me breakfast in bed would be after . . ." He flashes a devilish grin.

"Those meds have given you a dirty mind, Mister."

He locks eyes with me as I give him another forkful of eggs. "Hey, I wanted to ask you something."

"Sure."

"How did I win?"

"Win what?"

"You. How did I beat the other guy? I'd really like to know why you picked me."

"Isn't the fact that I chose you enough?"

"No, of course not. Don't you realize that my fragile male ego needs this? Guys have to savor their victories, especially with a prize like you. So how did I win?"

"Well, the other guy treated me very well, and you two were very close. But it came down to the way you looked at me on the dance floor."

"Really? Just a look?"

"Just a look. Yours went right into my soul."

"I could say the same about you."

"And, also, you're damned impressive with your shirt off."

"I'm sure you are as well."

"Will you stop it?"

"Hey, you started it. So that's when you decided? On the dance floor?"

175

Dammit, I can't tell him I made up my mind in the waiting room while he lay dying. "Yep. That dance in the rain. That's our song now, you know."

"Okay. I was worried that my current situation might have something to do with it. I, uh . . . didn't want you to choose me because you felt sorry for me."

Good God, now I'm getting it from him.

I put the fork down, reach out and take his face in my hands. "There's nothing to feel sorry for. You're gonna get well and dance with me again, Officer."

"This doesn't scare you, Madison?"

"What?"

"Having a relationship with someone who could die at any time? That every goodbye kiss in the morning could be your last?"

"I could walk out of here and get hit by a bus, Marino. We never know when our number's up. That's why it's important to live every day to the fullest. And right now I choose to share this particular day with you."

Bumper is purring on my lap on Friday night when the phone rings. It's Steve, Nick's partner. "Are you free tomorrow morning?"

"Yeah. What's up?"

"Just talked to the doctor."

"I was there a few minutes ago. Must have missed you. So what did the doctor say?"

"He would like those closest to Nick to be there when he gives him the prognosis."

My heart sinks. "Uh-oh. You know that can't be good."

"I wouldn't think so. If he was going to tell Nick he'd be completely normal he wouldn't need us around. Anyway, I'll pick you up at ten, if that's okay."

"Sure. See you then."

Nick's face lights up as Steve and I enter his room and move to the sides of the bed. I take his hand and give him a kiss. "How you feelin' today, Marino?"

"A little better each day. But that may be the painkillers talking."

"Well, you look better. You're getting a little color back in your face."

"Thanks." He turns to his partner. "Good timing with the two of you here at the same time while I'm awake."

"I, uh, ran into Madison in the lobby. Guess we're on the same wavelength."

A gentle knock on the door announces the arrival of the doctor, who gives me a quick nod as he moves toward the bed. "How are you feeling this morning, Officer?"

"No pain. And a little stronger. Think my friends could smuggle in some real food, Doc?"

He laughs a bit. "Sure. I've seen the stuff from the kitchen and don't blame you. I, uh, wanted to talk to you about your prognosis."

I study the doctor's face.

This isn't good.

I look back at Nick, who seems ready for anything.

And all I can think of is Gary Cooper playing Lou Gehrig in *Pride of the Yankees* saying, *"Give it to me straight, Doc. Is it curtains?"*

Nick smiles at me as I take his hand. "Well, don't keep me in suspense."

The doctor looks down at the floor. "One bullet did a lot of damage. And it might be permanent. While it's too early to tell, there is a chance you may never walk again."

His words are a punch to the soul. I squeeze Nick's hand as my eyes instantly well up.

He slowly nods, but incredibly shows no emotion. "So, what are my chances?"

"Again, much too early to tell. But I wanted you to be prepared. You may be able to eventually walk normally with a lot of physical therapy. But for right now, you'll be in a wheelchair when you're released in about a week." The doctor's medical explanation fades into the background as I stare at Nick, who still remains calm. No anger, no depressed look. I'm a wreck over this and he's not even upset. The guy is a rock. A single tear runs down my cheek. He notices and brushes it off with his thumb, then smiles at me.

He turns back to the doctor. "Okay, doctor. Thanks for being honest with me."

"Sure. Now, when you are released, do you have family that can attend to you and a place that is wheelchair accessible?"

"I live in a second floor apartment with no elevator. And I don't have any family. My parents are gone and I'm an only child."

"Well, I can get you into a special facility, but it's expensive. I'm not sure if your insurance will cover all of it, but I'll see what I can do."

"We'll raise the money," says Steve. "Whatever it takes."

I realize I have to take charge.

"No." I stand up, still holding his hand. "He can stay with me."

Nick looks up at me. "Madison, you can't—"

"You're not going into some *facility*. You're staying with me. End of story. And it is not up for discussion. You're not going to live with people who don't even know you for who knows how long and eat more awful hospital food. And you do have family. Your friends are your family."

"What about your job?"

"Don't worry about it. I'll work something out. I'll hire a live-in nurse if I have to. I can afford it and I've got a big house."

The doctor turns to me. "It *is* much better for the patient to be surrounded by friends and family. Can your home handle a wheelchair?"

"By the time he gets out of here it will."

Nick pulls on my hand. "Madison, you don't have to do this. What are you gonna do, knock down walls in your house?"

"Steve, please tell your partner to shut the hell up." I look down at Nick. "All I have to do is widen a couple of doors and build a ramp from the driveway. It's time for the damsel in distress to say thank you to her hero. So stop arguing with me. You're moving in and that's that."

The doctor chuckles a bit. "You've got a tough one in your corner, Officer, which is good. And it sounds like that's settled." He heads for the door. "I'll leave you all to discuss your plans."

"Very nice of you, Madison," says Steve.

I'm still looking at Nick. "He'd do it for me."

"Yeah, he would."

Nick gives me his usual soulful look. "I don't know what I did to deserve you."

"I do. And let's get one thing straight right now. You *are* going to walk again and dance with me. Meanwhile, I've got some remodeling to do."

By mid-afternoon I've already got the plans underway. A.J. brought her cousin Angelo the contractor who is busy taking measurements so he can widen the door to the guest room and the adjoining bathroom, while Tish and Rory are busy arranging furniture to create pathways for a wheelchair. (Bumper will have to develop new routes, but he's a resourceful kitten and all the bubble-wrap will keep him from getting hurt.) The sound of a power saw drifts through the open window as Steve has a bunch of off-duty cops already busy building a ramp from the driveway to the back door. We've got about a week to get things ready, but it shouldn't be a problem. It's really not all that much.

The problem is going to be my job. I've got a bunch of vacation time and comp days built up, but I know my boss isn't going to let me take the time off all at once, especially during an election year. I have a way to do my job and take care of Nick, I'm just not sure he'll go for it.

But if that's the case, I do have a trump card.

Chapter Twenty

The trump card is still in my hand, not having been played as I sit in my News Director's office waiting for him to return from corporate with a decision on my proposal.

I have the card and he knows it. Corporate knows it too.

There's no way he could fire me if I took all the time off. And if I got a flat out "no" on any parts of my proposal he knows damn well I'd quit and walk out. The backlash against a network not accommodating its most popular on-air person because she's taking care of a wounded hero would be devastating.

But he also has a good card in that we're in the middle of a presidential campaign and with our senior reporter on the shelf with a broken ankle, I'm the most experienced political reporter the network has. And the most popular thanks to the kittens and the adoption thing. There's no way they'll let me take off a solid month. And to be honest, I wouldn't do that to the network.

So I've asked for some reasonable changes to my schedule that will give me more time at home to take care of Nick until he gets well.

The only unknown factor is how long that will take.

Barry comes back into his office, shuts the door and sits behind his desk. "Okay, I think you'll agree this works for both of us.

And it's something I can live with. But I will tell you that it's the best I could do."

Of course when a News Director says that, it means he's got one more thing to offer beyond the first offer. "What's the deal?"

"First, you obviously can't take all your time off at once with the election so close."

"I realize that."

"That said, I can make your life a lot easier. First, as you know Jim Haller left the network two months ago and they never found a replacement for his spot on the Sunday morning political panel. They've been using substitutes every week and haven't found the right person."

"Barry, I can't go to Washington every weekend."

"I'm not asking you to do that. You can do the show from New York. The show's producer really wants you as a permanent member of the panel and is willing to have you participate that way, even if you never set foot in their studio. So that takes care of one day of your work week. Of course, that means getting up early Sunday morning, and I know how much you love rolling out of bed at the crack of dawn. But the good part is you're done at nine in the morning and it counts as a full workday."

Sure, that's a really fair trade. I nod, liking the idea that never crossed my mind. "Okay, sounds great. What else?"

"Since I already told you I was going to give you one day per week off the street to work the Senator Collier investigation I can let you do that from home since you basically work the phones anyway. So that's two days you don't have to be here."

"So far, so good, Barry."

"The other three days I need you knocking out your usual stories, so I do need you to be here. But how about this . . . we set up the portable background, camera and lights in your home and instead of having you do live shots from the field or sitting on the set, you do it from your house. We leave the gear in place and all the photog has to do is show up, turn things on and frame up the shot. This way we keep your presence on the newscast and you can go home as soon as your story is in the can. The photog I'm assigning will love it since the guy lives down the street from you. And since you're so organized and usually done by four, it would get you home a lot sooner."

"Can I do my Sunday morning live shot from the house as well?"

"I don't see why not. We can set up the portable background for that show as well. No reason for you to drive here. So that's the deal. Three days a week here and you go home early. One day working the Collier story from home and the Sunday morning show from home. Is that acceptable?"

"Yeah, Barry, I think that's very fair. I really appreciate you going to bat for me and making all these concessions. It will really help."

He smiles and leans back in his chair. "Okay, it's settled then."

"So what else did you have in your pocket?"

"What do you mean?"

"Every negotiation I've ever had when the boss says *it's the best I can do* always means there's something else he can offer."

He laughs a bit. "Now I see why you're such a good negotiator. And while that is a common tactic when it comes to money and contracts, or so I've heard—"

"Uh-huh."

"I was being totally honest with you. Considering the situation, Madison, there is no way I was going to play games and treat you like you're in a car dealership."

"Thanks, I appreciate that. I think what you've offered is terrific."

"Glad you're happy. And now I must say how impressed I am with you."

"For what?"

"Moving your new boyfriend into your house, remodeling it and taking care of him. That's a big undertaking."

182

"I can handle it."

"Have you ever done anything like this before? Taking care of a person with a physical challenge?"

"Nope. I do have a special needs kitten, though."

"You must really like this guy, huh?"

I can't help but smile. "Yeah. He's really special."

"What happened to the guy you brought to the office party? I thought you were pretty serious about him."

"He turned out to be very selfish. Funny, I never would have found out without those kittens."

"Well, it's really wonderful what you're doing for that cop. You've changed so much lately."

"I know. Sometimes I don't even recognize the person I used to be. It's almost like that was another life. But to be honest it also feels like I'm getting back to the real me, the person I used to be."

"It's a good look for you, Madison. And about the best compliment I can give you is that I hope my daughter turns out like you."

I heard from the doctor that Nick will be released Saturday morning barring any unforeseen setbacks. Thankfully A.J.'s cousin pretty much dropped what he was doing and will have the house ready to accommodate the wheelchair.

Meanwhile, a little will be coming off my plate tomorrow, as the kittens go to their furever homes. So I'll be going from four cats and no humans to taking care of one cat and one human. But I like the trade. And I really like the human.

I do feel bad about breaking up the litter and often wonder if the little guys will miss their siblings, but at least each one will receive undivided attention instead of the twenty-five percent I've been doling out. (Okay, I admit Bumper has been getting a lot more. So sue me. I love the little guy.)

Of course the fact that the kittens will be relocating necessitates another live shot, as the country is desperate to find out how the story turns out. People are also clamoring for cat videos, like I have time for that, but after being bombarded with requests I finally shot a few minutes of the little guys playing and it quickly went viral. As it turns out, their fifteen minutes of fame will not end, as one of the world's biggest cat food companies contacted me and wanted a photo of all four to put on a bag of their kitten food. Once again, I held the trump card.

Only this time, I played it.

"Hello, Miss Shaw? This is Jim Dwyer, Marketing Director at the Fluffy Cat Food Company."

"Hi. Jim. What can I do for you?"

"Well, we would love to feature a photo of your kittens on a bag of our cat food. Would you be amenable to that?"

"Certainly. And when can I expect your check for fifty thousand dollars to arrive at my local animal shelter?"

They overnighted the check.

If only contract negotiations with my network were that easy.

I'm beginning to think my fur babies have become so famous they can raise a ton of money for good causes.

Hmmm . . .

Rory, being camera shy, is very nervous as the hit time for our morning show live shot with the kittens grows near. I'm sitting next to her on the couch holding her hand. We're still a half hour away but she's already pale with her jaw and fists clenched, staring straight ahead. "Will you please try to relax?"

"Millions of people are going to see this? What will they think of me if I screw up?"

"How are you going to screw up? You sit there, smile and hold a kitten. I'm gonna ask you why you chose this kitten and you answer. That's it."

"I look like shit."

"Oh, gimme a break. You never look like shit. Men fall all over

184

you because it is impossible for you to look like shit. You can roll out of bed and look cute as hell. Have you forgotten you were prom queen and head cheerleader?"

"That was ages ago. I am way past my expiration date. High def is going to make my face look like an old catcher's mitt."

"Actually, right now you look like you're about to face a firing squad. Sweetie, once this live shot is over I'm going to be deluged with calls and emails from men asking if you're available."

The door opens as A.J. and Tish arrive. My eyes widen at A.J.'s attire, as she's in a gorgeous red cocktail dress. "What's with the outfit? You got a date at six in the morning?"

"Nah. Coming home from one."

"Sorry I asked. I assume you had a good time."

"If I'd had a good time my dress would be on backwards."

Tish has her usual lawyer garb on, a super conservative suit, hair up, horn-rimmed glasses. But she's wearing a big smile. "I've got a great name for my kitten."

"And that would be?"

"You'll have to wait for the big reveal. But it has to do with my office address."

"You're gonna name the cat *Empire State Building*?"

"Nope. Something very clever. You'll see."

The photographer cues me as the live shot begins and I hear the anchor's question in my earpiece. "So, Madison, I guess this is the big day for the country's most famous kittens as they are moving to their forever homes."

"Right, Kayla, and I know they're going to good homes because these are my closest friends in the whole world. Rory, A.J. and Tish." I wrap one arm around Rory's shoulders as she wears the classic TV deer in the headlights expression. Actually, the proverbial deer might be more relaxed. "Rory has been my best friend since high school and I want viewers to know she's been providing kitten day care while I've been at work. She lives across the street and has done a terrific job helping to raise the fur babies." I turn to her. "So, since you did the most work I gave you first choice. Why did you pick this kitten?"

She stares into the camera and answers like an android. "It's cute."

"Well, they're all cute. Do you have a name for it yet?"

"No."

Interviews like that are known as a "dead fish" because a reporter feels like she's been handed one. Time to move on because she's obviously not going to talk. "Sitting next to Rory is A.J., who runs the best delicatessen here on Staten Island and I'd have to say that your kitten turned the tables and chose you since it always jumps in your lap when you visit."

"I think it smells my usual perfume . . . *eau de cold cuts*. It's a very perceptive kitten and knows it will never starve. And no, I haven't come up with a name yet."

"Ah, but I do know our other cat parent has already named her kitten. That's Tish at the end of the couch, who is a lawyer in Manhattan. Now you wouldn't tell me the name of your fur baby before, so I'm waiting for the big reveal."

"Well, my office is in the Empire State Building, which is situated on Fifth Avenue. That street is also the home of the famous department store, Saks Fifth Avenue. And since this kitten has white socks, I think it is only appropriate that I name her *Socks Fifth Avenue*."

By the end of the day the Twitterverse is going wild over the kittens. I must admit that the name Tish came up with for her kitten is incredible, and its "account" on Twitter (@SocksFifthAvenue) already has a ton of followers. Of course as soon as she set it up I was pretty much forced to set up an account for Bumper (@BumperCat) and he is also attracting followers in droves. He'll probably have more than I do by the end of the week.

Tish must not have had a busy day because Socks Fifth Avenue has been tweeting every hour. (Either that or she delegated it to her secretary.) With stuff like this:

@SocksFifthAvenue
Training my human. Looked sad while she was eating salmon so she shared. And what did YOU have, @BumperCat?

I could see this could turn into a full-fledged Twitter war between Socks and Bumper, so I called her and told her I didn't have all day to spend as a ghost writer for a cat. Which resulted in this:

@SocksFifthAvenue
Yo, @BumperCat, you too lazy to tweet more than once a day? Already turning into a diva?

@BumperCat
Spotted a fly in the house and busy chasing it on behalf of human. At least I have a job, @SocksFifthAvenue

Meanwhile, the actual department store Saks Fifth Avenue thought the whole thing was cute and donated a chunk of change to a local shelter, while asking Tish if Socks could be their spokes-cat for a promotion in the future.

But adopting out the kittens has left my house pretty quiet, with just me and Bumper until Nick gets here this weekend. The kitten seemed a little bored when I got home so I've been busy playing with him. I guess he misses his friends so I'm going to schedule a play date with Rory's kitten.

Stop looking at me like that. I'm not obsessive.

Okay, I'm obsessive.

Mea culpa.

Chapter Twenty-One

Everything looks perfect as we prepare for Nick's arrival on Saturday morning. A.J. has brought a ton of food as the house will be filled with a bunch of cops within the hour, while Rory, Tish and I have been decorating. A huge banner hangs across the dining room reading "Welcome Home."

Of course, I don't know if that means home for good, home till he gets better, or maybe both.

Meanwhile, the guest room has been transformed to make things easier for him, while the living room now looks like a TV studio, with two backgrounds set up in the corner while a camera and lights are in the middle with cables running everywhere. The curtains are still doubled over the rods while the bubble-wrap remains a fixture.

And Bumper has his own room as well.

"Sure doesn't look like your house anymore," says Tish, as she sits on the couch and turns on the TV. "All this because of a bunch of kittens."

"Yeah, I don't think I'm making *Better Homes and Gardens* anytime soon." I sit next to her as A.J. grabs the seat on the other side. Our network's cable operation is covering Nick's release from the hospital, as his story of heroism has gathered national attention. I decided not to be there as this is his moment, and we both agree our relationship should remain private. Besides, if I were there it would be yet another step toward sainthood, and that's not why I'm doing this.

A.J. points at the TV and sits up straight. "Here he comes."

I lean forward and Tish turns up the sound as we see Nick being wheeled out of the hospital by his partner toward a waiting horde of media people. He smiles as he comes to a stop near the special van that is on loan to us by a local car dealership.

A reporter shoves a microphone in his direction. "How are you feeling, Officer Marino?"

"A little better every day. I want to thank all the doctors and nurses for saving my life and treating me so well. It's great to be going home."

"Officer, I understand you were clinically dead for a short time."

"That's correct. I met your great grandfather and he said you need to call your mother more often."

The media laughed and peppered him with more questions, all answered in an upbeat manner.

Tish pats my hand. "He's amazing. To have that kind of attitude. He's good for you, Madison."

"Excellent choice," says A.J. "If he can handle this with that much grace, he can handle anything."

I turn off the TV as the news conference ends and I see him loaded into the van. "Yeah. I don't think anything fazes him. Hopefully he'll stay that way."

"It will be a lot easier with you taking care of him," says Rory. "And please don't hesitate to ask us for help. This is going to require a lot more effort than taking care of the kittens."

Nick beams as his partner wheels him in the back door and is greeted by a loud cheer. My home is a sea of blue uniforms, as most of the cops from his precinct are here. I hang back and let all his fellow cops shake his hand and slap him on the back, then move forward, lean down and give him a hug. He takes my hands as I stand up. "I cannot believe you're doing this, Madison. But I can't thank you enough."

"Hey, what good is having a guest room if you don't have a guest?" Everyone laughs as I move behind him and push him up to the dining room table which is filled with food from A.J.'s deli. "But before I show you to your room, Officer, I know you want some real Italian food after all that hospital stuff."

His eyes light up as I dish out some lasagna onto a plate and slide it in front of him. "So, you cooked all this?"

"Yeah, right. Once the leftovers are gone you might wanna leave. Hope you like peanut butter and jelly. Though I do make a mean macaroni and cheese."

He takes a bite of the lasagna and closes his eyes as he savors it. "Damn, this is good. Who made this?"

A.J. is next to me and raises her hand. "All from my deli. If you want more, don't hesitate to ask."

"The best compliment I can give you is that it's as good as my mother's." He looks up at the ceiling. "No offense, Ma. A.J., maybe you can teach Madison to make this."

A.J. leans forward and whispers in my ear. "See, the red hair even trumps my cooking."

I sit next to him as everyone starts dishing out the food. "So we ended up having dinner on the weekend anyway."

"Can't wait to take you out to a real restaurant. I just don't know when."

"Don't worry. We'll get there."

A couple hours later I notice his eyes are drooping and he's yawning. "You out of gas?"

"Yeah, I sleep too much. But the doctor says that's normal after what I've gone through."

"Don't apologize, you need it." I stand up and get everyone's attention. "Okay, the guest of honor needs his rest. You can come back and visit tomorrow." People begin filing by, shaking his hand and patting him on the back as they leave, like a receiving line after a wedding. Finally the crowd clears out and it's time to show him around. I get behind the wheelchair and push him toward the guest room. "Okay, time to give you the lay of the land."

For the first time he notices the network backgrounds and TV gear set up in the living room. "What's the deal with all that stuff?"

"I'll be doing live shots from here, so I can get home early and spend more time with you."

"Geez, Madison, I'm really putting you out."

"No big deal. And I get to work at home a lot more. You'll see." I navigate him thorough the new wide door into the guest room. "Okay, bathroom is to the left and you can roll right into the shower. We lowered the bed so it's the same height as the wheelchair seat and you can slide in and out. And you've got a pull bar over the bed to help you move around." I point at the TV. "You've got Netflix so you can binge watch, books to read. Your partner brought your clothes and computer and it's already linked to my internet. There's a bell and a whistle on the night-stand in case you need help. And the nightstand is actually a small fridge, with drinks and snacks if you want something."

He shakes his head as he uses the pull bar to slide onto the bed. "Damn, Madison, I don't know what to say. I can't believe you did all this for me. And honestly, we don't know each other that well."

I sit on the edge of the bed. "I know you well enough. Now, do you need anything?"

"I don't have to take any medication for a few hours. I'm good."

"Okay, I'll let you sleep. And I'm not going anywhere this weekend. If you want me, just whistle."

"What is this, *Casablanca*?"

"Actually the line is from *To Have and Have Not*. But same result. I'll come running."

191

He picks up the whistle and blows.

"I'm right here, Nick."

"You said to whistle if I wanted you."

"Very funny. I meant if you *need* me for something."

"I do."

"Okay, knock it off."

"Hey, you're the one who told me to whistle if I wanted you. Anyway, what's the deal with your job?"

"I'll have to go in Monday, Tuesday and Wednesday. Thursday I'm doing research on Senator Collier which I can do from here. Friday and Saturday are my days off and tomorrow morning I'm on the Sunday political show, live from my living room. But I'll be done with that by nine and then I'm free the rest of the day. On the days I'm at the network we've got nurses scheduled to be here. Rory will be checking on you from across the street and A.J. will be sending lunch over."

He bites his lower lip and his eyes well up a bit.

He doesn't have to say a word.

I lean forward and give him a kiss. "Get your rest, Mister. I'll check on you later and we can watch TV. Welcome home, and I mean that sincerely."

He's been asleep all day and it's dinner time. I peek in his room and see him waking up. "Get a good nap?"

"Yeah. I was out cold. What time is it?"

"Six. You hungry?"

"Of course."

"Oh, you have another visitor. If you can handle it."

"Sure." I walk in holding the kitten and he smiles as I hand it to him. "Bumper! Look at you, you got bigger."

"They grow up so fast. Then off to college and they never call you anymore. Just come home with dirty laundry."

He lays the kitten on his chest and begins to scratch him on the head. "So, you can't jump and I can't walk. We're quite the pair."

The kitten meows as I sit on the edge of the bed. "I already told you that you're gonna walk again. Anyway, you two catch up and I'll go get you something to eat."

"Are there leftovers?"

"Thankfully, we have a ton of food. Enjoy it while it lasts."

"I seem to remember an excellent dinner you cooked for me."

"That was with a lot of help from A.J. and it's the only recipe I have."

"Well, I've got a ton of them in my head. I'll teach you. Least I can do."

Three hours later Nick laughs as the movie we've been watching ends. "Not exactly my idea of taking you out for dinner and a movie."

"Hey, it's the company that counts. You up for anything else?"

"I know it's only nine, but I'm fading."

I turn off the TV and sit up on the end of the bed. "You need anything before you crash?"

"My medication."

"You already took it with your dinner. Did you forget?"

"Not that kind of medicine." He points to his lips.

"What?"

"Hey, you've been lying next to me for the past three hours. You think I don't want a goodnight kiss?"

"You sure you can handle it? Don't want to put a strain on your heart."

"You did that before I got shot."

Wow.

I can't help but smile as my own heart flutters. "Awww. Damn, Marino, I must say you're good with the compliments." I lean forward, gently take his head in my hands and give him a long kiss.

He strokes my hair as our lips part, gives me that same look I saw on the dance floor, then he pulls my head back toward his. Suddenly we're making out and the sparks I'm feeling are off the charts. I want to climb on top of him but have to resist in light of his condition. Finally he stops and runs his hand across my cheek as I sit up. He's wearing a big smile as he nods. "Yep. Just as I thought."

"Huh?"

"At least some things below the waist are working perfectly."

Color rushes to my face as I instantly blush. "Why Nicholas Salvatore Marino, you have a dirty mind. Young man, you're a long way off from *that kind* of physical therapy."

"Hey, I had to know. Just looking long term."

"Yeah, right. You get well first, Mister."

"By the way, how'd you find out my middle name?"

I point at his arm. "The hospital wrist band. Salvatore, huh?"

"Don't remind me. So if you call me by my full name, does that mean you're in charge at the moment?"

I gently pat him on the cheek. "Aw, sweetie, didn't you get the memo? You should have figured out by now that I'm *always* in charge. Too late now. You're stuck here, just like James Caan in *Misery*."

I start to get up but he grabs my hand. "Hey."

"What?"

"All kidding aside, someday I hope I'll be able to thank you."

"You already thanked me. Several times."

"Words aren't enough, Madison."

"Just dance with me again. That will be thanks enough. And that's what I really want. Dance with me."

Chapter Twenty-Two

I'm not in my body yet as I get ready to head back to the newsroom on Monday morning. While getting up at a ridiculous hour on a Sunday was not my idea of fun, the trade-off was great. Spending an hour sharing my opinions on politics rather than a full day at work is well worth the crack of dawn wake-up call. Besides, I needed to get up to check on Nick and make him breakfast. Bacon and eggs I can handle. Though I made a mental note that I'm going to run out of leftovers by Thursday and will have to start cooking. Which could probably send the poor guy back to the hospital.

But I'm bleary-eyed because he had a rough night, apparently having some sort of flashbacks that manifested themselves into a nightmare. Nick woke up screaming at four in the morning, so I spent the rest of the night in his bed, his arm around my shoulders, my head resting on his.

It felt so perfect.

But Rory's right. This isn't going to be remotely like taking care of the kittens.

Something bright and colorful catches my eye as I enter the newsroom. A huge bouquet of flowers on my desk.

And then it hits me.

195

With all that has been going on of late, I completely forgot it was my birthday.

But Nick obviously remembered. Geez, the guy is recovering from a nearly fatal gunshot wound and he manages to call a florist. And spend way too much money. I know what cops make, and this is out of his price range.

Still, it's very sweet.

I pick up the pace, suddenly energized as I always am when I get flowers. I reach my desk and lean into the bouquet, breathing in the beautiful fragrance, then grab the card.

And when I open it, my joy disappears.

To a very special woman . . . Happy Birthday!
-Jamison

Well, so much for being "just friends" as it is clear the guy isn't giving up, nor is he respecting my decision. His phone number is still in my cell, so I quickly call him, waiting with narrowed eyes and a clenched jaw for him to answer.

"Hey, Madison, how are you?"

"Jamison, I told you the other day I couldn't date you anymore. Did you not get the message?"

"I told you I understood your decision. Why are you so upset?"

"Well, if you understand my decision then why are you sending me flowers? I told you I've chosen someone else."

"Oh, damn. I know what happened. Madison, I'm so sorry. I ordered them a couple of weeks ago when you told me this was your birthday. It slipped my mind and I forgot to cancel. Please don't take this the wrong way. I wasn't trying to get between you and the other guy."

Oh.

I exhale my tension, shaking my head at myself for getting angry with him. "No, I'm the one who should be sorry. I didn't mean to get upset with you. I just assumed . . . well, you know what they say when you assume."

"Not a problem, I certainly understand what you thought.

Listen, if you want to give the flowers to someone else—"

"No. They're beautiful and I appreciate the thought."

"Is everything okay, Madison?"

"Just didn't get much sleep last night and I'm kinda cranky when that happens."

"I'm the same way. Well, see you in a few days for that public service announcement."

"Thanks for being so understanding. Again. Bye."

I roll my eyes in disgust as I sit down, having chewed out a guy who was just being nice and cared enough to remember a special day.

Yeah, happy birthday.

I pull into my driveway around four thirty and have a live shot at six, so I've got some time to check in on Nick. I find Rory in the living room talking with one of the nurses who has volunteered to help out. "Hey guys."

Rory grins, steps forward and gives me a hug. "Happy birthday Freckles. Gift's on the table."

I smile back at her. "Thanks. So, how'd he do today?" I say, turning my attention to the nurse, a pretty blonde around forty who is married to a cop.

"I little rough," she says. "Tried a little of the physical therapy I showed you but couldn't do too much. He still has a long way to go. Maybe you can try again a little later."

"Is he up?"

"He was still asleep a few minutes ago."

"I'll go peek in on him." I head to the guest room and crack the door. What I see makes me smile.

Nick, sleeping peacefully, with Bumper curled up next to him, one paw over his hand.

I say goodnight to the photographer after the live shot, then head to Nick's room where he is just waking up. "Hey, sleepyhead. How ya doin'?"

"Slept a lot today."

"You needed it after last night."

"Yeah, about that. The dream was so real. Sorry to wake you."

"Don't worry about it." He grabs the pull bar and sits up. The movement wakes up the kitten. "And I see you've stolen my cat."

"Hey, those of us with challenges stick together."

"You ready for dinner?"

"In a minute." He pats the side of the bed and I sit on the edge. "I've got something for you."

"Is this another clever ruse to get a kiss?"

"Nope. Though I won't complain if that's the result." He turns and leans over to the other side of the bed, then hands me a beautifully wrapped gift. "Happy birthday. Rory told me it was today."

"So you went out shopping when I was at work?"

"Hey, I've got a phone and a credit card." He points at the box. "My C-I told me you might like this."

"Your what?"

"C-I, means *confidential informant.*"

"Ah. And I wonder who *that* could be?" I tear open the wrapping paper and see it's something from the little shop in town that sells handmade chocolate. "Oh, yeah. Something from Chocolate Heaven. You have discovered the way to my heart." I open the box and see a dozen huge chocolate dipped strawberries. "Damn, Nick, I love these." I pick one up and take a bite. "Oh. My. God."

"I take it they're acceptable."

"Perfect. You're amazing, you know that? Recovering from being shot and still getting something for my birthday. But I want something else." I finish the berry, lean forward and give him a long kiss.

"And the clever ruse works."

"You don't need to be clever to get a kiss from me. Right now you can't get well fast enough because there are other things I'd like to do to you."

"Ah. Quite the recovery incentive."

"Anyway, thank you so much for the strawberries. You want one?"

"They're yours. Besides, it will spoil my dinner."

"Won't spoil mine. Let me go get you something to eat and then we can relax a bit."

Between the lack of sleep, a very busy day at work, fixing dinner for Nick (okay, so heating up leftovers isn't terribly strenuous) and spending time playing with Bumper, I'm out of gas by nine o'clock. But Nick looks alert, so I figure I might try a little of that physical therapy the nurse taught me. "You up for a little exercise on those legs?"

"Sure. I couldn't get through much this afternoon. Though it's not like I have to do most of the work. I already got through the upper body stuff pretty easy, but everything below the waist is still hard."

"Yeah, you said that after I kissed you." I flash a wicked grin.

He blushes a bit. "I meant *difficult*. And you say I'm the one with the dirty mind."

"Are the exercises painful?"

"Somewhat. But let's try. Can't let those muscles atrophy."

"Okay." I pull back the sheets and see he's wearing sweatpants. I move to the foot of the bed and grab his ankles. "Feel anything?"

"Unfortunately, not a thing. But go ahead."

I go through the routine taught by the nurse, keeping a close eye on his facial expressions while I put each leg through the regimen. After about ten minutes I see him grimace. "Enough?"

"Yeah. For today. Puts a strain on the core muscles. But you got a lot farther than we did this afternoon. I feel bad that you have to do this."

"Hey, it's a good workout for me too. You're a big boy. But lucky for you I'm not a ninety pound waif. Besides, it saves me a trip to the gym."

"Tell you what, when I'm back to normal we are going out for a real birthday celebration."

199

"Today was fine, Nick. Like I said, just the fact you thought of getting me a present while you're recovering is amazing in my book. And you actually got something I love."

"Well, you deserve a lot more."

I stifle a yawn. "It's been a long day and I'm gonna turn in. Do you, uh, want me to stay here with you?"

"I do, but purely for selfish reasons. Seriously though, you won't get any good rest. If I need anything, I'll just whistle."

"Uh-oh. I may have created a monster with that." I lie next to him, pull up the covers, turn out the light and rest my head on his shoulder. The moonlight spilling through the window lights up his smile. "As for getting a good rest, this is the best place for me."

Most nightmares are scary. Some feature demons or have you facing your worst fear. A popular recurring nightmare among TV people is being on the air totally naked while the teleprompter goes out. I've had that one numerous times.

Nick's nightmare the night before had him re-living his near death experience of being shot.

Mine started when I woke up.

A nightmare doesn't have to be scary in itself. It can trick you, then make you deal with the demon it has planted in your head after it's over.

My dream was an incredibly pleasant one. Living a life of luxury in a gorgeous oceanfront home, sailing on crystal clear blue waters, being treated like a queen with dozens of roses every day.

Of course the dream had me with Jamison and not Nick.

Obviously getting the flowers from Jamison and talking to him on the phone got stuck in my subconscious and triggered the dream.

And when I got up, the dream cued the guilt I have about hurting Jamison.

Along with a scenario I hadn't considered.

When I first made the decision about Nick, my friends wondered if I had painted myself into a romantic corner. Let's face it, if I suddenly realized the guy was wrong for me, which is not going to happen, how could I break up with him in his current condition?

But the dream made me think about something else.

Suppose Nick comes to the realization that *I* am wrong for *him*? He couldn't exactly get up and leave. He's in a corner that *I've* painted him into.

Still, I'm one-hundred percent sure about my decision. You may think it's odd to make such a commitment after three dates, and I would agree if I was twenty-one. But when you're thirty-six, pretty much tired of the same small talk, and can size up a guy after an hour, you simply *know* if a guy is right for you.

So now I wonder . . . does Nick *know*?

Meanwhile, it doesn't help that Jamison is still in my life, making me feel guilty. And for the immediate future, I have no way to get him out of it.

Chapter Twenty-Three

On Wednesday I pull into my driveway exhausted from a three-day work week. I know, that sounds ridiculous, but Nick had another rough night, Bumper started howling for no apparent reason and I got little sleep. The days of coming home and turning into a couch potato are now over.

However, as we say in the news business, it's a good kind of tired.

Thankfully, I'll be in research mode tomorrow at home which isn't remotely stressful.

And as I walk toward the door, I see something that perks me up.

Bumper, waiting for me in the window, meowing through the screen.

I head inside and immediately pick him up. He greets me with a lick on the nose, then starts to purr.

And then I see another uplifting sight.

Nick, sitting in his wheelchair, at the kitchen table which is covered with papers. "Hey, you're up."

He shoots me a smile. "Felt better today. And I need to spend more time out of bed anyway." He cocks his head toward the kitten. "He's been waiting for you. I think he's got a clock in his head. He only got up in the window ten minutes ago."

I stroke his fur. "Awww, you missed me. I missed you too, kitty." I toss my purse on a chair and take a seat next to Nick with Bumper in my lap. "What's all this?"

"Cold case I was working on. Steve dropped by with this figuring I was bored. He was right. Daytime television isn't exactly riveting. How the hell does anyone watch that garbage?"

"Hey, I work in TV and I can't stand it." I look at all the files and see a box filled with plastic bags. "So this is how you guys do it. And that's physical evidence in the box?"

He nods as he pulls out a bag. "Yep. Everything relating to the case is in these files or that box. Right now it's a puzzle that doesn't fit together, but I've got nothing but time to work on it."

"How old is this case?"

"Six years. Unsolved murder that got a lot of news coverage. But every lead turned out to be a dead end."

"Hmmm. Any way I can help?"

"Well, how about I show you what I've got and then you share what you're working on with Senator Collier? Maybe different points of view and a fresh set of eyes might help. And I'm sure your process is a lot different than mine."

"Sounds like a plan. You wanna eat first? It's the last of the leftovers night."

"Bring it on."

Three hours later I feel like a kid putting together a jigsaw puzzle. The way police work a case is so different than my method of investigating a story, and I'm learning a lot while considering new ways to work on the whole Collier affair. Nick seems fascinated at my approach, and has a gleam in his eye now that he has a different method of looking at the evidence. And being "back to work" in a sense has really lifted his spirits.

But someone doesn't find this fascinating and has gotten bored. Bumper lets us know it's time to quit. He climbs out of my lap and stretches out on top of all my research on the

Senator. He meows at me, as if to say, "Enough of this paper-work. Pet me."

Nick scratches him under the chin and is rewarded with a lick. "I think he says it's quitting time."

"I apparently will have to divide my time between the two of you."

"Cats don't like to share."

"No, apparently not. Anyway, I'm ready to crash but the good news is I don't have to go in to work tomorrow and we can work on this in the morning."

"I'm a little tired myself."

"You seem to be doing a lot better today."

"Yeah, feel like I've turned a corner. The physical therapy didn't hurt as much, so I'm making progress. And it helps to do something productive."

"Still got nightmares, though, huh?"

"Yeah. Steve says it's normal to have post-traumatic stress. He got shot years ago and had nightmares for a few weeks. It goes away for some and not others."

I lean over and kiss him. "Pleasant dreams, Officer. You need help getting into bed?"

"Nope, I've got that part down. You need help getting into bed?"

"Not if you leave me enough room."

Big smile. "Hey, I love to share. Oh, one more thing on the to-do list for tomorrow."

"What's that?"

"Besides our investigations, I'm gonna teach you how to cook."

"Uh, I'll be busy."

"You won't be *that* busy."

The grandfather clock strikes noon and I realize we've been going through Senator Collier's documents for three hours since we got up. "Wow, lunch time already. Peanut butter okay?"

Nick leans back and smiles. "You forgot. Cooking lessons begin today."

I'm really not in the mood. "I can order a pizza."

"Sorry. You want an Italian man in your life, you need to know about food. Though I plan to do most of the stuff in the kitchen, I need your help because I can't reach the cooktop. However, I do not expect you to wait on me."

"Does that mean you plan to wait on me when you get well?"

"Absolutely. I've commissioned a pedestal and will put you up there. Peel you some grapes when you so desire them."

"Well, if you put it that way. So what's on today's menu?"

"Fettuccine Alfredo."

"Whoa, you're gonna start me on something exotic?"

"It's simple. Five ingredients."

"Oh, come on. There's gotta be more than five."

"Nope. Cream, butter, Parmesan cheese, egg yolk and of course, fettuccine."

"Seriously, that's it?"

"Yep."

There's a way out of this. "Well, fine, but I don't have all the ingredients."

"Yeah you do. I called A.J. yesterday and she brought 'em over. Fridge, top shelf."

Curses, foiled again.

I open the fridge and see a bag from A.J.'s deli. "That little sneak."

"Trust me, you'll love cooking once you get the hang of it. We'll need a pot for the pasta and a small saucepan for the Alfredo. And a cheese grater."

"I don't have one of those."

"You do now. In the bag."

"We have to grate our own cheese? I thought it just came in one of those shaker cans."

"Well, before there was processed cheese people actually grated

205

their own. You know, when dinosaurs roamed the earth. Trust me, it's fresher and has more of a kick this way."

Ten minutes later I have the water boiling in the pot (Nick said I got an "A" for that) and the saucepan is simmering with the cream, butter and cheese. "Okay, so what's the deal with the egg yolk?"

"First, we need to separate the eggs."

I take the two eggs from the bowl and move them to opposite ends of the table.

Nick wrinkles his nose at me. "Very funny, Madison." He grabs a small bowl, separates the eggs, and whips the yolks with a whisk. "Now add this to the sauce and blend it fast with the whisk because the yolk will cook instantly and you don't want any lumps."

I follow his directions and can see the sauce beginning to thicken. "Okay, now what?"

"Put the fresh pasta in the pot. Two minutes."

"That's it?"

"The fresh stuff cooks up very fast."

Five minutes later I shove a forkful into my mouth. "Damn."

"You like?"

"That's awesome. Who knew something like this was so simple."

"So cooking isn't that hard, huh?"

"No, not at all. Thank you for teaching me."

Bumper walks into the kitchen sniffing the air. He turns to me and meows.

"Sorry, kitty, I don't think this rich food would be good for you." I reach down and lift the kitten into my lap.

"Maybe he just wants his share of your attention."

"Okay, kitty, I'll have to divide my time for you."

"Y'know, that reminds me of something about Senator Collier's elections."

"What's that?"

"Dividing attention. You ever notice that every time he runs for re-election, the Republicans always have a strong candidate. And then some extreme right-wing whack job gets in the race as an independent and takes enough votes away from the legitimate Republican candidate so Collier wins. The Senator must love it when the Republicans divide their support."

I stop eating for a moment to consider it. "You're right. And every time polls have come out showing the race is close until the third candidate gets on the ballot. And then . . ." The wheels start turning.

Nick stops eating and locks eyes with me. "You thinking what I'm thinking? Is that even possible?"

I start to nod. "It's possible. Collier bankrolls the third party candidate. Damn, that would be ingenious if it's true."

"Is that even legal?"

"Pffft. It's politics. There are no rules. You'd be amazed at the stuff they get away with."

"If it were true, how would you prove that?"

"Just follow the money. But doing that is easier said than done. I need help on the inside. And I know just who to call."

I'd heard that cats hate riding in cars.

Oh. My. God.

Bumper will not stop howling.

He was fine for the one block trip to the vet, but taking him to Manhattan to shoot a public service announcement on Friday morning is an assault on the ears. I'm trying to calm him down, sticking my finger through the grate in the pet carrier while keeping one hand on the wheel. (Is there a petting-while-driving law, like the texting one?) But he won't stop. I knew he had a loud meow, but this is a low, blood curdling wail that sounds like he's being tortured.

My cell rings and I hit the hands-free device on the steering column. "This is Madison . . ."

"Hey, Madison, Brad Dexter returning your call."

Oooooowwwwwww . . .

"What the hell is that?" asks the Congressman.

"My cat."

"What are you doing to the poor thing?"

"Taking him to Manhattan for a commercial shoot. He apparently hates riding in cars."

Ooooooowwwwwww . . .

"So does mine. You'll get the same reaction if you ever have to bathe him. Of course you'll need peroxide and a ton of Band-Aids if you do."

"You put Band-Aids on a cat?"

"No, that's for you when it rips you to shreds while bathing it. Anyway, what can I do for you?"

"Can you get me the campaign financial disclosure forms for Collier's last three elections? I need both the Senator and the independents who ran against him. I could get it myself but I know Collier will slow-walk my request and you'd be faster. Besides, I don't want him to know I'm digging into this particular element."

"Sure, no problem. I'll have it for you in a few days. You got something?"

"Just a hunch about a creative accounting trick. It's a long shot, but I need to check it out."

Finally I come to a stop in the parking garage next to Jamison's production studio and Bumper calms down.

Can't wait for the drive home. Gotta ask the vet if there are such things as kitty tranquilizers. Chauffeuring him around if he's going to be a long-term spokes-cat will not be much fun.

The walk is short and Bumper is now curled up in the carrier taking a nap. The non-stop howling must have exhausted him. Jamison greets me at the door with a soft smile. "Hi, Madison. Good to see you."

"You too."

"You doing okay?"

"Yeah. Again, sorry about the other day."

"Not a problem. My mistake."

"Don't be ridiculous. It was a nice gesture." I note his face is sunburned and point at it. "Let me guess . . . you haven't been in an editing booth all week."

"Yeah, took the day off and went sailing yesterday. Didn't have my first mate to remind me about the sunblock."

Geez, more guilt? I need to put a stop to this. Today.

He gestures toward the studio. "Anyway, we're all set up and ready for you."

An hour later we're done. Bumper was terrific, doing his little paw-in-the-air thing and providing us with lots of cute video. Of course the minute I tried to get him back into the carrier he turned into a Tazmanian devil cat, stretching out all four paws sideways like a damn flying squirrel and latching onto the sides of the carrier to prevent me from putting him inside. From now on, any commercials featuring my cat will be shot at my house.

Jamison walks me to the door, his hand lightly on my back. He's been looking at me with sad eyes the whole time, and I can tell I've hurt him. Not sure it was a good idea to keep doing commercials with the guy, but what choice did I have with this being charity work? I'm not sure this will work. Actually, I'm sure it won't.

He stops at the door and looks at his watch. "Hey, you gotta get back to the station?"

"No, I'm off all day."

"Care to join me for lunch? No strings."

One look in his eyes tells me there are definitely strings. "Well, if I didn't have Bumper with me—"

"You can leave him here. The staff loves him."

"Eh, not a good idea. It's a strange place with people he doesn't know. And he's pretty attached to me." Thank you, kitty, for providing me an escape route.

"Well, okay. Maybe next time when we shoot the adoption spot and you don't have a cat with you."

"Sure." Not a good idea either. Not happening.

"So, you still on the wild goose chase?"

"Huh?"

"Senator Collier."

"Yeah. I've got a hunch I'm following. Nothing concrete."

"You know, I had lunch the other day with a friend at an ad agency that handles his campaign. Said everything was on the up and up. And he's one of those religious, straight-laced guys who wouldn't work for a client who broke the law."

"Interesting. Well, gotta go."

"Nice seeing you Madison." The sad eyes return.

"Yeah. You too." I turn to head out the door when he takes my arm.

"Hey, almost forgot." He reaches in his pocket, pulls out a check and hands it to me. "Little donation to your favorite charity."

My eyes widen as I see it's for ten thousand dollars made out to the animal shelter. "Wow. Jamison, that's really nice of you."

"Hey, you know what they say. Do well, then do good."

"You already do the commercials for free."

"That's just donating my time. This is a little extra."

"Thank you, it's very kind. Well, see you next time."

"Bye, Madison."

I head out the door and the guilt slaps me in the face. I hurt a really good guy. And I know the only way I can feel better about this.

Find him someone else.

I've got just the person in mind.

Chapter Twenty-Four

Tish shakes her head as the bar waiter hands her a glass of wine. "Not just no, but hell no."

"Aw, c'mon, Tish, you already met Jamison and you liked him."

"It doesn't seem right, Madison."

"What, you think he's one of my leftovers?"

"No, that's not it."

"So what's the problem? You talked with him a lot at the party, you had good things to say about him and you thought he was awfully cute."

"He is awfully cute."

"Who else is on your dance card right now?"

"I've got two trials coming up."

"Not trials. Men."

She shakes her head. "I have been using my peremptory strikes of late."

"So you just excuse them like jurors you don't want?"

"Basically."

"Your standards are too high. They can't even get out of the starting gate. C'mon, you saw how he treated me, what a gentleman he is."

She shakes her head. "Fine. I know you're not gonna drop this."

"Great. He might be your soul mate."

"I know what you're up to. This is just using me to get the guilt monster off your back."

Dammit, she figured it out. "How—"

"Madison, when you prefaced this whole idea with the fact you feel guilty about hurting the guy and that he's still carrying a torch, you basically tipped it off. But whatever. I guess I could use a night out with a decent guy. Did you already talk to him about me?"

"Uh, no."

"So how does this work?"

"Haven't figured that part out yet."

"Wonderful. I guess I'll have to come up with some reason to invite him to lunch." She looks at her watch. "Where are A.J. and Rory?"

"They'll be here soon."

"I guess girls night out is easier now that you have a permanent cat sitter at your house."

"Don't really need one for Bumper anymore. He's pretty self-sufficient. Although very demanding of attention."

"So is Socks. And who's keeping an eye on Nick?"

"His cop buddies. Poker game at my house."

"Ah. So how's it going? I mean, you guys are basically living together now."

"It's nice coming home and having him there. And since there's no possibility of anything sexual right now, we're really getting to know each other a lot better. It's not the typical relationship progression . . . a few dates and then hop in bed."

"Never thought of it that way. Though you're not the type to hop in bed after a few dates anyway."

(I know what you're thinking. Don't say it.)

"Madison, are you still comfortable with your decision?"

"Absolutely."

"But you miss Jamison."

"No, I feel bad about hurting him. I really need to get him out of my head. I think if I knew he had moved on it would help."

I arrive home at eleven, surprised to find the poker game still going on. I note Nick has the most chips in front of him. "Ah, I can see who's winning."

One of the cops gets up. "Gotta run, I'm on overnights this week."

A groan from the other players. "I hate playing with four," says Steve. He points to the empty chair. "Madison, we need a fifth. You play poker?"

"Sure, why not. I like card games." I take the empty seat. "How much are we playing for?"

"Nickle, dime, quarter. Very high stakes."

I reach in my purse and pull out a twenty, then give it to Steve. "Okay, I'm in." He passes me a few stacks of chips.

Nick starts dealing. "Five card draw. Madison, you know the game?"

"What, you think girls don't know how to play poker?"

"Just asking."

I pick up my cards and decide to have a little fun with an old stereotype. "So, are lots of kings good in this game?"

Big groan again, as three of the cops toss their cards on the table and drop out.

Nick studies my face. "You are so full of it. She's bluffing, guys."

I put on my innocent little girl face. "Just asking a question about the rules."

"Bull. How many cards do you want?"

I toss two in his direction. "Two."

He deals two cards and three for himself, then tosses a blue chip into the pot. "Quarter."

"So, is it okay if I bet more than a quarter?"

"Oh, give me a break, Madison."

I toss two blue chips into the pot. "I raise you a quarter."

He adds another blue chip. "Call. Waddaya got?"

I lay down my cards. "Full house. Kings over aces."

"Sonofabitch."

Steve pats Nick on the back. "Yeah, right, she's bluffing." He turns to me. "But you *are* full of it, young lady."

I rake in the chips and the cards as it's my deal. I execute a shuffle with a flourish, fan the cards on the table and flip them like a magician, then begin to deal. "Seven card, low in the hole, roll your own, no choice on last."

Steve turns to Nick. "Partner, you've got no shot in this house."

It's nearly one in the morning when the game breaks up. I help Nick get comfortable in his bed, then sit on the edge and run my fingers through his hair. "You're starting to look like your old self. I can tell you're really starting to feel better."

"Yeah. And the poker game really cheered me up. I missed the guys and the camaraderie."

"Good to see you smile and laugh."

"Though I'm not sure I wanna play poker with you again."

"What, you didn't like getting your ass kicked in front of your friends?"

"I think you were a con artist in a previous life."

"I'm just a girl who likes to have fun."

"Yeah, right. Hey, do me a favor before you turn in?"

"Sure. Waddaya need?"

"Scratch my right foot. It itches like hell and I can't reach it."

"Sure." I move to the end of the bed, pull back the covers and start to scratch his foot. "Better?"

"Yeah, much."

He's wearing a huge grin. "What?"

"For a network reporter, you sure miss the obvious."

"Huh?"

"I just told you might foot itches. Wait for it . . ."

And then it hits me. My eyes widen. "Oh my God! You've got feeling in your foot?"

"A little."

"When did this happen?"

"While we were playing poker. I leaned forward to get the cards and all of a sudden got this tingling in my feet."

I'm euphoric.

I move quickly back to the head of the bed, take his hands and lock eyes with him. "You're going to walk again. Nick, I'm so happy for you." My eyes start to well up.

"Still got a long way to go, but it's a start."

We both sleep late after staying up past midnight. It's a beautiful day, sunny and warm, and with Nick feeling better I'm going to suggest we go outside for a while. Poor guy has been cooped up inside since he got shot and I think the fresh air and sunshine will do him good. He rolls into the kitchen as I'm making coffee. "Sleep okay, Marino?"

"Yeah. Great. I think knowing there's light at the end of the tunnel helped."

"You still have feeling in your foot?"

"There's more this morning. Check it out." I look at his feet and see him wiggling his toes and flexing his ankles a bit.

"Wow, that's great." I lean over and give him a hug. "I think you're gonna be walking sooner than we thought."

"It really helps to have your support, Madison. You have no idea what it means for me to recover here instead of some hospital."

"Don't worry, I've got all your back rent on account."

"What do I owe you so far?"

"You'll see when you get your final bill." I run one finger down his cheek. "Though I might take it out in trade." I pour two cups of coffee and set one down on the kitchen table in front of him. "Hey, I was thinking it would be nice for you to get some fresh

215

air. It's gorgeous outside. How about we go down to the park on the corner? We can even take Bumper."

"You mean the park that doesn't allow dogs?"

"Right. It doesn't say anything about cats."

"Probably because no one ever thought to take a cat to a park. You really want to take Bumper? How are you going to keep him from running away?"

"I've got a harness for him. He won't get away and the poor thing has been sitting in the window a lot. I know he's dying to get outside. And since dogs aren't allowed he'll be fine."

Had I known walking a cat on a harness would attract men in droves, I would have tried it years ago.

Of course I don't need anyone since I've already got my guy with me, and he's attracting his share of attention as well. The whole neighborhood knows about Nick from all the publicity, so between him and Bumper we've been surrounded since we arrived.

Kinda funny that I'm the one on TV and the two of them are getting all the attention. But I don't mind. It's really nice to not be the center of attention for a change.

Bumper is having a ball, swatting at the occasional insect, wanting to explore everything within reach while stretching the six foot cord attached to the harness. And he's lapping up all the attention as several people wanted selfies with America's most famous kitten.

An hour later we're back home. Nick is invigorated and the moment I release Bumper from the harness he moves quickly to his favorite spot in the window and looks outside. Deep down he's obviously an outdoor cat, but he'll have to be content with little trips outside.

Nick wheels over to the kitchen table, still cluttered with research from his cold case and my Collier investigation. "Hey, want to show you something. I cracked a cold case."

My eyes widen as I sit next to him. "Really? The six year old murder?"

216

"Not that one, something else I've been working on. Actually, I started before I got shot and finally got around to following up on some leads."

"Okay, let's see."

He pauses a moment, then gives me a serious look. "Madison, I hope I haven't overstepped here and invaded your privacy."

"What the hell are you talking about? I told you how much I like having you here."

He shakes his head as he hands me a sheet of paper. "Not about that. The cold case. I think I found your birth certificate."

My jaw drops as I look at the copy of an official document from the State of New York. I quickly scan it, looking for the names of my parents.

He takes my arm. "Madison, you okay?"

I keep staring at the paper. "I don't know what to say."

"You're not mad?"

"Of course not." I find the line on the form listing the parents. Next to "father" the word "unknown" is typed.

And next to "mother" I read the name.

Caitlin O'Leary.

The place for the baby's name reads "unnamed."

I look up at him. "How the hell did you find this?"

"I pulled the original police report, talked to the two cops who found you along with the witness. Back then police resources were tight and the cops got pulled off the case since you had been placed in a home and were okay. Anyway, the key was that the witness remembered talking to a teenage girl around sixteen with a heavy Irish accent. So I did a search of all the babies born in New York around the time you were found. There was only one with the address of the mother listed as Ireland. The age is right. Madison, that's gotta be your birth certificate."

I look back at the document. "I can't believe you found it after all these years."

"Well, that's not proof it's yours, but everything seems to point that way. But there's one way to find out for sure."

"What's that?"

He hands me another sheet of paper with an address. "I found the woman listed as your mother. She lives upstate."

Chapter Twenty-Five

Mid-afternoon. Jaw and fists clenched, eyes narrowed, looking through the windshield at nothing as Rory drives me out to a small town north of the city on the Hudson River. I'm too emotional to be behind the wheel and I want her with me for this.

After all these years, I will finally meet . . . make that confront . . . my birth mother.

Rory reaches over and takes my hand. "Hey."

"What?" I keep staring straight ahead.

"You sure you want to do this?"

"I have to know."

She pulls one of my fists apart and entwines her fingers with mine. "You know what you're gonna say?"

"I've rehearsed it for years. First question: Why did you throw me away?"

We get off the Henry Hudson Parkway and the GPS tells us we're just a few blocks away from the address Nick provided. My heart rate jumps as Rory makes a few turns and pulls to a stop in front of a small house.

The door is open.

I turn to her. "Please come with me. I can't do this alone."

"Sure, Freckles. I was planning on it."

We get out of the car and head up the front walk. Rory notices I'm shaking a bit and wraps one arm around my waist. I knock on the door. "Hello? Anybody home?" My usually powerful broadcasting voice cracks from the emotion.

A male voice answers. "I'm in the living room."

"Might be her husband," says Rory.

We head inside and move down the hallway, past a small dining room. I can see a TV and sofa at the end of the hall.

But when we get there, I don't find a husband, but an old priest crouched down around a bunch of boxes. He stands up and smiles. "Hello. Can I help—" He studies my face and his eyes widen.

"I'm looking for Caitlin O'Leary."

He bites his lower lip. "I'm so sorry."

"What?"

"She passed away a few days ago."

My heart sinks.

The priest is still staring at me. "I was about to contact you, Miss Shaw."

"Huh?"

"You're her daughter."

His name is Father Anthony, a tall, slender man in his sixties with thick white hair, pale green eyes and a Boston accent. He sits in a reclining chair while Rory and I are on the couch. "How did you find her?" he asks.

"My boyfriend is a cop and tracked her down. But obviously I'm too late."

He slowly nods. "Yes, my fault."

"I don't understand."

"Caitlin . . . your birth mother . . . realized you were her daughter when you testified before Congress. But by then she was in her last days. We talked about contacting you. She wasn't sure and neither was I. Obviously the fact that you're here tells me I made the wrong decision."

"Don't blame yourself, Father. Do you know her whole story?"

"Yes, and I'm the only one who does. I've known Caitlin since she was a teenager. The church took her in after you were born. I was a rookie priest, right out of the seminary, and found her in my church one night, curled up on a pew, crying. She was only fifteen. She didn't tell me everything until a few years later." He smiles as he studies my face. "Seeing you in person . . . you are a carbon copy of her. Same eyes. Same color hair. All those freckles. And from what I've seen on television, same good heart."

I'm puzzled by that last part. "But she threw me away."

He slowly nods. "And that, in a strange way, turned her into an amazing person. She had gotten pregnant and after you were born the father took off. Left her with nothing, no place to live."

"The birth certificate said she was from Ireland."

"Her parents had moved to this country a couple of years earlier and she was a runaway. Abusive family situation. She ended up with a man who took advantage of an innocent teenage girl and then left her. She didn't want to be sent back to her parents so she used her old Ireland address and lied about her age at the hospital so they wouldn't track down her family."

"Do you know who my father is?"

"He apparently died shortly after. He was a criminal. Not a good man. She never told me his name."

"I see."

"So she left the hospital and panicked when she couldn't find the father. Remember, she was fifteen, alone in New York City, and scared with a newborn baby she couldn't take care of."

"Why didn't she just go to the police, or social services?"

"She thought she'd get in trouble and the father would be charged with statutory rape, which he would have been. And she was worried they would find her parents. Even though your father abandoned her she still cared about him and didn't want to see him go to jail. She was just a kid. So she went to a busy park in the richest neighborhood in Manhattan, thinking some wealthy family would find you and take you in. I know, it doesn't make any sense, but when you're young and desperate you don't think clearly. But she knew you'd be found."

"And after that the church took her in."

"Right. And I was put in charge of her since I was overseeing an at-risk youth program. When she was about eighteen . . . that's when she found her calling."

"Calling?"

"She felt so much guilt about what she had done that she decided to devote her life to doing charitable acts." He points at all the plaques on the wall. "She spent her life working for various benevolent organizations, every one of them involving children. You can see the result."

I study the plaques, all from well-known children's charities. Saint Jude. Shriners. Her name on each, many reading "volunteer of the year." I spot a framed photo and get up to get a closer look.

It's like a photo of myself. The priest is right. Dead ringer.

Another photo shows her with a few children. I turn back to the priest. "So, does she have a husband? Are these her kids?"

He shakes his head. "Caitlin never married. She was so devoted to charity, it filled her life. She was especially committed to helping at-risk children. It really enriched her, gave her purpose."

That makes my eyes well up as I move back to the couch. "You said you weren't sure if you should contact me when she was still alive."

"Caitlin and I discussed it after she realized you were her daughter. She was afraid you would despise her and so was I. She was terminal and I wasn't sure if she should die knowing her only child might hate her. You have to understand that while she was an incredibly giving soul, what she had done to you haunted

222

her. But it drove her to do good. She attended Mass and prayed for you every day, even though she had no idea who you were or even if you were alive. She finished every prayer with *please watch over my daughter.*"

Tears begin to roll down my face and Rory wraps an arm around my shoulders. "You were probably right not to contact me when she was alive. I'll be honest, Father, I came here today without good intentions. And I did hate what she did to me. I simply had to know why she did what she did. I did not come here looking for a loving reunion. I was going to ask her why she threw me away."

The priest nods. "And that's certainly understandable. After hearing your story about the foster homes, I don't blame you for being angry."

"Now I feel awful about it."

"Don't. She actually died peacefully, knowing you had turned out so well. She said she was proud of you and all the good you were doing. I guess charity runs in the family."

Rory pats my hand. "Madison is the kindest person I know."

"I wasn't always this way, Father. Did she have any relatives?"

"No. Only child." He pulls some papers covered by a blue folder from an end table. I recognize it as a legal document. "I need to tell you about this. When she found out she was terminal six months ago, she had a will drawn up and left everything to the church, earmarked to build a children's home. I have no doubt that once she discovered you were her daughter she wanted to leave everything to you, but she never got around to it. You certainly have the right—"

"No, Father. You keep it. She should have a legacy. And it will help children in need."

"Very generous of you." He reaches out and grabs a box, then slides it over to me. "I've been packing this up for you. Photos, some of her favorite things. The cross she wore every day, rosary beads. Her medical records, DNA tests and such, in case you need family history." He then takes an envelope from the table. "And she wrote you a letter before she died."

He hands it to me and my emotions are hung up in my throat. I turn it over in my hand and see "Madison" written in beautiful handwriting. "I think I'll read this later, if that's okay."

"Sure."

I reach into the box for a worn, silver crucifix on a chain, pick it up and put it around my neck. Then the dam holding my emotions back breaks. I begin to cry and hug Rory for dear life.

Nick looks up from his book as I enter his room carrying the box. "You were gone a long time. So that was your mother?"

"Yeah."

"What did she say?"

I put the box on the floor, sit on the edge of the bed and pet Bumper who is curled up at the foot. "She had just passed away." My eyes start to well up and Nick pulls me close, hugging me while gently stroking my hair.

"I'm sorry, Madison. Maybe I shouldn't have—"

"No, actually it's very good that you did. All my questions were answered, and more." I tell him the story, then grab a photo from the box and hand it to him.

"Wow. Talk about a family resemblance. I'd swear this is you."

"No kidding." I reach into the box and take the letter. "And she wrote to me before she died."

"What did she say?"

"I haven't had the nerve to look at it yet. Would you read it to me?"

He takes it from me. "Sure, Madison." He pulls me close as he leans back. I rest my head on his shoulder and wrap my arms around him while the kitten crawls onto my lap. He opens the envelope and starts to read.

Dear Madison,

It seems strange to address you in that way, as I only learned of your name a few days ago when I realized your story matched mine. By now Father Anthony has told you everything and why I did what I did.

When I saw you testify before Congress I was devastated by what I had put you through. And then I was proud that you had accomplished so much, overcoming such adversity, using your position to make the world a better place. I wanted to tell everyone, "That's my daughter!" but of course I had no right to do that. While I gave birth to you I was not your mother in a traditional sense. And while what I did was such a terrible thing, not a day went by that I didn't think of you and pray that you were safe and loved. Obviously some of those prayers went unanswered, and I am sorry your childhood was such an unhappy one.

Madison, I can never write an apology that will make up for my actions, and I certainly don't expect your forgiveness. But please know that I spent the rest of my life trying to help children in need.

I am so happy you turned out to be such a beautiful, successful and compassionate woman. I wish you all the happiness in the world, and am hopeful when we do meet in Heaven that you will accept me. Until then, I will watch over you since I finally know who you are . . . a woman with a beautiful and kind heart.

Love and peace,

Caitlin

Nick gently folds the letter like a priceless heirloom and puts it back in the envelope, then sets it on the nightstand. He takes my chin and tilts it up, noting the tears are flowing. "Beautiful letter."

"I feel awful. I went up there wanting to hate her and now . . ."

He kisses the top of my head. "Madison, you couldn't possibly hate anyone. You're not wired that way. The last line in that letter is spot on. You're a woman with a beautiful and kind heart.

Actually you have the biggest heart of anyone I've ever met. I thank God every day that I met you."

His words send me over the emotional edge. I bury my head in his chest and cry it out. He holds me, saying nothing, simply stroking my back. Finally I'm all wrung out and look up at him.

He brushes away my tears with his thumb. "Your mother prayed that you would be safe and loved. I can take care of that."

Chapter Twenty-Six

I'm already awake, looking at Nick who's still asleep as the sunlight spills onto his face. I actually slept well, probably because my emotions had drained me.

Or maybe because of who I was sleeping with.

More important, did Nick tell me he loved me last night?

Too much to sort out right now. At least the mystery of my mother has been solved, painful as it was.

Bumper wakes up, moves up from the foot of the bed and meows.

Nick's eyes flicker open. He yawns and smiles. "Morning, gorgeous."

I give him a sly smile. "Flattery will get you nowhere, Mister."

"I was talking to the cat."

I sit up straight. "Hey!"

He reaches up and runs his hand across my cheek. "Look at that, I made you smile."

"Thanks. And thank you for last night."

"My job, remember? Damsels in distress."

"And I was in serious distress."

"Sleep well?"

"Yeah. When you get a thirty-five year old demon out of your head, it helps."

"I can imagine." He looks at the clock. "You better get going on your Sunday morning show."

"In a minute." I lay back next to him and he wraps an arm around my shoulders. "In a minute."

No longer in need of a cat sitter and with Nick able to take care of himself, Sunday brunch moves back to one of our favorite restaurants. I've let everyone read the letter from my mother, and of course they were all touched.

My brain must resemble one of those lottery machines, with thoughts bouncing around like ping pong balls. Finally finding my mother, my guilt about hating her all these years, what Nick said to me last night, memories of foster homes dredged up. I want to send my brain on a vacation, spend a week doing totally mindless stuff that requires no thinking. If you've got a big book of Sudoku puzzles, I'm your girl.

"I think Madison has been taken over by the pod people." Tish jolts me out of my trance.

I look up at her. "Sorry. I've had a lot to process in the last twenty-four hours."

Rory pats me on the shoulder. "But you got some sense of closure. The question that had been haunting you all these years was finally answered. Now you can move on."

"I guess. But there's something else right now that has moved to the front burner. I think Nick told me he loved me last night."

A.J. shakes her head. "What do you mean, you *think* he told you he loved you? Did he say *I love you*?"

"Not exactly."

Tish stops eating. "He either said it or he didn't."

"Okay, you all read the letter. That line where my mother hopes I will be safe and loved. Nick said, '*Your mother prayed that you would be safe and loved. I can take care of that.*'"

Tish nods as she considers it. "What did you say?"

"Nothing. I went to sleep."

228

"Did you not respond because you weren't sure what to say, because you didn't want to tell him you loved him?"

"I don't know. I was exhausted and emotional. It didn't really hit me till I woke up and thought about it."

Rory pats me on the shoulder. "He loves you, and we all know it. But you're doing what you always do, Freckles. Acting like a man."

"What are you talking about?"

"Every time a guy makes a commitment he always has this little voice in his head wondering if he could have done better, even if he's dating the most beautiful woman in the world. A man could have Nicole Kidman in his back pocket and still wonder if Miss Universe is available. And you've played the *what if?* game your whole life, both with romance and your career. You have always second guessed your decisions."

"I know, but—"

"She's right," says A.J. "By the way, I think he told you he loved you."

"Yeah, I think you're right. I needed it, too. I didn't want to be alone after what happened yesterday. And if he wasn't around I would have come over and crawled in bed with you."

A.J. flashes a wicked grin. "There wasn't a vacancy next to me."

Tish studies my face. "Do you love him?"

"Yeah, but you know how hard it is for me to say the L-word. I love having him there when I get home. We get along great. He's incredibly thoughtful and so sweet to me. He's funny and smart and we have a lot in common. I'm more physically attracted to him than any man I've ever dated."

"I think I've figured this out," says Tish.

"What?"

"Rory's right. You sneaked off and had a sex change. You're now a man who can't commit."

"Very funny."

"Oh, by the way, I'm having lunch with Jamison tomorrow. I

called him up with some bogus stuff about needing a video produced for my law firm. So maybe I can get the guilt monster off your back."

My cell rings the minute I walk into the newsroom on Monday morning. I see it's Congressman Dexter's office calling. "Madison Shaw . . ."

"Hi Madison, Brad Dexter. Wanted to make sure you were in the newsroom today."

"Yeah, at least until I go out on a story. You got something for me?"

"I'm not sure you want it, but I've got it. You'll be buried in paperwork."

"I'm not on a timetable. Can you email everything to me?"

"I've actually got a messenger outside in your parking lot. I didn't want an electronic paper trail and wanted to make sure it was hand delivered to you and not simply left at the desk. I'll tell him to make the delivery."

"Thanks, I really appreciate that. Did you have time to look at it?"

"Only enough to know that there's a pretty big haystack for you to sift through in order to find the needle."

"Well, if it's there, I'll find it. Thanks so much for your help."

"If you need any more, just call."

The call ends and I head down to the lobby, expecting a typical young bike messenger in shorts and a helmet. Instead I see a middle-aged man in a dark suit carrying a large box. He sees me and heads in my direction. "Miss Shaw, this is for you."

He hands me the box which weighs a ton. Obviously the Congressman wasn't kidding about the size of the haystack. "Thank you. Do I need to sign anything?"

"No." His suit jacket is open and I can see a shoulder holster inside. He's obviously a Fed, probably one of Brad Dexter's FBI friends.

"Okay. Appreciate you doing this."

"I'm not really here. Have a nice day, Miss Shaw."

He turns and leaves the building. I decide to take the box to the parking lot rather than leave it sitting on my desk all day. Reporters are too damn nosy and I don't want anyone knowing what I'm working on. I reach my car and lock the box in the trunk.

Can't wait to get home and start digging.

Tish shows up after dinner, looking like she needs to talk. "C'mon, let's take a walk. Need to tell you some stuff."

"Sure." I turn to Nick, who's watching television. "Tish and I are going for a walk."

"Okay. Be back by ten. And I want your Algebra homework done, young lady, or no video games."

"Very funny."

We head out the door and start down the block. "He looks like he's in good spirits," says Tish.

"He's getting more feeling back in his legs every day. Doctor says the prognosis is looking up."

"That's great, Madison. I'm happy for both of you."

"So what's up?"

"Had lunch with Jamison today."

"And . . ."

"I have good news and bad news."

"Uh-oh. What's the good news?"

"He picked up the check."

"What's the bad news?"

"You know that torch the Statue of Liberty has? The one he's carrying for you is bigger and burning bright as hell."

"Aw, shit."

"Madison, I took my best shot. Really. Tried to flirt, even had my hair down and glasses off."

"Damn, you *are* a good friend. For you that's like showing up naked."

"Anyway, the majority of the lunch conversation was about a certain redhead. How's Madison? Is she still serious about this other guy? Is there anything I can do to get her back? I told him there was no way but that didn't seem to get through. Sorry, kiddo, he really misses you and wants another chance. I could have given the guy a lap dance and it wouldn't have helped."

"Well, thanks for trying."

"Oh, this was interesting. I noticed that when he took out his wallet to pay the bill, he had one of those police courtesy cards from the Commissioner. He must be well connected."

"Considering he gave me ten grand for the animal shelter, he probably just made a big donation to some police charity."

"Yeah, that makes sense. Oh, almost forgot. He said he had someone who could help you with your story."

"Huh?"

"Your Senator Collier investigation. He's gonna have a friend of his with inside information call you. Said it should keep you from wasting your time chasing a dead end."

"Yeah, he did mention he knew someone in the campaign. Anyway, thanks for trying, Tish."

"Maybe A.J. would have more luck. She's a little more, shall we say, *forward* than I am with men."

"I dunno. He might start getting suspicious with all my friends hitting on him."

"Well, anyway, I guess you'll have to deal with it. Meanwhile, you've got a terrific guy waiting for you at home. Sweet, smart, funny, a real-live hero, awfully cute, and obviously in love with you. Most women would kill for that, you know."

I nod. I need to focus completely on Nick, stop worrying about hurting Jamison and bury the past. "You're right."

We finish our walk and head back to the house, finding Nick in the living room playing with Bumper. He's got a ball of aluminum foil tied to a yard stick, holding it inside a shoe box with a hole cut out in the side. Bumper is having a ball reaching through the hole trying to catch the foil. Nick looks up and smiles. "Oh, hey. I invented a game for him since he can't jump." He turns his attention back to the kitten.

Tish leans forward and whispers in my ear. "If he'd do that for a kitten, imagine what he'd do for a child."

I can't help but smile as I watch this tough-as-nails cop play with a special needs kitten. It speaks volumes. "Point taken."

"So, can the defense rest now?"

"Yeah. The verdict is in on the L-word."

"About damn time. Case dismissed."

Nick and I are sitting at the kitchen table, going through the mountain of papers sent to me by the Congressman.

But that's not occupying my full attention.

Incredibly, a kitten has once again helped me make an important decision. If he was a black and white kitten I would change his name to *magic eight ball.*

For the first time I'm perfectly relaxed. Jamison is out of my head. Yes, he's a great guy who would no doubt treat me like a queen while offering an incredible lifestyle, but it doesn't matter. Seeing Nick playing with my kitten . . . well, that's an intangible quality which goes deep into my soul. The fact that a man who can't walk, who is recovering from a near-fatal gunshot wound, would take the time to create a toy for a kitten . . . well, a woman can't ask for a better man.

We've been going through papers for an hour and my eyes are getting tired. I reach over and take his hand. "Hey, how about we take a break. I'm getting cross-eyed looking at all this."

"Sounds good to me. You wanna watch TV for a while?"

"Actually, I wanted to talk to you about something."

"Sure."

I lean back in my chair. "By now you know that I'm a rather stubborn, strong-willed woman who likes to be in charge."

His eyes widen. "Seriously? I had no idea. I'm outta here."

233

"Very funny. But there's something I wanted to ask you. About moving you in here."

"What about it?"

"That day in the hospital when I basically told you that you were staying with me. I guess I've always wondered how you felt about it. I didn't exactly ask for your opinion at the time."

"It's been great, Madison. I shouldn't have to tell you that."

"I don't mean *since* you moved in. I meant . . . did you feel pressured to come here? Was I out of line taking charge of your life?"

"Not at all. I was thrilled. Even if I had family to take care of me, I'd rather be here with you."

"Thanks. I just wanted to be sure." Another loose end tied up.

"Y'know, Madison, you worry about the smallest details. If I could change one thing about you, I'd want you to simply relax and accept things as they are without analyzing every little detail. It's like trying to explain why I'm attracted to you, why any two people are attracted to each other. Some things you just accept without trying to figure out why."

I slowly nod. "You're right. I do over-analyze things."

"By the way, I have a confession to make. I've been worried about something. I mean, since you brought up the moving in thing."

"What are you worried about?"

"Well . . . if I get to the point where I can walk normally, it's going to be awfully hard for me to move out."

"I think you've just gotten spoiled having a woman wait on you."

"Trust me, I'd much rather be waiting on you." He locks eyes with me.

"Ah, that's something I must consider. So, regarding that apartment of yours. When is the lease up?"

"Next month. Why?"

"Tell you what, Marino. Why don't you call the landlord tomorrow and tell him you won't be renewing."

"You serious?"

"Yeah. Last night you told me I was safe and I was loved. I want you to know that you are too. I love you lots, Marino. More than you know. Welcome home."

Chapter Twenty-Seven

By Thursday morning I have sorted through most of the papers on Senator Collier and the third party candidates and weeded out the useless stuff. It's clear campaigns are buried in paperwork required by the federal government, but that also offers them the opportunity to hide stuff with creative accounting. While I'm no expert in finance, when it comes to something illegal involving money I'll know it when I see it.

But the investigation pales in comparison with my personal life the past few days since I came to the realization that Nick is the one for me and I really do love him. The Jamison dreams have stopped, and I'm no longer second-guessing myself. Funny, it took seeing him play with Bumper to make the light bulb over my head turn on. The image of a real-life hero playing with a kitten plays on a loop in my head, reminding me of the kindness of this man.

I'm up early on my day off, sipping coffee as I study the now smaller haystack on the kitchen table. Nick rolls into the kitchen, stops next to me and gives me a kiss. "You're actually up before me. I'm shocked."

"I've been sleeping so well, I guess I don't need as much."

"Probably because for the first time in your life you're at peace. About your mother, I mean."

"Well, that . . . and having you in my life." Bumper meows from a sun square on the floor. "And yeah, you too, kitty."

Nick rolls toward the coffee machine and the kitten backs up to give him room. He's learned to give the wheelchair a wide berth, obviously not wanting to have his tail run over. Nick fixes a cup of coffee then leans down and brings Bumper onto his lap. "How ya doin' fur ball?"

"I'm glad he's not a one-person cat, because you're getting more time with him than I am. I still think you're stealing my pet."

"He's great company when you're not here." He cocks his head toward the papers. "Find anything since last night?"

I shake my head. "I'm stuck. If only I could find out where the PAC money for the third party candidates comes from."

"What's a PAC?"

"Political action committee. Clever way for rich people to stash money in a campaign, very often off the books or done in a shady manner. Basically it's a slush fund for politicians."

"So that's how the third party candidates funded their campaigns?"

"That's a big part of their contributions. I've tried to find out who put money in the PAC but someone or some organization really covered their tracks."

He looks down at the cat. "Maybe you're looking in the wrong direction."

"What do you mean?"

"Well, Bumper goes in reverse gear when my wheelchair is moving. Maybe you need to reverse the way you're looking at the campaign. Since you can't find the source of the money, see where it was spent. You know how politicians love kickbacks. There might be one that would lead you back to the original donor."

My jaw hangs open. "Why the hell didn't I think of that?"

"Because you're a reporter and I'm a cop. Or maybe because I just saw the cat walk backwards. We look at evidence in a different way. Hey, you've helped me a lot with my cold case just by sharing your techniques."

I quickly grab a set of papers with the campaign expenditures of the third party candidates, and start to scan through the expenses.

And then the air is knocked out of me as I see the one common denominator in all three.

Nick takes my arm. "You find something?"

I slowly nod, still staring in disbelief at what I'm seeing. "Oh my God . . ."

Right there in black and white. Multi-million dollar expenditures for each campaign.

To Jamison's production house.

I quickly start what will be a thorough search into the life of the man I was dating. While I have already figured out the obvious (how he is able to afford his oceanfront home, fancy car, classic sailboat and limousines), I need more. Much more.

And I'm pretty sure what I'm going to find isn't going to be good.

More important, how the hell did I miss something like this? Am I that bad a judge of character?

A simple search of his name turns up several people named Jamison Rogers. So I narrow it down to New York.

The top hit is a photo that is a punch to the soul.

Jamison standing next to Senator Collier, who has his arm around him. I click on the link to bring up the caption.

Jamison Rogers with stepfather Senator Joe Collier

I lean back as my jaw drops. "You gotta be friggin' kidding me." I shake my head and continue digging, discovering that Jamison is the son of Corinne Rogers, Senator Collier's third wife.

"Something good?" asks Nick.

"Something incredible." *Yeah, the guy I was dating and almost picked instead of you is a criminal.* "The person who produced the commercials for the third party candidates is Collier's stepson."

"Whoa." He looks at the papers. "Wait a minute, why would the guy's stepson—"

"It's ingenious. Think about it . . . Collier bankrolls the third party campaign, takes money from his own campaign and funnels it somehow through the other candidate to his step son. Millions of dollars for running a campaign that only required producing a few commercials. Basically he's taking campaign contributions and giving it to his own family, at the same time tampering with an election."

"Is that last part illegal?"

"If not it's unethical as hell." I pick up my cell. "I gotta call Congressman Dexter. I need the FBI's help on this. The story isn't complete until we get a paper trail back to Collier. I need that smoking gun."

Picture the most excited child you've ever seen on Christmas morning. Now multiply that by ten and you'll know how a reporter feels when she's about to break a major, and I mean *major*, national story.

So those lottery ping pong balls which have gotten a rest are bouncing around in my head as I sit in the doctor's waiting room while Nick is getting checked. This story is almost too much to process; while getting the smoking gun on Collier is huge, what I'm experiencing knowing that Jamison was part of it lies somewhere between hurt and anger.

I haven't told Nick that Jamison was the other guy, and not sure how or even if I should do that.

The door to the exam room opens and Nick wheels into the waiting room wearing a big smile with the doctor right behind him. I get up and shake the doctor's hand. "Good to see you again, Doctor."

239

"You too, Miss Shaw." He pats Nick on the shoulder. "I must say, I'm pleasantly surprised at how well he is recovering."

Nick looks up at me. "She's a good nurse. Really works my tail off with physical therapy."

The doctor nods. "Well, it shows. And it's time to take things to the next level."

I'm at one end of two long, parallel steel handrails. Nick is at the other, seated in his chair. The physical therapist, a muscled, thirtyish guy with huge biceps named Joey stands next to him. He looks at Nick. "You ready?"

"Let's rock."

The therapist gets behind Nick, places his hands under Nick's arms, and helps him to a standing position. Nick grabs the rails and rolls his head. "Whoa. Little dizzy."

"That's because you haven't been standing for a while. Take your time. I'm right behind you so you won't fall. Now brace yourself with the handrails and let's see if you can walk a little. Your goal is to make it to that hot redhead waiting for you at the end of the room."

Nick smiles at me. "That's all the incentive I need." He pushes himself up straight, then grimaces as he slowly swings one leg forward. He shakes his head as he catches his breath. "Harder than I thought."

"It takes time," says the therapist. "Let's try another step."

I clap a few times. "C'mon, Marino. Your best girl is waiting and she desperately wants to give you a hug. You've gotta come here to get it. Let's go, Officer."

Nick nods, pushes himself up again and swings the other leg forward. He pauses, then takes another step. Then another. And another. Beads of sweat cover his forehead.

"You're doing great," says the therapist, still standing right behind him with his arms on Nick's waist.

I extend my arms as he gets closer. "Just a few more."

Nick takes two more steps and reaches me. I quickly wrap my

240

arms around him and give him a strong hug, laying my head on his shoulder as tears of joy stream down my face. "You did it. You're gonna walk again."

He leans back and looks at me. "No. *We* did it."

Chapter Twenty-Eight

One week later I'm sitting in a nearly empty restaurant, waiting to meet Jamison for a late lunch at two o'clock.

No, it's not what you think.

I'm wearing a wire in return for an exclusive and the FBI has agents masquerading as waiters.

The Feds have pretty much what they need to take down Collier, but they want ironclad proof from his son so the Senator can't have the popular "plausible deniability" that many politicians use to get out of jams. Having Jamison admit the whole thing on tape will make the case a slam dunk.

I'm pretending to look at a menu when I see Jamison enter the restaurant. He spots me and flashes a big smile as he quickly moves to my table, but I do not get up to greet him. "Right on time, Jamison."

He takes a seat. "I must say, I didn't expect you to call me so soon. I got the impression last time that you wanted to avoid me."

I shrug and smile. "Well, you know, things change."

"So, the other guy—"

"Don't want to talk about him. I'm here with you, aren't I?" Big smile.

Got him. That was easy.

He leans back in his chair, totally relaxed. "I'm really glad you called me, Madison."

"Well, I'm in a good mood. About to break a big story. Well, maybe."

A bit of concern creeps into his eyes. "Oh, really?"

"Yeah, finally got the goods on Senator Collier." His face tightens, his eyes instantly filled with concern. "Oh, relax, Jamison, I haven't aired the story on your stepfather yet."

His jaw slowly drops. "How did you find out?"

"I'm an investigative reporter with a wall full of Emmy awards, sweetie. Why didn't you tell me? It wouldn't have made a difference."

"Uh . . . I don't like to use his name. Always wanted to make my own way in life."

"Ah." *And stealing millions is making your own way. Right.*

"So . . . what exactly are you going to air on television?"

"Oh, I haven't even decided if I'm going to use it. I might sit on the story."

He looks around then drops his voice. "What exactly did you find, Madison?"

"The way you can afford your current lifestyle. I must say, the whole thing is ingenious. Funneling millions to a member of your family while controlling an election."

His fists tighten a bit and the muscles in his neck go taut. "Madison, please—"

"Oh, relax, Jamison. I said I might sit on the story."

"I would really appreciate that. You have no idea."

"Hey, you're a great guy and have always treated me well. And, ya know, I've been thinking of late that I'm getting tired of the reporter grind. Might want to do something else. Since you and I get along so well, I had an idea . . . well, that you might want a partner."

His eyes widen a bit. "A partner?"

"Yeah. You know, what you did for your stepfather we could

do with other politicians. Why stop at one since the system has worked so well for so many years? Of course, I'd have to be paid a lot more than what I make at the network. I mean, let's put it this way . . . a good job offer from you and I'd clean out my desk today. Which means the story never hits the air."

He slowly nods. "I see. So you're basically blackmailing—"

"Jamison, that's such a terrible word. I'm giving you a business proposition. Let's be partners, in business and in life. I might even throw in a bikini for the next ride on that sailboat of yours." I run my toe up his leg and steal his breath.

"And . . . how much more would you need to make?"

I shrug. "Everything's negotiable. But I think, oh, a half-million base salary per year would be a good starting point. Considering you make considerably more. I could bring a lot more politicians into the fold. So maybe there could be some bonuses as well for clients I recruit."

He slowly nods, obviously figuring out he has no choice. "Okay, Madison, you've got a deal. You'll clean out your desk today?"

"Consider it done." I lean back and pick up the menu. "Okay, while I understand the process, I've gotta know . . . who came up with the idea and the way to do it? You or Senator Collier?"

"My stepfather. He knew I was frustrated as a reporter and wanted a way to take money from his campaign and keep it in the family. So he came up with the idea of a slush fund that would bankroll third party candidates to guarantee his re-election while depositing several million dollars into my bank account. Of course I kick back some to him through the same shell corporation that's in my mother's name. I'm amazed that you found it. My compliments."

"Thank you."

"The way I look at it, Madison, is that people contributed to the Collier campaign because they wanted him to win. And he spent the money to do just that. The fact that he kept money in the family makes no difference to the people who supported him. For them, the bottom line was keeping him in office, and they didn't care how it was done. It's a win-win situation for our family."

"Interesting way to look at things. But it does make sense. The ends do often justify the means."

"Glad you can see it from my point of view." Jamison smiles at me as an FBI agent dressed as a waiter arrives at our table. He looks up at the agent. "Oh, can you give us a few minutes?"

I stand up. "I don't need any more time. I know what I want." I nod at my photographer who has been sitting at a table in the corner. He picks his camera up from the floor and begins shooting video as I get out of the way.

The agent pulls his ID from his pocket and flips it open in front of Jamison. "I'm Special Agent Kirk Butler, FBI. Jamison Rogers, you are under arrest for embezzlement and violation of federal election laws. You have the right to remain silent."

The color drains from Jamison's face as another agent arrives. They finish reading him his rights, handcuff him and start to lead him out of the restaurant. I'm at the door, smiling with my arms folded. Jamison stops and locks eyes with me. "How could you?"

"Because you're nothing more than a common thief. And I'm a reporter after a big story that will make the world a better place. This is a win-win. For me."

I arrive home around seven-thirty after breaking my story. I stayed at the studio since a major story like this demanded I be on the set. Besides, Nick is up and around, having traded in his wheel-chair for a walker, so he hasn't needed me to rush home.

I find him along with Rory, Tish and A.J. wearing party hats and blowing noisemakers as I walk in the door. Rory pops a bottle of champagne as they all cheer for me. "You kicked the Senator's ass, Freckles! Congratulations!"

"Finally got your great white whale," says Tish.

"She harpooned the sonofabitch," adds A.J.

Nick moves forward and gives me a hug with one arm as he braces himself on the walker. "Really proud of you, Madison."

"Hey, without your idea to look in the other direction it never would have happened."

"Actually, Bumper gave me the idea. So don't forget to thank your cat."

I pick up the cat from his spot in the window and he meows. "You're quite the detective, kitty." I look at the dining room table and see it filled with goodies from A.J.'s deli. "Okay, enough of this, I'm starved. Let's eat."

Nick is on the phone talking to his partner in the other room, which gives me a chance to chat with my friends about the final loose end in my life. "So, what do I do about Jamison?"

Rory laughs. "You don't have to do anything. He's going to jail, right?"

"Yeah, but not for as long as he should. The FBI agent said he 'flipped like a pancake' on his stepfather in return for a reduced sentence. So he will be out eventually."

A.J. takes a seat on the couch with a glass of wine. "Yeah, but Jamison will have moved on by then. He'll make a new girlfriend in prison."

Tish wrinkles her face. "Ewwww. Anyway, Madison, Rory's right. You don't have to do anything."

"I meant about Nick. Do I tell him? And if I do, how?"

Rory shakes her head. "I vote no."

"Me too," adds A.J. "Leave it alone."

Tish takes my hand. "There's no reason to do so. You wouldn't tell him about old boyfriends anyway, so why bother?"

"Good point."

Nick comes back to the living room. "So, now that you've broken the ultimate story, what will you do to top it?"

"I've got an idea."

I head into Nick's bedroom carrying two glasses of champagne, finding him sitting up on the bed reading a book. "Help me finish this, will ya? It's no good once the fizz is gone."

He takes one from me. "Thank goodness I'm done with the medication." He clinks my glass. "Cheers to the best reporter in America."

"Thank you. You didn't tell me you were done with the pills."

"Yeah. Rory took me to the doctor this morning and he said I didn't need them anymore. And other than the fact that I still need a walker for a while, he gave me a clean bill of health. I can start desk duty at the precinct next week."

"Hmmm. Y'know, when I talked to him last week he said you would still need some physical therapy."

Nick shakes his head. "Nope. Doc said I'm done going to that facility."

"I wasn't talking about that." I put my glass on the nightstand, sit on the edge of the bed, lean forward and give him a long kiss. "There are some different exercises you need." I swing one leg over him and straddle him. "This is home-based physical therapy. We need to get your heart rate up. Y'know, some cardio would be good for you."

His hands come up, slide under my blouse and rest gently on my waist, his touch sending my pulse rocketing. "Ah. The doctor didn't tell me about this."

"Well, this isn't exactly something you'd find on webMD.com." I give him another kiss and run my hands under his shirt, savoring the touch of his toned chest while stealing his breath.

"Madison, I'm not sure my legs are strong enough—"

"Shhh." I put one finger on his lips. "Let Madison do all the work. You do know I like to be in charge, right?"

"Right."

"Good. Now lay back, relax and let me take you. That's an order, Officer."

Chapter Twenty-Nine

One month later . . .

MADISON SHAW NAMED
"MOST ADMIRED AMERICAN WOMAN"
By Kelly Driver

She bottle feeds orphaned kittens, nurses a seriously wounded cop back to health, provides key testimony for the newly-passed adoption bill, and oh, in her spare time, breaks the biggest political story of the year that takes down one of the country's most powerful United States Senators.

It's no wonder that America admires network reporter Madison Shaw.

"Honestly, I'm humbled by that title, but I'm nothing special," said Shaw upon learning of the poll that has people looking up to her. "And to be honest, if I hadn't taken in those kittens none of this would have happened."

By now the country is familiar with the story of the driven journalist who basically "got stuck" taking care of a litter of orphaned kittens, discovered while on a Friday night story. And the resulting events that took place as a result. What people might not know is how this simple twist of fate changed her. "I will admit I was a total bitch in the newsroom before I found those kittens and most of my co-workers probably hated me. My career was all that mattered. But the cats gave me a wake-up call about what was really important in my life. I'm a completely different person now. I'm not real proud of the way I used to be, but glad I saw the light."

While the story of the bottle-fed kittens went viral, what wasn't known is that Shaw was channeling Florence Nightingale as she nursed her boyfriend, a New York City cop, back to health after being shot. "We really didn't know each other that well," said Officer Nick Marino, who nearly died after a shootout left him temporarily unable to walk. "We'd only had three dates yet she moved me into her house, remodeled it to accommodate a wheelchair and got the network to let her do live shots from her living room so she could spend more time taking care of me. As long as I live I'll never be able to repay her for that. She's the finest person I've ever known with an incredible heart."

Shaw is also revered among some Congressional circles, as her emotional heartfelt testimony was instrumental in passing the adoption bill. But the icing on the cake was her takedown of Senator Joe Collier, long known as "Teflon Joe." Her investigation resulted in a veteran member of Congress and his family receiving jail sentences for embezzling campaign funds. "He was my great white whale," said Shaw. "So many reporters had tried to find the smoking gun on the guy over the years; I'm just glad to expose a common criminal. Of course the idea for where to look came from my boyfriend, who got it from the cat."

She laughs when asked about the upcoming special election to fill Collier's seat. "A few political bigwigs actually contacted me suggesting I run. But I think that was a clever ruse to get me out of the media. They don't want me digging up dirt on anyone else. Too bad, you guys will have to keep looking over *your shoulders if you've broken the law because I'm not going away."*

Shaw seems at total peace as she strokes the fur of the tortoiseshell kitten she adopted, named Bumper, who is blind in one eye and can't jump due to a deformed leg. "This kitten is really attached to me. He waits for me in the window to come home every day. And I can't wait to see him. It's amazing how everything that happened came about because of the kittens. I met Nick when I ran a stop sign trying to get home to feed them and he pulled me over. Shelters got a ton of donations and pet adoptions are up. Kids that might not have homes are getting adopted. And a corrupt United States Senator is in prison because Bumper walked backwards to get out of the way of Nick's wheelchair and he gets the idea for me to reverse-engineer Collier's financial statements. They need to change the name of the butterfly effect to the kitten effect. At least in my case."

As for what the future holds, Shaw no longer considers it. "When you're in love with a cop you live every day to the fullest and take nothing for granted. The present is all that matters. I love my job, have a terrific boyfriend, great friends and a pet that turned my house into a home and me into a real human being. They say you can't have it all, but I do. I have it all."

Nick is busy fiddling with a long wand at the kitchen table, obviously making another toy for Bumper as I finish the article. "Wow, that was really nice. You read it already?"

"Yeah."

"Well?"

He puts the wand on his lap and shrugs. "I thought it was nice."

I sit down next to him. "Nice? That's all? Seriously? That was about the most glowing thing anyone could write."

250

"Yeah, but I hate it when reporters have errors in their stories. Or leave stuff out."

"What got left out?"

"Well, it would have been nice if you said we have the best sex ever. Since you say it to me every night."

I slap him on the shoulder. "That's private! I'm not going to tell that to the whole world!" I drop my voice a bit. "Though I did tell Rory after she heard me scream from across the street."

"Well, at least *someone* knows."

"Typical man, wanting the world know you're a stud in the bedroom. Meanwhile, what errors are you talking about?"

"The part about me. The writer called me your boyfriend."

"You *are* my boyfriend." Suddenly my face tightens. "Aren't you?"

He pulls the wand from his lap and holds it up, dangling something shiny on the end of a string in front of me.

An engagement ring.

"Madison, I think the term *fiancée* is more accurate. Don't you?"

I reach for it and he yanks it away. "Hey! I'm not a cat! Gimme that thing!"

He holds it in front of me and I pull the ring off the thread holding it. A beautiful antique platinum ring with a solitaire diamond, probably about one carat. "It's my mother's. I hope it's okay. I don't make a lot on a cop's salary and can't afford to get you what you really deserve. Maybe someday."

My eyes well up as I look at him. "It's perfect, Nick. And I don't need outrageously expensive jewelry if I've got you." I hand him the ring. "Put it on me."

He takes the ring and smiles as I extend my hand. "So I assume that means *yes*? That you'll marry me?"

"Yes, okay? Now put it on me before I change my mind."

"I can't get down on one knee—"

"Oh for God's sake, shut the hell up and ring me!"

He slides the ring onto my finger, a perfect fit. I extend my hand into a ray of sunlight, and smile as it sparkles. "It's gorgeous. And I'm honored to wear your mother's ring." I get up and slide onto his lap, wrap my arms around his neck and give him a long kiss. Bumper meows and I reach down to pick him up.

"We're one big happy family, huh?"

"You know, come to think of it, the article *was* a bit premature."

"Huh?"

"Actually, I misspoke when I said I had it all. I was premature."

"So now you have it all."

"Almost. I need one more thing." I put Bumper down, get up and turn on the stereo to play our song. Belinda Carlisle's voice fills the room as I extend my hand to Nick. "C'mon. Dance with me."

"I'm not that steady yet."

"You can lean on me. Always." I take his hands and pull him out of the chair, then wrap my arms around his waist. He puts his arms around my shoulders as we lock eyes, swaying to the music. "*Now* I have it all."

Acknowledgments

This is a work of fiction. Any resemblance to any cat, living or dead, is not coincidental and is purely intentional.

Most writers use this part of a book to thank an editor, cover artist, family and friends. But since this is a book about cats, I felt it would be proper to spotlight the two real cats who inspired the kitten named Bumper.

Bumper is a kitten facing challenges, as he is an orphan who has to be bottle fed. This part of his character comes from our Siamese cat Pandora, who was with us for seventeen years. My wife found her, abandoned by the mother cat, when she was just a few days old. We fed her first with an eyedropper and then a bottle. Since my wife is a teacher and I was a reporter at the time, I was able to run home during lunch to feed her. I got to spend more time with her as a kitten. When she opened her eyes she imprinted on me and became very attached, a true one-person cat. At the time we didn't know she was a Siamese, as that breed is born all white and gets the points (mask, socks and tail) as they become adults. Pandora was a highly entertaining cat, exhibiting two personalities depending on our house guests. She would either be a sweet, purring cat or turn into the Tasmanian devil. One friend said we should have named her "Sybil" after the literary character with multiple personalities. But Pandora fit her well since she was more curious than any cat I've ever had.

Bumper is blind in one eye and runs into things, which is a trait shared by our current cat, Gypsy. The little tortoiseshell tabby showed up at our house one day, meowing at me through the window and looking hungry. I fed her and she stuck around. The vet guessed she was about five. She was already fixed so she either ran away or was abandoned. She's been with us about six years and is an incredibly sweet cat. We named her Gypsy because when she first arrived I would often see her all over the neighborhood.

A while ago I noticed she started walking around the perimeter of rooms rather than taking a direct path across them. I thought it was one of her cat quirks until I moved some furniture one day while cleaning and saw her walk face first into a door when she took a different route. The vet confirmed that she had cataracts in one eye, which affected her depth perception. She no longer jumps, as she can't really judge distances correctly and was missing her targets. So we do our best to keep things in the same place so that she can get around without any problems. She's very demanding of attention, and spent a good deal of time on my lap while I wrote this book.

I've always had cats since I was a kid, and perhaps being an only child I understand their independence more than most. To me I've always thought they were angels keeping an eye on us, reporting back to Heaven about how we treat little animals. While that is speculation, what's clear is that in my case, a home without a cat is just a house.